'Gripping from the off: sexy, scandalous brilliance, this book is a genuine must-read *****' – Heat

'Takes you to the most glamorous corners of the globe while keeping you on the edge of your seat' – Glamour

'A gripping, pacy read with a few dark twists I did not see coming. The perfect end-of-summer novel' – Daily Mail

'Excellent . . . A dark and devious psychological thriller but with all the glamour you'd expect from Tasmina' – Red

'A book to cancel plans for – we were completely gripped' – Closer

'Well-drawn characters and a twisty plot make this page-turner a must-read' – Good Housekeeping

'Beautifully descriptive and achingly romantic, this absorbing tale is a pure delight.' ***** – Heat magazine

'I love Tasmina Perry's novels. Trust me, pick one up and you'll be hooked.'

This edition published by Sunflower Press 2021

ISBN 978-1-911297-28-4

Also available by Tasmina Perry:
Daddy's Girls
Gold Diggers
Guilty Pleasures
Original Sin
Kiss Heaven Goodbye
Private Lives
Perfect Strangers
The Proposal
Deep Blue Sea
The Last Kiss Goodbye
The House on Sunset Lake
The Pool House
Friend of the Family

www.tasminaperry.com

The Singles Table

Tasmina Perry

Sunflower Press

Prologue

The Wedding of Miss Vanessa Louise Farringdon

&

Mr Timothy Michael Jameson

Seating plan version 22

Table 14

Mr. Adam Stowe

Miss Sophie Wallis

Mr. Ali Malik

Ms. Lucy Cotton

Mr. Paul Hobbs

Mr. Hugo Crabb

Ms. Zara Stephens

Dr. Cherie Akinowa

THERE WAS SOMETHING wrong. Vanessa stared down at the chart, running a finger down the list of names.

'Oh no,' she said, trying to swallow.

Tim glanced up. He was sitting back on his chair, chai latte poised in one hand, thumb scrolling with the other. All around them in the café were thirty-something men in similar poses, blanketed in Sunday papers and croissant crumbs, wives negotiating with toddlers or flicking through the homes section. As the late spring sunshine slanted in across lime-washed floorboards, a feeling of warm contentment floated through the room like dandelion clocks. And why wouldn't it? This was the Belvedere, Wandsworth's finest brunch spot, bang in the centre of *everything*. There was turmeric frittata on the menu and all was right in the world.

Only it wasn't.

'How did I miss this?' Vanessa locked eyes with her fiancé.

Finally sensing that his attention was required, Tim craned his neck to look at the seating chart spread out on the table, the corners weighted down by local honey and reclaimed glassware.

'The Singles Table?' he said. 'What's the problem?'

The problem, thought Vanessa, was precisely that. The problem was that Tim didn't think it was a problem.

'Can't you see?' said Vanessa, tapping a polished nail on the paper. 'Boy, girl, boy, girl, boy, *boy*.'

Tim showed her his even teeth, recently whitened by Dr. Patergee in readiness for the big day.

'Boy, boy? So? We're modern,' he said.

'Not funny, Tim,' said Vanessa.

Tim slumped back and made a flapping motion with his hand. 'So move them,' he said.

Vanessa curled her hands under the table, rubbing her engagement rock like a genie's lamp.

'I can't 'just' move them,' she hissed. 'You know

why.'

Tim looked unmoved.

'Your friend Ali, that's why,' said Vanessa, lowering her voice. 'Because of his... *wandering hands.*'

Tim gave a low, dismissive laugh and Vanessa pulled air in through her nose. He'd been like this with the flowers and the invitations too. If Vanessa hadn't pushed him, Tim's ushers would have been wearing their *own ties*.

'Why don't you move Jessica from our table,' Tim was saying. 'She's single, isn't she?'

Vanessa barked out a laugh.

'You *are* joking? Jessica is one of my *actual* friends.'

Tim looked blank.

'If I put her on the Singles Table, I might as well be saying to Jess that I have no confidence in her ever finding a husband.'

Tim sipped his chai. 'But she could meet someone there. Isn't that what the Singles Table is for? How about Adam?'

'Adam.' She repeated, her voice flat.

'Alright, not Adam – someone else. Hugo?'

'I love Hugo, but he's hardly husband material is he? Plus he's at least twice Jessica's height.'

'What's wrong with that? It's a wedding, Vee, not some Nazi breeding programme.'

Vanessa pressed her lips together. *Men think differently about weddings.* That's what her mother had said – no, that's what she had warned her about the morning of their announcement. *And he'll change, darling.*

She turned back to the window. *If only.* The Belvedere really did have the best view of the common, all those happy weekend families strolling in convoy, Nunas and Babyzens gliding past like yachts in the Solent.

And they were part of it now – Tim and Vee, their new neighbours. The terrace on Rackman Avenue was theirs at last, paper stripped, every blank wall a Little Greene patchwork of sap green, calamine and French Grey. Vanessa had known it would be perfect the moment the estate agent had unlocked the door. Those original tiles in the hallway, the untouched dado rails in the living room and the cutest nursery right at the top of the stairs. Because a nursery was the next step, wasn't it? First the wedding, then the honeymoon, then the tiny moulded feet of Grace or Beatrice or Katie. Maybe even Clara at a push, but Imogen bloody Peters had called her stupid yapping Shih Tzu 'Clara', hadn't she?

She glanced at Tim, hunched over his iPhone, his face as creased as his Crew shirt. Had *he* picked out names? Had he ever thought beyond 'I will'? For one sharp moment Vanessa considered what her husband-to-be wanted from their life together – and came up empty.

'Tim?'

'What?' he said, not looking up. She let it hang in the air. Tim didn't like silences.

'What?' he repeated, his blue eyes cutting her way.

'Are you alright?' said Vanessa. 'You've been very

quiet.'

He shrugged, eyes down again. 'Catching up on the cricket.'

'No, I mean for the past few weeks. Since all this.' She gestured at the seating plan. Say it. *Say it.*

'You do still want to get married?' She tried to say it lightly, but it came out in a rush, slightly shrill and she could feel spots flaring in the centres of her cheeks, like a child playing dress-up.

'What? Of course I do.' He was looking at her now, but Vanessa saw his eyes flit back to the seating plan and a penny dropped with an almost audible 'chink'.

'The wedding? The *wedding* is the problem?' she said quietly, her voice now audibly wobbling.

Tim smiled. 'Don't be daft.' And there it was: that glassy, fixed look.

The look she had seen on his face before. Tim Jameson the ad man, the slick manipulator of words and emotions: but unable to lie to save his life.

'Just tell me.'

Tim sighed and put his phone down, carefully. 'Look Vee, it's not about us…'

He trailed off and looked at the table, staring at that stupid little hourglass egg-timer they gave you to make sure you didn't over-steep your orange pekoe. Vanessa felt as if she were one of those grains of sand, stuck, hanging in the air. Neither here nor there. Her future a coin toss at best.

'All this wedding stuff,' said Tim. 'It's just…'

Tim took her hand, the platinum band of her engagement ring digging into her knuckle.

'I want to be *married* to you, Vee. I just could do without the hoo-ha.'

'Hoo-ha?' she said, her words cracking. 'Our wedding is "hoo-ha" now?'

'Yes!' He was smiling, but Vanessa's face felt rigid, fragile. Spun glass.

'You know what my ideal wedding would be?' he said, squeezing her fingers. 'Just you and me on a beach. No place settings, no cufflinks, just us swearing our love or whatever you do – then that's it, we get on with our lives together. Doesn't that sound good?'

Vanessa nodded, because she could tell that was the correct answer.

But it didn't sound good. It sounded awful. Because Vanessa loved the wedding. She loved the place settings and the co-ordinated ties and auditioning the organist and sampling the canapés. And she had loved being a bride-to-be, had loved being caught in that golden Polaroid moment when everything was possible, every path untrodden. Because what *was* after 'I will'? What happened when the confetti had been swept away? What would they say to each other? Who would they be?

'All I want is for us to…' said Tim, turning back towards the table, reaching for his phone, his hand catching the rim of his latte glass. It hung for a half-second then fell, the cinnamon-dusted milk spilling across the seating chart.

'Ohshitshitshit!' he hissed, grabbing Vanessa's blush pink cardigan from the chair to swipe the foam from the plan.

'Tim, stop! It's cashmere!'

But it was too late, at least for the table plan, which was now a mushed ball of paper, grey milk and matted wool.

'Sorry Vee,' he said, his head sunk into his chest. At least he meant it.

'Doesn't matter,' she said, looking at what was left of the Table 24 plan. 'It'll be fine.'

But Vanessa wasn't sure it would be. She wasn't sure at all.

Chapter One

ADAM JOLTED AWAKE, his head thudding against the train window. Eyes squinted against the sudden light, he tried to focus on the green countryside scrolling by outside. Rasping a hand over his chin, he peered out at the blurred hedges, sheep hunched into the landscape. *Where the hell am I?* he muttered, taking off his headphones.

'Milbourne'.

Looking up, Adam saw the amused smile of an attractive redhead opposite. Green eyes, a sharp bob and the kind of chunky rings meant to indicate 'interesting' or 'poetic'. She looked back down at her phone.

'I'm sorry, what?' said Adam, pulling the buds from his ears.

'Milbourne,' she repeated. 'We've just left Milbourne. I didn't want to wake you.'

Adam rolled his shoulders and there was an audible crack in his neck.

'Sleeping like a baby, huh?' he said, massaging the spot and trying not to grimace.

'Snoring, actually.'

'Oh.'

Adam shivered and tried to gather his thoughts. Where was Milbourne? How long had he been asleep? And what was the likelihood this girl might be open to a spur-of-the-moment invitation to a wedding at a country house hotel? Adam looked at her. She really was pretty.

'Where does it stop?' asked Adam. 'The train?'

The girl didn't look up from her phone.

'Depends. Where are you going?'

'A wedding. Friend of mine. We were at school together, but I haven't seen him in a while.'

'Why not?'

The girl finally looked up. It was a serious question.

'He went off to Uni, made new friends. I had a job in London. I suppose we drifted apart.' Adam shrugged, trying to make it sound as if this happened recently, not almost twenty years ago. She didn't ask, so Adam filled in the gap.

'I'm a music journalist. I write for *Cream.*'

Her face remained blank and Adam tried not to look as disappointed as he felt. Surely she wasn't *that* young.

'You know, *Cream.* The rock magazine…' he began.

'Huh.' Her eyes dropped back to her phone.

Adam took a deep breath. There had been a time, not so very long ago – really not that long – when the words 'music journalist' had been like catnip to girls. Adam had been cool, connected, *dazzling*. When he walked into one of those sweaty, black-painted indie venues he would see girls whisper to each other: *there he is*. Adam Stowe, he's *that writer*. But recently that had all changed. Or maybe it wasn't so recently, now he thought about it. Adam knew the girl was right: no one read magazines any more. Adam might as well have said he was a chimney sweep.

'So what do you do?' he asked.

'Instagram,' she said. He waited, but that was all. He felt the gap stretch wider between them but wasn't quite ready to give up yet.

'I'm DJing at the wedding, actually.'

'Why?'

It was Adam's turn to look blank. Wasn't being an international DJ one of the top career choices for today's hipsters, just a few notches below reality TV star and social media influencer?

'I mean, why do you need a DJ?' said the girl. 'Why not just put on a playlist?'

'Because…'

'Why do they even call it DJing?' she continued, as if she was pondering a difficult philosophical question.

Adam coughed. 'Well, DJ stands for "Disc Jockey" – someone who plays discs…' But even as the words left his mouth, he knew the full horror of what the girl was going to say.

'Discs?'

This girl was mid-twenties. Tops. So actually, the maths added up; by the time she would have been old enough to care about music, vinyl was long gone and even CDs were being replaced by downloads. She might have spotted a reissued Blondie album in Urban

Outfitters, but there was a decent chance she had never seen a single or didn't even know what a *45* was.

'Anyway,' he said, rushing on. 'The wedding's at Haslop Hall, but tonight I'm going to see Belasco at that festival in...'

'Haslop Hall?' That brightened her up. 'That big house in Playborough?'

'Yes...well, I think so.'

'Then you'd better get off, hadn't you?'

His eyes darted left. He'd been so engrossed in trying to impress her, he'd missed the fact that the train was slowing, sliding into a station. *Playborough* read the sign.

He jumped up, thumping his head on the luggage rack. *Great.* So cool.

'Listen,' he said. 'If you're around tonight, maybe I can get you in to see the band?'

For a moment, Adam feared he might have to explain what a 'band' was. It was obvious she wasn't interested, but for some reason, Adam couldn't let it go. It was suddenly extremely important that this total stranger find him funny and interesting and desirable. He felt like he was attempting to audition for RADA while being engulfed in quicksand.

'*Playborough station, this is Playborough. Please ensure...*'

Fumbling, Adam pulled out a business card, and gave it to her: *Adam Stowe, Editor at Large.*

'Give me a bell?'

'You'd better go,' she said, glancing at the card, then out at the station. He scraped his arm as he clunked his holdall and record case down from the luggage rack, trying not to groan as he jockeyed it towards the door.

He looked up at the train as it began to move, knowing – just knowing – that the pretty girl would have already forgotten him. And yes: she was laughing on the phone, not looking his way. It was as if he was invisible.

'Give me a bell,' he muttered, shaking his head. He could have been talking in iambic pentameter. His shoulders rounded, Adam followed the exit signs, climbing up a flight of concrete stairs that gave directly onto a road. No barriers, not even a ticket office. Playborough was only a fifty-minute journey away from Waterloo, but it felt like another country, another time.

He looked up and down the two-lane tarmac strip: nothing in either direction, just unkempt embankment and something flat, which might once have been a badger.

'Oi! Clooney!'

Adam turned at the shout, which was followed by a long blare of a car horn. A blond man was leaning out of the window of a shiny black 4x4. Adam's frown turned to a wide grin.

'Tim!'

Adam had texted his friend when he was leaving Waterloo but hadn't for a second expected a lift to the hotel.

'Who else, loser?' he grinned.

Adam threw his stuff in the back of the car and slid

into the passenger seat, immediately struck by the fresh smell and the pristine finish. Cream leather, walnut trim. No empty crisp bags, no coffee cups; it was like Tim had driven it off the showroom forecourt.

'Wow, nice. Is this new?'

'Don't take the piss,' said Tim, flipping down his sunglasses and gunning the engine. 'I've got the new Tesla on order. You need something decent if you're doing that nightmare commute every day.'

Adam nodded vaguely, thinking about his own Lynx-and-sweat scented tube grind from Walthamstow to the outer reaches of Hammersmith where Cream's publishers had recently re-located. He ran a fascinated finger along the polished dashboard.

'You drive this into the City every day?'

'The City? Didn't I tell you? We've moved out to Canary Wharf. Everyone's there these days.'

Everyone. Adam looked away, pressing his lips together. What he'd said to the girl on the train was true. He and Tim had drifted apart and Adam thought you could trace a good portion of their estrangement back to that one word. *Everyone.* After school, after Adam had joined the staff of *Cream*, while Tim had gone to Bristol University and fallen in with a posh crowd who were only interested in what 'everyone' else was doing. 'You have to come skiing, everyone's going.' 'Did you go to Cassie's party? Everyone was there.' Everyone it seemed, except him.

'So, how's it going? How's work?'

Tim was creative director for Glasshouse, a high-end advertising company that positioned itself as cutting-edge, but whose clients seemed to be exclusively corporate: Ross Oil, Zenosoft computing, many of the big banks.

'Great actually,' he said. 'Had our best-ever year, which means a nice bonus. Just as well, with the cost of the honeymoon.'

'Congratulations, mate,' said Adam. 'And are you still enjoying it?'

Tim glanced across.

'Does anyone really enjoy their work? Jonty's been doing contract law for fifteen years. Can't imagine that's too stimulating. But as he says, "just look at the balance at the end of the month."'

Adam suppressed a grimace. *Jonty.* Jonty was one of Tim's Uni 'pals', the worst example of the sort Tim had taken up with at Bristol. Adam didn't have anything against rich or posh people: after all, pop music was littered with public school alums. No Bedales, no Lily Allen, no Marlborough, no Nick Drake. And no Joe Strummer either, which would obviously be a deep, deep tragedy. But Jonty? Tim's friends? They wouldn't be able to name a single Clash song. Like, *not a single one.*

'So, who's coming?' said Adam. 'To the wedding.'

Tim glanced across. 'No one from school, if that's what you mean. Thank God.'

He nodded in agreement. While Adam didn't fit into Tim's new world, the one thing they had always agreed on was the joy of having left their roots behind. Adam couldn't speak for Tim, but he had barely seen anyone else from Harling Comprehensive since that blessed afternoon he'd walked through the gates and torn off his tie. Adam's idea had been to set it on fire like Jimi Hendrix, but his disposable lighter had failed to do much more than scorch the end, so he'd thrown it over a hedge instead. Embarrassingly, it was returned to his mother two days later – there was a name-tag sewn on the back and due to the world-class standard of bullying at Harling Comp, the local residents were used to having things thrown into their gardens.

'Actually, Ali's coming,' said Tim, opening the sun-roof.

'Ali Malik? Really?'

Tim glanced at him.

'Why not? You've seen how well he's doing in Silicon Valley?'

'But doesn't Vanessa hate him?'

'No, why?'

'I thought he tried to cop off with her.'

Tim waved a hand.

'Ali tries to cop off with everyone.'

'But at the engagement party?'

Adam saw Tim's jaw clench.

'If I ruled out all my friends who might embarrass me, I wouldn't have anyone on my side of the church, would I?'

Adam tried not to react. *It's his weekend, remember?* Instead he reached over and flicked on the car's music system. Immediately the car was filled with swelling violins and the rumble of kettle drums. Adam stared in disbelief at the glowing read-out on the dash.

'*Classic FM?*' he said.

'Vee likes it,' said Tim, stabbing a finger to turn it off.

He looked at Tim, flashing onto the memory of the two of them at seventeen, queuing in the rain outside some indie dive, their Saturday job money pooled for tickets and one shared pint, the anticipation of the night ahead the biggest buzz imaginable. Music had been everything back then, the glue that held them together, the script for their dialogue, *everything*. Adam sighed to himself. It wasn't Tim's fault, not really. How could you hold onto the 'real you' when life wore you down with its drip-drip-drip, day by day? And it wasn't as if Adam's rock'n'roll lifestyle had brought him any particular happiness lately – or even the smug satisfaction of ideological purity. The music industry was home to plenty of Porsche-driving idiots too.

'So how was the stag?' asked Adam, keen to change the subject.

'Pretty good,' shrugged Tim. 'Shame you couldn't make it.'

Adam could have made it. He just couldn't afford it. The stag had been held at a golf resort in Marbella and he wasn't about to spend his meagre savings swinging a nine iron or whatever it was you did in those places.

'So why don't we do it properly?' said Adam suddenly, turning in his seat.

'Do what properly?'

'The stag. Let's do it the traditional way.'

'What? When?'

'Tonight of course. The Stag Night is supposed to be held the night before the wedding, isn't it? Your actual "last night of freedom", not two months before at some flash corporate hotel.'

'It was very nice actually.'

'Yeah, but… come on, this could be epic.'

Tim paused.

'In Playborough?' he said dubiously. 'Not exactly Vegas, is it?'

'But that's the point, isn't it? It's old school. Cider in the bus shelter, smoking banana skins, sniffing Tipp-Ex. Like the old days.'

Tim looked at him meaningfully.

'The old days were shit, Adam.'

Adam laughed. 'I'm *joking*, Timbo. Look, Belasco are playing up the road at a festival at Malvern Castle tonight. Declan, the singer? He's a mate. I can get us all on the guest list. What do you think?'

He glanced over at his friend, hoping to see a flicker of admiration.

'Belasco? Are they still going?'

'And you're into street-level grime all of a sudden? Come on, what else are we going to do the night before your wedding? A couple of G&Ts in the hotel bar, then an early night? This is your *actual* last night of singledom, Tim.'

Tim puckered his lips, obviously mulling it over.

'Why not?'

Adam raised an eyebrow and laughed.

'Why not? Well, Vanessa won't approve, for one.'

Tim flashed him a quiet smile.

'As you say, I'm not married quite yet.'

Adam slapped him on the shoulder, making the car swerve dangerously.

'That's the spirit. I'll check in, have a quick shower – then we'll break out the mankinis.'

Chapter Two

'Danger: Ducks crossing'.

SOPHIE FELT HERSELF tense as Christa turned her battered Renault into the car park. The sign – artfully weathered, paint peeling – had a picture of a family of ducks in silhouette and the slightly skew-whiff subtitle nailed below: 'Slow down, ducklings ahead'.

'Where's the ducks?' asked Hattie, Christa's four-year-old, struggling to peer out of the steamed-up window. 'I like ducks.'

'I'm not sure there actually are any ducks, darling,' said Christa as the car bumped across the pothole-strewn car park. 'I think it's to let us know the hotel is all cutesy and quaint.'

The Swan did actually look pretty boho and stylish from the front. Bow windows with honeysuckle curling around the pastel-painted frames; there was even a dovecote with cooing beaks poking out. It was charming, you had to give it that. Maybe the weekend wouldn't be the complete disaster that Sophie had been imagining.

'Now have you got everything?' said Christa,

yanking on the handbrake. Sophie's younger sister was, by nature, erratic and disorganised – you only had to glance at the inside of her car, decorated as it was by a thick layer of snack wrappers, paperwork and Hattie's discarded socks – but when it came to the welfare of her family Christa was laser-sighted.

'I'm 37 years old, Chris,' said Sophie, glancing across. 'And this is not my first day of school. I *am* a grown woman.'

Christa nodded, but she didn't look convinced.

'Can I go to the wedding with Auntie Sophie?' said Hattie hopefully. Hattie was going through a hardcore Disney addiction and had spent most of the journey from London filling Sophie in on the various wedding gowns of cartoon princesses. She had a well-loved Barbie version of Ariel – sea green dress – clutched in her grubby hand.

'No, sweetie,' said Christa firmly. 'We're just dropping Soph here, then we've got to get back for Theatrebugs, remember?'

Hattie considered this. 'Will you bring me some cake?' she asked.

'Of course, munchkin. And I promise I'll take lots of photos of the wedding dress,' said Sophie, although she was secretly hoping it looked like an over-filled sack. This seemed to satisfy Hattie and she went back to brushing her Barbie's now-threadbare nylon hair.

'And you've asked for an accessible room?' said Christa.

'Yes,' smiled Sophie, rolling her eyes. 'I made a note on the booking and I called up to confirm it.'

Christa peered at her, one of her 'incisive' looks. 'You're really sure you're up for this?'

Sophie let out a breath. 'Chris, it's just a wedding. A ceremony in a church, a nice meal and maybe a jazz band. There'll probably be a few old friends there from uni. I promise I'll avoid any competitive jostle for the bride's bouquet and I will be here waiting for you, after breakfast on Sunday.'

Christa looked as if she was weighing up what to say, but Sophie had a pretty good idea what was going through her sister's mind, anyway.

'I just don't know why you want to put yourself through this, Soph,' said Christa finally.

Sophie could see the concern in the sister's face and it made her heart swell. The two of them hadn't always seen eye-to-eye – in fact it had been quite the opposite in their teenage years, when Sophie had always been the high-flier, the girl with the perfect grades, the cups, trophies and medals, while Christa had been the rebel, the arty one, the slacker smoking behind the science block. But since Sophie's accident, Christa had been fiercely protective, taking up the slack, being cheerleader, PA and therapist to Sophie all in one, and now they had a fierce, tight bond between them. It had almost been worth it. Almost.

'Look,' she said, with more confidence than she felt. 'You're the one who's been telling me for years that I've got to get back into the game, to hook up with old friends and start living.' She raised a hand towards the pub. 'Well, here I am.'

'Sure,' said Christa, with a cynical look. 'I'm just

not sure that your ex-boyfriend's wedding is the best place to start. Of course I want you to find closure and move on, the question is, *can* you get past it?'

'Past Tim or past the accident?'

'Both.'

For the first time, Sophie noticed how tired her sister was beginning to look: faint lilac crescents were under her eyes and there was a thick double frown line between her unplucked brows. Christa already had her hands full, spinning plates as a working mother and wife to Annoyingly Handsome Dan. It had been so good of her to drive Sophie all the way out here, and she had no desire to add to her burden, and keep her at The Swan longer than necessary.

'Look. You'd better get off to Theatrebugs,' she said quickly.

They got out of the car, took her case out of the boot, and Hattie hopped out to say her goodbyes.

'You have a good time, okay?' sighed Christa, pulling Sophie into a hug. Just the right amount of pressure – not too tight so that it hurt, but enough to tell her that she loved her. 'Say hello to Tim. And wish him well for me.'

Sophie raised one eyebrow. The last time the groom's name had come up in conversation, Christa had expressed a desire to 'punch him in the nuts'.

Christa didn't miss the point.

'Well, it *is* his wedding day,' she said. 'Even if he is a toad.'

SOPHIE STOOD IN the car park and waved as Christa pulled away, feeling very alone. What she'd said back there: 'I'm a grown woman', it was a half-truth at best. Christa was a grown woman. She had a food processor and a milkman and a subscription to *Newsweek*. Sophie lived in the converted garage of their parents' house.

'Come on, you can do this,' she muttered, psyching herself up as she headed for the pub. She had made the decision to come and now she had to go through with it. Her suitcase bumped and bucked behind her as she dragged it along the stone path. It was either missing a wheel or Sophie had one leg shorter than the other – and she was pretty sure they were both the same length. They measured those sorts of things in hospital: they measured *everything* in hospital, from how much you weigh to the volume of one breath, which Sophie had always found rather poetic, especially considering how disgusting the tube tasted. At 37, many parts of Sophie were slipping, but aside from an imperceptible limp, her legs were inch-perfect: she was sure of that.

She made a mental note to buy a new case. As a travel agent – or rather an 'experience concierge' as her boss Selena insisted on referring to her minions – she possibly should have something better than a battered twenty-year-old Samsonite. Caroline in her office had a beautiful cream Globetrotter case for her many glamorous fact-finding trips to exotic resorts. Then again, Sophie rarely left the office. The commute from Wimbledon to Putney three times a week was as much as she could stand: the idea of sitting still on an aeroplane was enough to bring on a stress headache.

Much like now, she thought, as she banged through the doorway and into the lobby.

At first glance, The Swan was your standard Country English pub with rooms. It had slate floors and a dark-wood bar, but there were self-conscious style tweaks here too: the stuffed squirrel trapped under a bell jar and a stag's head above the dartboard suggesting a recent refurb by an interior designer.

'May I help?' said a thin woman, with a severe black fringe and matching Slavic accent.

'Yes, I'm checking in. Sophie Wallis.'

The woman snapped an ancient-looking computer monitor towards her; hopefully all part of the retro vibe.

'Wallis…' she said, her pencil-thin finger clicking on the mouse, click-click-click. Sophie stared at the iPhone tattoo on the girl's wrist and imagined her trying to explain it in twenty years' time.

'Wallis, Wallis… no.'

She looked up, peering at Sophie suspiciously.

'What was the name, again?'

'Sophie *Wallis*.'

She bent closer to the screen.

'Sorry, here we are. We have you in Room 12. Nice quiet room in the eaves.'

'The eaves?'

The woman smiled at her, revealing a dot of red lipstick on her front tooth.

'Don't worry, the ceilings are quite high, lots of room.' She paused, considering. 'Unless you want to sit up in bed.'

'Actually, I did ask for an accessible room,' said Sophie, feeling horribly English. Nice girls didn't make a fuss.

'Accessible?'

The woman leant over the desk, her narrow eyes running up and down Sophie, then turned back to the screen.

'No note about that on the system,' she said, clicking liberally on the mouse. 'We do have accessible rooms but they're for people with *disabilities*.'

Sophie turned to follow the woman's gaze: a mobility scooter was sitting in the corridor.

'We have someone staying here with *no legs*,' she whispered for emphasis. 'And we are fully booked this weekend. The wedding, you see.'

Sophie took a deep breath.

'Do you have a lift?'

The woman's expression did not change. 'No,' she said, holding out a key attached to a block of wood.

Sophie manoeuvred her case through a side-door towards the stairs leading to the inn's rooms. She stood at the bottom, staring up. *Fifteen stairs*, she counted, feeling her heart sink.

After more than a decade of rehab, Sophie could walk fine. No four-minute miles, but a stroll to Waitrose she could manage. Stairs, however? Still not her friends. She could feel the ache in her back just looking at them. Spotting a door marked 'Ladies', Sophie pushed through. A splash of water on her face might perk her up before the ascent.

As she caught sight of herself in the mirror, she

groaned. Harassed from the journey, her long chestnut hair was sticking out at all angles, her face was pink and blotchy and her make-up had slipped off her face somewhere along the A3.

'And what *are* you wearing?' she whispered to herself, eyeing the dress and blazer she had bought online the week before.

The look she'd been after was Wimbledon Week Pippa Middleton: clean, sporty, successful. Instead, she looked like an air hostess just after evacuation drill.

'Fifteen years', she said, shaking her head, trying not to give in to the wave of hopelessness that was looming like a tsunami.

Fifteen bloody years, that's all I had to prepare.

Lying in her hospital bed, the thought that had kept her going had been fantasising about what would happen the next time she met Tim Jameson. Tim, her college sweetheart. Tim, the man who had dumped her in hospital. Tim, the groom at tomorrow's wedding.

She had always imagined what she would be wearing when she next met her startled, regretful ex-boyfriend. She had planned the witty comebacks she'd use to cut him down to size. And she had imagined him begging her to come back. In these endlessly nuanced scenarios, Tim would look at Sophie and immediately know that he'd made a mistake leaving her, because she was gorgeous, successful, connected and famous – any of the above. Which was why she had chosen the dress and jacket. Sophie had imagined herself looking like one of those kick-ass super-together women they feature in *Harper's Bazaar*. One glance at her and Tim would think 'there goes a woman with a second home in the Cotswolds and an amazing backhand.'

Instead, Sophie looked like a woman in her late thirties who worked in a travel agent, twenty years after people had stopped going to travel agents.

'Sophie?'

Sophie jumped, looking up. A woman in a brightly patterned dress was standing behind her.

'Sophie, it *is* you!'

In a rush, Sophie realised this woman was Tim's mother, Jennifer.

'Jenny,' she muttered, cheeks flushing. 'Just arrived. Long journey, been sitting down too long.'

She felt awkward, but not quite as awkward as their last encounter a few weeks earlier by South Kensington tube.

Sophie had just been to meet her old friend Emma at the V&A, which she did every couple of months, and had been in the queue for the ticket machines on the way home when Jennifer had spotted her.

'This must be fate,' Jennifer had said sweeping her up into a hug. 'Tim's been trying to track you down for weeks. He's been desperate to invite you to the wedding but didn't know how to find you.'

Utterly thrown by the news that her ex was even engaged, Sophie had blushed and stuttered and exchanged contact details, then spent the next week obsessing over Jennifer's words: Tim had been *tracking her down*? He was *dying* to invite her? To his wedding? What did it all mean? It was only when the stiff white scalloped invitation had dropped onto her mat that Sophie was finally sure she hadn't hallucinated the whole thing.

'How are you, Jenny?' Sophie said now. Here in The Swan's ladies' room, it sounded as forced as it felt: Tim's mother was the last person she wanted to see. What Sophie wanted – no, what she *needed*, was to get to her room, get out of these ridiculous clothes and try to stop her hands from shaking.

'How am I?' said Jennifer with brittle laugh. 'Anxious if I'm honest. It's not every day you send your eldest son off into the world.'

Sophie knew how she felt. She might have talked a good game in front of her sister but Sophie was highly apprehensive about the entire weekend and had surprised herself that she had even got this far.

'So how *is* Tim?' replied Sophie. She tried to sound casual, but was surprised to feel her heart quicken at the mention of his name. 'He's not too nervous, I hope?'

'Oh please,' said Jennifer. 'Timothy lives for moments like this. Everyone looking at him, paying attention. He was that way when he was a toddler standing on top of the climbing frame shouting, "look at me, Mummy! Look how high I got!" He hasn't changed a bit.'

'Well, I'm sure it will all go smoothly on the day,' said Sophie with a nervous laugh.

'Oh yes,' nodded Jennifer. 'Vanessa has made sure of that. She has spent the last six months matching flower petals to the place cards. Nothing has been left to chance.'

'I suppose I'll see you tomorrow at the church?' said Sophie, backing away, hands feeling for her suitcase.

Jennifer frowned.

'But you'll be up at the house tonight?'

'The house?'

'Haslop Hall. Where the reception is being held tomorrow. Except tonight Vee's having the bridal shower there or whatever they call it these days; it was a "Hen Night" in my day. Everyone is going to be there.'

Everyone except me, thought Sophie.

'As I say, I've had a long journey. My back, you know…' she said.

Mention of her injury always brought on a sympathetic look – head tilted to one side, a murmur of 'oh yes, I totally understand'. After all, what was the point in having a catastrophic, life-changing accident if you couldn't use it to get out of social engagements? But there was no concerned look from Jennifer, no tilt – and Sophie remembered too late that Mrs Jameson had spent three decades as a schoolteacher. She could undoubtably spot a fake sick-note at fifty paces.

'You don't get off that easily,' said the older woman. 'Besides which, Vee's party will be dull as ditchwater and I don't want to be sitting there on my own, listening to them blather on about diets and pedicures and how hard it is to find a decent vegan caterer.'

Despite herself, Sophie laughed.

'I'll collect you in an hour and will drive you myself,' said Jennifer firmly. 'We'll stay just long enough to eat a velvet cupcake but you must promise not to leave me with Vanessa's mother.'

Jennifer's expression softened as she touched Sophie's arm.

Sophie had the unsettling feeling that Jennifer could see right inside her head. Or maybe all teachers were like that, an evolutionary development to help survive teenagers.

'I know you probably don't want to speak to half of those people,' said Jennifer kindly. 'But isn't it better you face them tonight – with me there as your wing-man – than to be overwhelmed by it all tomorrow at the wedding?'

It did make sense, Sophie had to admit, but it was rather like choosing to have your fingernails pulled out tonight in order to save your toenails from the torturers tomorrow.

'Believe me, I don't want to go either,' added Jennifer. 'I'm missing *Bake Off* for this.'

Sophie sighed.

'Fine, I suppose you're right.'

'Great,' said Jennifer, clapping her hands. 'Now you go and make yourself beautiful and I'll see you downstairs at six-thirty. How does that sound?'

It sounded horrible, thought Sophie, forcing her way back through the door. It sounded like hell on earth.

Chapter Three

Adam turned left and right, jiggling his key impatiently. 'Room 6, room 7... room 11? Where's room bloody eight?'

The twisting corridors of the inn seemed to defy logic. Lit only by thirty-watt bulbs in dusty shades, they were an obstacle course of sudden steps and hidden sharp-cornered tables, like stumbling through a funfair haunted house without the ghosts.

Maybe if he hadn't booked the cheapest room he wouldn't be fumbling around in the dark; perhaps The Swan had a Royal Suite with wide, well-lit corridors and his 'n' hers clawfoot baths; if it did, then Tim would almost certainly be in it. But there was another reason Adam was stumbling about in the semi-darkness. He had also requested 'a quiet room' away from the smug families with their double buggies and travel cots and the endless grizzling through the paper-thin walls. Adam didn't want that sort of distraction, especially not when he was 'entertaining'. Which was all just a matter of time, obviously.

Adam smiled to himself. He was usually cynical about all the 'death us do part' stuff, but he was secretly excited about the weekend. Bridesmaids in cocktail dresses, flushed on romance and free prosecco, dancing about as Adam spun the tunes. It was going to be epic.

'That's if I ever get out of here,' he muttered. Taking a random right turn, he saw a sign pointing up a steep flight of stairs. He craned his neck to read the door numbers. Room 8 and Room 12. Pure logic. Squeezing up the narrow stairway bumping his bag behind him, he opened the door.

'Great.'

It was exactly the sort of room you'd see in a horror movie full of sinister dolls and possibly the malevolent spirit of a murdered nanny.

There were no dolls here, just a built-in wardrobe and an ancient-looking chest of drawers with a flowery ceramic jug perched on the top, presumably to brighten up the place.

It wasn't working.

Adam dropped his bag and record box and crossed to the window. If he leaned forward all the way, he could just see the tops of some trees and big patch of sky as grey and flat as cement.

'What were you expecting?' he sighed. 'Miami Beach?'

At least there was some natural light. Adam had recently stayed in a hotel which had the curtains permanently sewn shut to disguise the fact that behind them was a smooth plastered wall. It was hard to believe that on his first day at *Cream*, Adam had been given an assignment to fly with soft metal legends Def Leppard to Canada in their private jet and the editor had taken him to one side and warned him: 'the life of a journalist might give you a taste for a life you can never afford'. Recently, cut-price hotel rooms like this were far more common than private jets. Not that he was planning on spending much time here, lounging in his bath robe.

'Let's get this party started,' he whispered to himself, holding up his phone: one bar, which was one bar more than he'd been expecting.

He scrolled through his numbers and stopped at 'DeclanSuperStar' – *the* Declan, Declan Hawsley, singer with indie pop stalwarts Belasco. Adam could still picture the moment he'd tapped the singer's number into the phone, high on bonhomie and free backstage booze, schoolgirl giggly that an *actual pop star* was swapping numbers with him. People assumed that musicians and journos were always hanging out together, but outside of formal interview situations, it almost never happened. The world of music was governed by a rigid structure, with the pop hack marginally above the level of the fans queuing at the stage door. Even the guys providing catering backstage were closer to the artists than the writers, especially if they served edible vegan food: all rock stars liked to believe they were spiritual, even if they were in Motley Crue.

DeclanSuperStar's number rang once, then went to message.

He took a deep breath. 'Hey Dec, it's Adam. Adam Stowe. From *Cream. Cream* Magazine. Listen mate, I'm in the area with a few mates tonight. Thought we might swing by for the show, maybe hook up afterwards if you're not shooting off? Can you put… uh, four on the list? Give me a bell, yeah?'

Give me a bell. Again. He quickly left his number, repeating it twice, just in case Dec had a new phone, then hung up before he could say anything else idiotic. Sitting down on the bed, his eyes darted towards the mini-bar, before telling himself he couldn't afford it. He had just remembered the brandy in his bag when the phone rang.

Adam jumped and scrambled for the phone buzzing against his thigh.

'Declan, that was quick,' he said. 'I wasn't sure if you'd be soundchecking…'

'It's Tony. Who the hell's Declan?'

Adam felt his heart sink, immediately recognising the voice. Tony Robb, entertainment editor on the *Sunday Chronicle*. Tony had started out at *Cream* at the same time as Adam, but when Adam had been hanging out with musos and hacks at venues in Camden and Islington, Tony had been in the wine bars and clubs of Soho, cosying up to TV people and advertising execs, amusing them with his insider gossip, flattering them, oiling their tiny wheels. Which, irritatingly, had worked. Tony had landed a column on a Sunday supplement, which had led to a presenting slot on a Channel 4 youth show – and finally to his current gig on the *Chronicle*, gleefully breaking all the latest scandals rolling in from the world of show business. It was like watching a Vegas magician make an elephant levitate: you really had no idea how it happened.

'Listen Tone, I'm at a wedding in the middle of nowhere. It's a miracle I've got enough signal to talk to you. What's up?'

Tony gave an exaggerated intake of breath.

'I'm after a quote about *Cream*,' said Tony.

'What for?' said Adam, opening his bag and rummaging around inside for the brandy.

'You don't know?' said Tony.

'Know what?'

'It's folded.'

'What's folded?' Adam said it slowly, trying to process the information.

'*Cream*, you numbskull. It's closed, shut up shop. They've just sent out a press release. This month's issue is the last one. Ever.'

There was a pause during which Adam tried and failed to swallow.

'I've not been in the office today.' His voice was barely a croak. 'I'd heard rumours, of course.'

That part was a lie. He'd heard nothing of the sort. Privately he'd wondered how long *Cream* could survive given that the sales figures were just a fraction of what they'd been in the heady days of awards ceremonies and lavish lunches at Quaglino's, but still…

'I know. Amazing it's taken this long, really,' said Tony. 'But I thought I could get a quote from you. You're an insider, you've been there forever. Why do you think the magazine went down?'

Adam could imagine Tony sitting in his chrome

and glass office, gloating smile, stubby fingers pressing the 'record' button on some flash digital audio device.

'Adam? You there?' said Tony. 'What do you think?'

'What do I think?' repeated Adam, looking down at the bottle in his hand, head swimming. What he thought – what he *really* thought – was that *Cream* was just like every other magazine on the news-stand. It was a dinosaur, a lumbering, wounded beast peering up in surprise as the burning meteor of the internet squashed them flat. Print was static, it was black and white, it was boring. The worldwide web was shiny, lightning fast, it was gaudy and fun. Why would anyone want to read what some pompous rock hack thought of the new Rihanna tune, when you could listen to it on YouTube accompanied by a gyrating million-dollar video? Paper, staples and critics, they were all redundant.

'And so am I,' whispered Adam.

'You're what?' asked Tony.

'I'm going,' said Adam, and tapped the red circle on his phone, ending the call.

For a moment, Adam just stood there. The most he could do was try and force air into his lungs. His hands still shaking, he clicked onto his email in-box and was surprised to see that he had no new messages, no chatter about *Cream*'s demise, no consolatory missives from his colleagues. Or was he? Was he really that shocked? Earlier that year he'd had his hours cut to three days a week by *Cream*'s incoming editor Ellie

Simmons, a twenty-something former social media manager brought in by the ageing board in a last-ditch effort to inject some 'digital dynamism' into the brand.

At the time, Adam had shrugged off the pay-cut, telling himself that the part-time role would give him more time to write something important and incisive; a novel or era-defining non-fiction. He wanted to write about his generation, the last generation who really cared about music and movies and the mad joy of *living*, before everything became about you, about how many likes and how many friends you had. Because it used to be about something bigger.

In his early days as a struggling hack, Adam had toured the pubs of Camden playing the quiz machines, paying the rent with the prize money because the questions in the 'music' section, assumed to be near-impossible to the average pub-goer, were easy to him. Nirvana's first single? 'Love Buzz': next. Bassist on 'Walk on the Wild Side'? Herbie Flowers – obviously. Elvis' dead twin's name? Jesse – duh. It was like asking a painter to name the primary colours. And yes, right now, that sounded hollow and childish. But it was all that knowledge, all those deeply felt enthusiasms that had led Adam to London, and onto all those tour buses and VIP areas in the first place. Sure, he'd only been an observer, an urchin lifting the flap of the circus big top to peek inside, but he'd been there. In Real Life, as they said on the 'net.

But none of that helped now did it? However much fun it had been, the party was over. Ten years ago, he could have strolled into another gig on another music paper but ten years ago there *were* other music papers. And ten years ago he was ten years younger.

Now here he was on the edge of forty, highly skilled in an occupation no one wanted, like a telegraph operator in the age of fibre-optics. Aside from being awesome on the pink square in Trivial Pursuit, he had next to nothing to offer and the idea of retraining for a job in IT filled him with dread.

Adam grabbed the brandy he'd bought for Tim, twisted off the cap and took a swallow.

'Christ,' he coughed. Sweet oblivion felt attractive right then, but spirits had always made him heave. He wiped his lips with the back of his hand and forced himself to think. Maybe there was an upside to *Cream*'s closure. A redundancy cheque, maybe? He had no idea whether he qualified, but he wouldn't mind finding out.

He looked down at his mobile: who would know? Who could he call? *Cream*'s editor, Ellie Simmons?

He barely knew her and besides, he had never got round to asking for her number. She seemed very uptight and in today's jumpy work environment, he feared she might get the wrong idea.

So who?

Ten years ago, *Cream*'s editorial staff had been like family. He'd even lived with a couple of them in the early days – their big Camden house-share had been the scene of many raucous New Year's Eve parties and post-pub drinking sessions, but one by one, that gang had moved on. Adam Stowe was the last man standing. Well, almost.

He scrolled down to 'Nick B', his thumb hovering over the number.

Nick Baker was – had been – *Cream*'s features director and the nearest thing Adam had to a mate on the magazine. He wasn't quite the old guard, but he was the next oldest member of staff.

So call him.

Adam let out a long breath, shaking his head. He knew exactly what he would get: rage. Nick was a grumpy character at the best of times, and he was still furious for being overlooked for editor. All Adam would get from calling him would be a huge rant about what idiots the *Cream* management were for handing the reins to such an inexperienced bean-counter like Ellie. Adam pulled a face. He only had one option.

'Lauren,' he sighed, scrolling to her number. Adam had been having an on-off 'thing' with Lauren for the past few months. Pretty and switched-on, Lauren worked in *Cream*'s advertising department. She would definitely have the inside track, but the uncomfortable truth was that Adam had been avoiding Lauren for the last few weeks. Not so much 'ghosting' as a long drawn out exorcism.

Tensing, he pressed 'call' and listened to the electronic facsimile of a ringing telephone. Once, twice – then relief: it went to message.

'Hey Lauren, it's me. Adam. Just heard the news. Could you give me a call? Cheers.'

He clicked off and was reaching for the brandy when his phone chirped. He looked at the screen: a message.

'You're on the list. We're on at 9.30. Dec'

Slowly, Adam began to smile. Tentatively at first, then spreading into a grin. Anticipation and relief. His best mate was getting married tomorrow and it was up to Adam to show him a good time. There might be free booze at the festival. There would certainly be women. One last night of glory – after all, that was the point of a stag do, wasn't it? Adam sniffed one armpit and recoiled. First he needed a shower.

He put down the bottle, pulled off his shirt and dropped his trousers, hopping as he levered off each sock. Leaving his boxers in a pool, Adam grabbed a couple of towels from the bed, opened the bathroom door and stepped inside.

He heard the scream first. A loud scream. He blinked at the sight in front of him, frozen halfway between horror and detached fascination. Somewhere deep in his cerebral cortex, Adam was calmly processing the information: *There is a woman here in front of me. She is naked. And so am I.*

'WHAT the HELL are you doing in my room?' she yelled.

Adam clasped one towel to his crotch and handed her his other one, trying not to look.

'I'm really sorry. I thought this was my bathroom...'

'Well it's bloody *not,*' she replied, wrapping the towelling sheet around her body.

'But my room is just there and there isn't any other shower...'

‘There’s clearly been some misunderstanding. Perhaps you’d like to sort it out with reception. In the meantime, do you mind if I have some privacy?’

‘Of course,’ said Adam, backing out of the room towards the open door.

‘You didn’t see anything?’ she asked before he shut the door.

‘You mean, you? Naked?’

She glared at him through the dissipating steam.

‘No,’ he said, noticing she was really quite pretty.

‘Liar,’ said the girl and slammed the door in his face.

Chapter Four

SOPHIE COULD SEE why they called it the Big House. Haslop Hall was huge, a Georgian mansion in the classic style: a towering white building with tall windows and wide steps, grand wings on either side like a dove in flight. There was even an ornate fountain in the middle of the gravelled drive. Right now, back-lit by a glowering sunset, the hall was even more impressive – and even more forbidding. The peacock fountain plume fell like rain, tiny diamonds stippling the pond's surface with a hiss, sculpted stone and water as an expression of wealth and power. *Eighteenth-century marketing*, thought Sophie. *Welcome to my kingdom, see how important I am.* She didn't doubt it was why Vanessa had chosen the luxury hotel as a backdrop for the nuptials. It was also why Sophie felt cowed, out of place. An imposter.

'I know what you're thinking,' said Jennifer as she squeezed her Mini into a space between Audis, Mercs and Range Rovers, their long shadows jostling either side.

'The last time you said that to me was when you read my palm that Christmas in Sheffield,' said Sophie, trying to deflect Jennifer as butterflies collected in her stomach.

Jennifer gave a low laugh as she turned off the engine. 'In my defence, it was Tim who gave me that *How To Read Palms* book,' laughed Jennifer. 'And I did vow to steer clear of alcohol at family gatherings after that.'

Sophie smiled. That had been her last Christmas before the accident. She had been thrilled that Tim had invited her to spend the festive season at his uncle's sheep farm in the Peak District. She had naturally been nervous, keen to impress his extended family, but it had been three perfect days of Yuletide joy. By day they had taken long walks through the snow-speckled Pennines, at night they would all take turns to cook, laughing and joking. It was a world away from the high-achieving Wallis clan who regarded Christmas as an unwelcome distraction from work. Sophie couldn't ever remember watching a post-Queen's Speech movie without the discreet rustle of papers or one of her parents disappearing to their study. 'Just trying to get ahead of myself' was the age-old excuse. Maybe they knew what was coming.

'You think that everyone's going to be looking at you, don't you?' said Jennifer, swivelling to look at Sophie. 'I can assure you they're not. I've seen the guest list and there are very few familiar names. Lots of Vanessa's work friends, people who won't know you or I from Adam.'

She knew what Jennifer was trying to say. Women loved to gossip and right here was a juicy story: Tim's ex-girlfriend had been invited to the wedding.

'Actually, it's not that,' said Sophie. 'I've had total strangers peering at me for years, so I've developed a pretty thick skin.' That much was true. In hospital, she'd been ordered to strip and bend over with such monotonous regularity that the word 'examination' lost its meaning after a while.

'In fact, someone even walked in on me naked in the bathroom back at the hotel and I just sent him on his way with a flea in his ear.'

She smiled to herself, thinking back to the cute guy in the next bedroom, idly wondering if she had been a little too harsh on him.

'Something's worrying you. What is it?' said Jennifer, touching Sophie's knee.

Sophie buttoned up her jacket.

'I'm just not sure I should be here,' said Sophie honestly. 'I haven't seen Tim or Vanessa for such a long time. I don't really know why they invited me.'

Jennifer nodded and looked across to the Big House.

'Well I know this: they can't wait to see you. Come on, let's go or the canapés will all be gone.'

Sophie opened the car door and took her time swinging her legs round so she could put both feet flat on the ground. As she levered herself up, Jennifer walked around and silently offered her arm. 'Sorry,' said Sophie, feeling her cheeks flush.

The day was beginning to lose its warmth, the sky ripening to an artist's palette of apricot and soft raspberry above the pitched gables of the house. And it was quiet, still, not a breath of wind, just low footsteps crunching on the driveway.

'You know I never really told you how sorry I was about everything that happened,' said Jennifer. 'I can't imagine how hard it must have been for you and your family.'

Sophie carried on walking in slow, steady steps.

'It's okay. It's all in the past now.'

Jennifer paused.

'I should have come to visit,' she said haltingly. 'Bill and I both wanted to, but…'

Sophie shook her head sympathetically. She didn't need to hear Jennifer's excuses and she understood Jennifer's more than most.

'Sheffield to London is a long way,' she said. 'Especially to see someone feeling sorry for themselves in hospital. Besides, I loved your letters. They always cheered me up.'

'I should apologise for Tim too,' said Jennifer, after another moment. 'He's a grown man now of course, but he is our son and we still feel responsible for everything he does – or did. Tim didn't behave well after the accident, the way he… finished things.'

'At least he waited until I'd come out of the coma.'

It came out sarcastic and unbidden, the acrimony surprisingly fresh. Her therapist – when Sophie could stand to see her – had explained that bitterness was so-called because it was poisonous. It only hurt you, not the person it was directed at.

'Sorry, that was unfair,' she said, looking down at her feet.

'No, you're right,' said Jennifer. 'Tim didn't behave… honourably.'

'Sophie, I'm so sorry.'

Jenny's eyes sparkled in the floodlights; she looked genuinely stricken and ashamed; motherhood in full effect. Tim had flown the nest a generation ago and yet here was the mother hen still watching out for him, still attempting to do his laundry. Sophie had seen a similar thing with Christa and Hattie, how her sister would defend her young daughter to the hilt, whatever she had done. Sophie wondered if she had ever felt that way about anyone – or if she ever would.

'Jenny, he was young, we all were,' she said. 'At twenty-two you don't think about what's right, you just think about yourself. Of course, I was angry and hurt when our relationship finished, but in those first few weeks, I couldn't walk, talk. I didn't expect Tim to hang around forever.'

'A few more months might have been nice,' replied Jennifer.

Sophie just nodded, quietly agreeing with her.

'I just wish it hadn't happened,' sighed Jennifer.

'I did a lot of wishing too,' said Sophie. 'But I always woke up on my back.'

They took the winding ramp rather than the steps and Sophie let go of Jennifer's arm, gripping the rail. She was nervous, jumpy, but couldn't quite say why. The unknown, she supposed. But there was something else too: a nagging feeling of anticipation, that something was about to happen. That something was about to change.

'Another sunny day tomorrow,' said Jennifer, looking up at the blushing red sky. 'Vanessa always gets what she wants.'

Sophie glanced up towards the top of the stairs. 'Looks like it,' she said.

Standing at the door of the hotel was a butler. Mid-twenties, crisp white shirt and dickie-bow.

'The Chippendales are one down tonight,' muttered Jennifer nudging Sophie with a sly grin.

'I'm Matt,' smiled the butler. 'I'll be looking after you this evening. If you'd like to come this way, your friends are through here,' he said, gesturing inside.

They walked through into a bar, softly lit and tastefully decorated in art deco-influenced shades of cream, peach and teal. Arranged across a range of plush sofas and stools were a handful of thirty-something women, all primped and dressed up as if for a night on the town: sequins, high shoes, unnaturally arched eyebrows.

But no Vanessa, no one from Bristol. In fact, no one Sophie even vaguely recognised. She felt her shoulders relax just a little.

'Jennifer, right?' said a pretty blonde woman jumping up from a bar stool. 'I'm Annabelle, Vee's MOH.'

She gave a self-satisfied smile. 'Maid of honour, that is.' Annabelle had waves of golden hair, an off-the-shoulder silk dress and the limpest handshake Sophie had ever experienced.

'So, where's the bride?' asked Jennifer.

'She's still in the spa with the others… oh,' said Annabelle, trailing off as her big, blue eyes flitted back and forth between Sophie and Jennifer. 'Didn't Vee tell you about it? We've been getting treatments all afternoon.'

Sophie and Jennifer exchanged a look: clearly the bridal shower had a hierarchy and they were in the lower leagues.

'She did mention the spa, but Sophie has only just got in from the city,' said Jennifer, recovering the higher ground.

Annabelle shrugged, clearly unconvinced. 'Well, I think Vanessa will be along any minute. I cut my treatment short. Hot stone, a little passé,' she said, leaning in, conspiratorially.

Sophie nodded, even though she had little idea what Annabelle was talking about; she had missed out on the rise of spa culture. Back when the seaweed wrap and the oxygen facial were becoming fashionable, Sophie was in real therapy, trying to get her legs to work, not toning her glutes for a bikini bod. She'd read about fillers and peels and tints in magazines of course, but in the real world, Sophie had never got past the mud packs she had bought in Boots as a student.

'Anyway – we've got so much fun on this evening,' said Annabelle. 'The dinner is going to be amazing. Gluten-free vegan in case you were wondering. And – oh! Speak of the devil, here's the blushing bride.'

At first, Sophie didn't quite recognise her. Vanessa Farringdon swept into the bar like an Egyptian queen, her chocolate brown hair falling in a slick corkscrew over one tanned shoulder. *Wow*, thought Sophie. *That's some spa.* Vanessa had always been on the fringes of their group at Bristol University, always hiding at the back on photographs, certainly not one of the big, memorable personalities. In fact, Sophie had always felt a little sorry for her. She was sweet, mousy and inoffensive – or perhaps that was just in comparison to their particular social gang, a collection of the confident, the quirky and the charismatic, every one of them obviously going places. Especially Sophie. She had been the most dazzling, the most likely to. Until – bam – she wasn't.

But what a difference two decades made: now Vanessa Farringdon seemed to glow with polish and accomplishment. Striding through the room in a shimmering green dress, Sophie couldn't help but notice the jelly bean sized diamond sparkling on Vanessa's ring finger; as she looked back up, their eyes locked.

'Sophie Wallis, is that you?'

There was a look of genuine surprise on Vanessa's face.

'Hello Vanessa,' she said, as the bride-to-be came across and leant in for an exaggerated air-kiss. As she stepped back, still holding Sophie's hands, she couldn't miss the glance up and down.

'I didn't know you were…'

'Walking again?'

Sophie was used to it. People who knew about the accident often expected to see her in a wheelchair, trailing a drip.

'Yes, I'm a miracle of medical science,' she said a little too brightly.

'You look fantastic,' said Vanessa, taking Sophie's arm and leading her to the bar.

'Anton? Do you think you could whip up one of those delicious apple mojitos for my friend Sophie?'

'Of course, madam' smiled Anton.

'Thanks *so* much,' said Vanessa. 'And it's *Mademoiselle* – at least for a few more hours.' Vanessa giggled at her own joke and Sophie smiled politely.

'It's so amazing to see you,' said Vanessa. 'What are you up to these days. Still in management consultancy?'

Sophie shook her head.

'I'm in travel now.'

'Same as Emily, my bridesmaid.' said Vanessa, nodding towards a petite blonde near the window. 'We're both in PR but she's at Harton Lane, do you know it? Very strong hotel client base. They do the Mandarin, the One and Only,' she held up a hand and whispered behind it. 'It's how we got this place. Not quite a freebie, but a deep discount.'

Sophie was aware of Harton Lane, a chic outfit with shiny offices in Golden Square. They couldn't be further away from Sophie's workplace, a grime-fogged shop front by Putney Bridge.

'The travel industry is such a perfect job for you, isn't it?' said Vanessa, sipping a freshly delivered cocktail. 'You were always rushing off somewhere exotic; I remember you raving about India. We thought about it for the honeymoon, actually. I told Tim we should get at least one big trip in before we start having kids.'

'Good idea, yes,' said Sophie, her smile freezing at the mention of children. Vanessa didn't seem to notice, chirping on. '...although Camilla Johnson was telling me that they took their one-year-old around New Zealand. But I can't quite imagine Timmy pushing a buggy up a glacier, can you?'

'They do a helicopter ride up Mount Cook,' said Sophie, almost automatically. 'That's supposed to be incredible, and without the hard work of climbing the thing.'

Vanessa touched her on the arm.

'See? You always know everything.'

Sophie nodded: she did. Lying on her back with only a single window for company, travel had become one of her fantasy escapes. *When I get out of here, I'm going straight to Fiji*, she had told herself, guidebooks face-down on the pillow. *When I get back on my feet I'm going to walk the Appalachian trail, drive across Utah, climb the Chrysler Building.* Except Sophie never had gone to the Polynesian Islands, Virginia or New York once she finally did get upright. She'd got a job organising wonderful trips for people like Vanessa and her friend Camilla instead.

'And where do you live these days?' asked Vanessa.

'Wimbledon.'

'The village?'

'Yes.'

Vanessa's nod suggested a brownie point had been won, so Sophie didn't mention she could only afford one of London's smartest postcodes because she lived in her parents' garage. An estate agent would call it a 'ground floor lateral conversion', but it did still have a faint smell of petrol, despite her parent's best efforts with laminate flooring and Colefax and Fowler wallpaper. Sophie knew she was lucky to be there of course – particularly given that any London flat she could afford would be in a loft or a basement and therefore an assault course of stairs – but it still wasn't what she had imagined for herself as she hurtled towards forty.

'Our friends Lizbeth and Tony have a place on the Common,' said Vanessa, tilting her head. 'The Paynes, you must know them?'

'No, I don't think so.'

Vanessa's smile slipped a notch: brownie point lost.

'Well, it's handy for the tennis,' she said and Sophie nodded, swirling the ice cubes around her drink, trying to summon up the girl she once was. *You used to be charming, witty, the life and soul*, she scolded herself. *Say something clever.*

'I hope you like your wedding present,' she said.

Vanessa's interest piqued.

'Did you get something from the list? Tim wanted it at Thomas Goode but I thought there'd be something for everyone at Peter Jones.'

Sophie shook her head.

'There was nothing decent left by the time I got to it. I didn't want to be the person who bought the sugar tongs so I went off-piste. It's a picture.'

Sophie had seen the small oil painting of the Hope

Valley a week before she had even been invited to the wedding. The green valley was where Tim had spent his early childhood, before his parents had moved closer to the city. He had once taken Sophie walking to the top of the ridge on a visit. It hadn't been particularly romantic – it had drizzled for most of the hike and Sophie had developed a vicious blister half way up a hill, but she could still remember the look on Tim's face when he reached the top. Happy.

The painting Sophie had found captured that view perfectly in swirls of green, ochre and blue, and although it had been expensive, although she wasn't usually the sort of person who would stray from the wedding-list, she had dipped into her savings to buy it.

'A picture? How lovely,' said Vanessa with a pretty shrug. 'Although Tim *was* after those sugar tongs for the drinks trolley. He's really into making old fashioned cocktails.'

Sophie felt her heart drop. Of course. Why *would* she know what Tim wanted? The old Tim, the fantasy Tim, he would have loved that painting; in fact, hadn't he said at the time that he wanted to bottle the view and take it home? But the real Tim? Sophie didn't really know him at all.

'Well, it's so good to see you,' said Vanessa, filling the gap. 'I can't remember the last time we talked.'

'It's been a while. Not since Verbier, actually,' said Sophie. She noted a flicker in Vanessa's eyes, just a second of discomfort, then she nodded. 'That was all so horrid, wasn't it? But I'm so pleased you're over it.

She said it with detachment, as if she was speaking

about something she'd read about in the paper. But at least it wasn't pity. Compassion, empathy – they were fine and Sophie had received those by the bucketload since her accident, but pity was something else. Pity was empathy tainted by superiority and arrogance. Not having to hear the words, 'You poor thing,' was one reason why Sophie had fought so hard to learn to walk again.

She felt Vanessa's eyes on her.

'Can I ask you something?' she said, her voice lower.

'Sure.'

'How did you manage it?'

Sophie frowned at her.

'Manage what?'

Vanessa was looking awkward now. 'How did you get back on your feet? I mean, you were paralysed.'

Sophie nodded, watching Vanessa carefully, but there was no hint of the mawkish concern or the noxious thirst for detail; Sophie had experienced plenty of both. No, Vanessa seemed genuinely interested.

'I focused on the problem. Worked hard with the therapists. Once the doctors had told me it was possible to walk again, I gave myself no choice. I just had to get better.'

Which, to Sophie's surprise, was the truth. She had done what she had always done, with exams, with her first-class degree and landing the plum job offers: she had decided what she had wanted and pursued it, studied for it, made it happen. It was what had attracted her to Tim in the first place. She had seen him flash his smile in the Students' Union during Freshers Week – the life and soul of the party, the one who didn't take life too seriously. But it was when she had seen him in the library stacks the following week, working hard with no distractions; when she recognised that he too was someone who knew what he wanted, *that* was when she had started to find him attractive.

'So, are you seeing anyone?' asked Vanessa, disturbing her thoughts. The question was so casual, so throwaway, but so loaded with meaning – or was that just Sophie's paranoid mind working overtime again? Certainly, Sophie wasn't about to blurt out the truth. At the same time, she didn't want to come across as the abject failure she really felt.

'Yes,' she lied. It was pathetic, but she couldn't stop the words coming out of her mouth.

'I'm so glad to hear it. You deserve to have someone amazing.'

'Vanessa, can I ask you something too?'

There were so many questions she wanted to ask. Had she planned it all? Had she seduced Tim while Sophie lay in a fog of morphine? Had she seen her future with Tim panning out like this, huge diamond rock and corkscrew hair and all? Was she happy? Would she – would they – live happily ever after? She looked at Vanessa and blinked.

'Where's the nearest loo?'

Chapter Five

ADAM WAS TRYING, he really was. He was trying to get on with Tim's friends, he was trying to laugh at their jokes, trying to set his aching face into a polite smile. But it wasn't working. At all.

Sitting across from him in Tim's suite were Jonty and Charlie K, Tim's 'Uni pals', the kind of banker-lawyers who boasted about their houses, cars and Peloton classes – although from their red faces and slumped beanbag bodies, it didn't look like Jonty and Charlie K were keeping up with the programme.

A peal of smug laughter brayed out and Adam flinched. *Get me out of here.*

In an ideal world, of course, it wouldn't matter that Adam didn't get on with 'Jonts' and 'CK', but this was Tim's weekend and these were Tim's friends, so Adam was doing his best, making a conscious effort. And praying Tim hadn't invited them on the stag.

'You ever been to Bali, Adam?' boomed Jonty. Blonde, thin and pale as paper, he didn't wait for an answer.

'Bloody nice place, isn't it, Timbo? Well, as long as you stay in the compound.'

Charlie belched and nodded his round head.

'Sketchy.'

Adam slumped a little lower in his armchair, trying to seep into the upholstery. He had fled from his room – and from what he was already thinking of as 'the shower incident' – seeking sanctuary in Tim's suite, hoping that his friend would reassure him, laugh it off. Instead, he'd found these two, drinking single-malt whisky and reminiscing about a Christmas trip to Indonesia they'd all gone on. Without him, obviously.

'You do know Beyoncé was in the villa next to ours?' said Jonty, waving his glass towards Adam. 'Milly spotted her going down to the beach. I'd never have recognised her myself.'

'Wasn't she with the husband?' asked Charlie, repeatedly clicking his fingers. 'What's his name? Kanye something.'

Tim hooted with laughter and from his position prone on the bed, jabbed a bare foot at Charlie.

'I think you mean Jay-Z, Chas. Kanye's married to Kim Kardashian. Isn't that right Ads?'

Adam nodded, forcing a smile. He appreciated Tim's gesture, but he didn't really need to have it confirmed. And this, of course, was why *Cream* had gone under: everyone knew about celebrity these days, they didn't need a magazine to tell them. There had been a time when Adam's tales of meeting Madonna or going on tour with U2 had people hanging on his every word. In his twenties, access to that rarefied world was remarkable. Now everyone 'followed' pop stars and actors on social media, getting daily updates on their movements: the stars seemed closer, the sky lower. But it was worse than that. Adam looked over at Tim and Jonty, who were now chatting about the infinity pool in Bali. Part of the appeal of Adam's stories had been that he had been allowed behind the velvet rope. He'd interviewed film stars at the Ritz Paris and the Beverly Wilshire, been fed petit fours and Krug from the tour rider. But now Jonty and Tim were drinking £100 bottles of Scotch, popping off to Bali on a whim and sitting next to Kim and Kanye in first class. Adam's one ace had been trumped and all he was left with was what? A rented flat in Walthamstow and a few hundred collectable records. Okay, a few thousand. But right now, it didn't feel like much at all.

'So how *is* the world of pop, Adders?' asked Jonty, looking over at Adam. 'Wacko Jacko still behaving himself?'

'Michael Jackson's dead, Jonts,' said Tim.

Jonty frowned, as if trying to recall the facts. 'Really?' he mused, then shrugged. 'Never liked him anyway. I mean, one glove? Bit dodge in the first place, wasn't it? Here, have a splash of this,' he said, leaning over to pour some whisky into Adam's glass. 'Fingleton '59. Oak-smoked.'

'Finlayson '58,' snapped Charlie with pious irritation. 'And it's aged in oak casks you Philistine.'

Adam thought of the brandy he'd bought at Sainsbury's Local and was glad he'd left it in his room. In front of Jonty and Charlie he might as well have turned up with a bottle of Lambrusco and a family pack of Wagon Wheels.

'Cheers,' said Adam, knocking the whisky back

and grimacing.

'Smooth, isn't it?' said Charlie. 'But with those big peaty notes on the finish.'

Adam expected an ironic laugh, but instead the others simply nodded solemnly and murmured their assent.

'We'd better get off,' sighed Jonty, levering himself up with a grunt.

'Where are you going?' frowned Tim.

'Heading back to the Big House. The girls have blockaded the entire ground floor for the hen so we're banished to our rooms. Still, there'll be hell to pay if we turn up three sheets to the wind.'

'Surely you can stay for one more,' said Tim, not hiding his disappointment. 'We could get some room service.'

Charlie shook his head. 'That's the plan back at the room, I think. Our suite cost a bloody packet, so Hannah wants to "make the most of it."'

'I'll leave this with you, Timbo,' said Jonty, thumping the whisky bottle onto the coffee table and clapping Tim on the shoulder. 'Your need is greater than mine and all that. We'll see you on the morrow for the big event, hmm?'

Adam stayed in his seat as Tim showed them out, listening as they exchanged over-hearty goodbyes. He leant across and picked up the whisky bottle, peering at the label. It certainly looked expensive, gold and embossed, lavished with words like 'matured', 'complexity' and 'traditional', phrases designed to make you feel grown up and sophisticated, as if you were an alchemist tinkering with ancient spells. Adam cautiously sniffed the neck and felt himself transported back to his childhood; Gareth Harris offering him a sip from a quarter-bottle of Bell's round the back of the Scout Hut, laughing when Adam spat it out. 'It's an acquired taste,' Harris had smirked, a thirteen-year-old connoisseur. Even now, Adam could still feel the shame of not being worldly enough to appreciate whisky and wondered now, as he had then, whether he ever would. Was it ever too late to grow up?

He looked up as Tim took the bottle from his hands and dropped into the chair opposite, sighing.

'Shame they had to go,' said Adam.

'Is it?' said Tim, glancing up as he poured himself a drink.

Tim knew how Adam felt about Jonty – and yes, in normal circumstances, it would have been a relief to see him walking out the door. But Adam could see his old friend was disappointed that his party was breaking up – and he could sympathise with that feeling. Over the past few years, Adam's friends had fallen into relationships and disappeared into the mysterious world of dinner parties and theatre visits, nightclubs and gigs being passed over for a 'quiet one' on their newly bought John Lewis sofa. There was nothing malicious about it, just people getting together and following the well-worn ruts of coupledom, but Adam felt as if he'd woken up one morning to find everyone else had emigrated.

'We should probably get moving too, eh?' he said, slapping the arm of his chair decisively. Tim just looked at him.

'Moving where?'

'To Malvern Castle of course – the festival. Belasco will be on in a couple of hours and it might take a while to get there.'

Tim took another slug of whisky.

'You're not still on about this bloody stag do are you? Why don't we just stay here? Big day tomorrow, I should probably have an early night. Well, early-ish.' He pushed the bottle towards Adam. 'Here, have another.'

'Better not,' said Adam. 'Spirits make me sick, you know that.'

'I remember,' grinned Tim. 'You bent over the garden wall at Suzie Carter's party.'

He could suddenly see a fragment of that evening with startling clarity. Tim and he standing by the record player – actual, real-life vinyl spinning round and round – singing *Rock 'n' Roll Star* at the top of their voices, Tim's face lit up like a pinball machine.

How did he remember it so clearly? He could see Tim drawing out the words 'shiiine' and 'starrr' like Liam Gallagher, making the most of the Northern accent that had long since disappeared, totally in the moment, utterly convinced they could go anywhere, do anything – and that they would be friends forever. Adam looked over at Tim and for a moment, Adam considered telling him about *Cream*, about losing his job, about how his career had blinked out like a blown pilot light. Would his old friend understand? Would he put an arm around his shoulders and tell him it'd be alright, just as he had that night carrying Adam home from Suzie Carter's? Or would he shrug and say, 'it's about time, magazines went out with Stephenson's Rocket?' Adam knew he wasn't ready to hear that. Tonight, he needed to keep running, to keep moving forward, even if he was stumbling. He needed to feel that mad energy they'd shared as teenagers one more time.

'Hey, just before I came down here, I found a naked girl in my shower,' he said with a shy grin.

Tim looked over.

'How naked?'

Adam smiled.

'Totally.'

'So? What happened?'

'Nothing much. I gave her a towel.'

'You handed her *your* towel?' he laughed, sitting forward. 'Sounds like the start of a porn movie. What was she like?'

'Couldn't say. There was a lot of steam.'

Tim paused as if to think. 'I wonder who it is? Can't be one of Vee's mates, they're all up at the house tonight. Poor girl's probably down in the pub bar right now, discussing the size of your knob over a bottle of prosecco.'

Adam winced. It was entirely possible.

'Either way, that's what we should be doing too,' he said, standing up and putting out a hand to his friend. 'Come on, one mad last night of freedom? It's *traditional.*'

A soft smile spread across Tim's face.

'Sod it,' he said, banging his glass down. 'Let's go. What's the worst that can happen?'

Chapter Six

SOPHIE STOOD IN the centre of the hotel's bar trying to look invisible. As a strategy, it was failing, in fact it was making her more obvious, like Sissy Spacek in *Carrie*, trying to do 'inconspicuous' while covered in three gallons of pig blood. Anton, one of the waiters, was circulating with the canapés again, but Sophie had engaged him in conversation last time he'd come around with his silver platter. There were only so many questions you could ask about blinis and bruschetta, and besides, the poor man looked rushed off his feet – small talk was not part of the job description when you had twenty-five hens to take care of.

She looked around in vain. Jennifer had disappeared with Vanessa, and everyone else at the bridal shower seemed to know each other and were merrily gabbling away about house prices, boutique hotels, baby yoga and nursery school catchment areas, while stealing occasional looks in her direction that said, 'who's she?' And Sophie had to concede it was a valid question. Who *was* she?

Sophie wasn't really sure how to answer that question any more. Growing up, she'd always had a strong sense of who she was and how she fitted in to the world – her over-achieving parents Michael and Vivienne, both Oxbridge, both barristers, had drilled it into her from an early age that you had to find your strengths early and maximise them. So, Sophie had discovered she was a scholar, a leader, an athlete and a problem solver. Music lessons, drama, creative subjects for which she had no natural aptitude were jettisoned and instead she planned out her future before she had even done her GCSEs. Top university, then a management consultancy job, business school – ideally Harvard, a place on a blue-chip board and then the CEO job. In that order and as fast as possible.

It had all been going nicely too: Sophie's confidence and organised mind caught the attention of her senior partners at McKinsey, there had been much talk of plum assignments and secondments to New York, until – wham! – that life had disappeared, melting into the snow.

And from that moment, Sophie had become defined not by her abilities or achievements, but by something else: her injuries. During her recovery, when Sophie had gone to all the support groups suggested by her doctors and therapists, she took encouragement and solidarity from the friends she found there, and in those darkest days of her life, she had still felt belonging, a sense of who she was. But Sophie didn't go to the support groups anymore. Her recovery – not an option for so many – left her feeling horribly guilty when her friend Dave was still in his wheelchair and aphasia had left Val's speech and thought process permanently muddled. Sophie would take her 90% mobility over the alternative, but she wasn't sure the doctor's beaming declarations she was 'back to normal' were anywhere near the mark. But where did that leave her? She was no longer disabled but she was certainly not the same person she once was. So, who was Sophie Wallis now?

'Am I just getting old or is socialising absolutely exhausting?'

Sophie turned to see the petite blonde Vanessa had mentioned. She was slender, with sharp features; even her eyebrows finished in precise points.

'You're Emily, aren't you?' said Sophie. 'One of the bridesmaids?'

'And you're…?' the girl frowned, feline green eyes barely wrinkling.

'Sophie.'

'Come on, let's sit down for a minute,' said Emily, gesturing towards an elegant sofa. 'I need to give my feet a break from these bloody things.'

Sophie perched next to her as Emily pulled off her five-inch heels.

'I see you've been sensible,' she said gesturing towards Sophie's chunky Mary Janes. Sophie nodded quickly, alert now. No one would seriously compliment her shoes.

'So how do you know Vanessa?' she said, trying to deflect.

'Barrecore,' sighed Emily.

'What's that?'

'Ballet classes. We call it "hard core", it's so tough on the glutes. Plus we were neighbours before Tim and

Vee moved out to Wandsworth. Have you been to their new place yet? It's straight out of *House and Garden.*'

Emily leant in. 'In fact, entre nous, Vee says *Living Etc* are coming round to shoot them for the cover.'

Sophie could certainly picture Tim and Vanessa in Wandsworth on their giant velvet sofa, drinking hot toddies or whatever retro cocktails Tim liked to put sugar cubes in. Saturday night soirées, fairy lights in the back garden, a caterer on hand, the sound of laughter. The life she'd always imagined for herself in fact. Emily looked at her Apple Watch, then angrily pulled her heels back on, her rest apparently over.

'Where the bloody hell is Vee? We're due in the screening room any second.'

'She disappeared with Tim's mum about twenty minutes ago,' said Sophie.

'Not another place-setting crisis?' said Emily. 'Tim's parents are such a liability.'

'Liability?'

Emily glanced around, then lowered her voice.

'They keep inviting all these randoms and messing up the seating plan. The mother even invited Tim's ex-girlfriend – can you believe that? Vee was furious, obviously; it caused a right old ding-dong when Tim agreed to it. Apparently, he felt bad because she's…' Emily whispered the word '…*disabled.* But still. It's a bit much, don't you think? Especially since the groom's side don't even pay for anything.'

Sophie watched Emily stalk off. What the bridesmaid had said, it had left her completely stunned. Jennifer had invited her, not Tim. Ever since she'd bumped into Tim's mother in South Kensington and been invited to the wedding, Sophie had been trying to make sense of it. Why had Tim wanted to track her down? Why had he wanted her to be at the wedding? Why was Jennifer so keen to make it happen? What did it all mean?

But the truth was, it meant nothing at all. Tim didn't want her here. And honestly? That made perfect sense. Why *would* he? Sophie wasn't just his past, she was a painful reminder of everything bad that had happened – and of everything bad that *could* happen. In the years after her accident, Sophie had often wondered why many of her friends had drifted away. She was less mobile, sure, but had she become less witty or clever, had her personality changed radically? It had taken Christa to gently point out that no one wanted to look at rotten luck. Sophie was living proof that your world could turn upside down at any moment – and that made people uncomfortable, whether they'd admit it or not.

Sophie was rattled by the clang of a gong.

'Everyone!' called Emily. 'If you'd just follow me through into the screening room, we have arranged some light entertainment.'

Twittering with anticipation, the hens around the table got up and streamed out of the room. Sophie watched them go. This was her chance: the time to slip away quietly. She hadn't just outstayed her welcome – she hadn't been wanted here in the first place. Pulling her mobile out of her pocket, she groaned when she saw it had no signal. Thinking she might be able to use the hotel lines, she moved towards the foyer, but there was no one in reception and Anton the waiter had gone. Just then, Emily appeared, waving her gong towards a pair of wide wooden doors.

'Come along. Chop, chop,' she called, her smile betraying a hint of irritation. 'Can't start until you're all inside.'

'Sure, sorry,' said Sophie, reluctantly walking past her into a room finished in dark wood and red velvet. Plush seats were lined up in rows just like a luxury cinema. In front of the wide screen were two bar stools and Emily was steering Vanessa onto the first. Sophie headed for the back row, away from Vanessa. Away from everyone.

'Now if you'll settle down please,' said Emily, clapping her hands as the women took their seats. 'We're all going to play a game. Or rather Vanessa will be.' She waved to Annabelle, the Maid of Honour who was now standing behind a desk at the back of the room, an open laptop in front of her. Suddenly the cinema screen lit up with a glittery logo and a vaguely familiar theme tune. It was a moment before Sophie realised it was from the Eighties TV show *Mr and Mrs.*

There was laughter and a flutter of anticipation, until Emily patted the air for quiet.

Sophie flinched as she saw Jennifer come into the screening room. She saw her glance around the room, then finally slid down in a chair next to Elspeth, Vanessa's mum. The double doors closed and Sophie knew that she was trapped.

'For those of us too young to remember, *Mr and*

Mrs was a cheesy TV game show where a married couple were asked questions about each other and won prizes if their answers matched. So tonight, I will be the quizmaster asking Vanessa the tough questions and…' She turned to the screen as a freeze-frame picture of Tim appeared. '…Tim will be giving his answers.'

'Hi Vee,' grinned Tim, as the film began. 'I know we're not supposed to see each other the night before the wedding, but Emily assures me this doesn't count. So, let's see how much we know about each other.'

His picture froze again and the room erupted in more laughter but Sophie couldn't take her eyes from the screen, her anger immediately forgotten.

She wanted to swallow, but somehow it didn't work. It was Tim, but not quite as she remembered him. Older, more confident, his hair different, but his eyes were just as blue.

Her mouth was dry, her breath shuddered. She hadn't seen him for nearly fifteen years. Obviously, she had seen pictures of him on social media, but this was the first time in this form, as a moving, larger-than-life reality.

Sophie tuned back into the room as Emily began reading a question from a card.

'Okay, question one, Vanessa: What would you say Tim's worst habit is?'

This was met by more laughter and cat calls.

'I'm supposed to guess what he thinks it is?' Vanessa asked.

'Yes' said Emily, with a wink towards the audience. 'But you can tell us what it *really* is too.'

Humming, thought Sophie. For no reason, she thought of a coach journey she and Tim had made from Bristol to Brighton. All the way there, Tim had been humming 'Barbie Girl' by Aqua. In the end, the lady in the seat in front had asked him to stop. They'd laughed about that for weeks.

'Well, he does like to sing,' said Vanessa.

'In the shower?' asked Emily, one eyebrow raised, triggering a low 'ooh!' from the audience.

'In the car when he's driving,' said Vanessa. 'Stupid jingles or pop songs. It's more of a hum, actually.'

Sophie blinked.

'Let's see what Tim said,' smiled Emily, gesturing towards Annabelle. Up on the screen, Tim was speaking again.

'Vee would probably say, "leaving wet towels on the bathroom floor." So that's my answer: messing up the bathroom.'

There were disappointed 'boos' from the crowd.

'Okay, okay. It's only the first question,' said Emily. 'We move onto question two: 'What fragrance does Tim think you wear?'

Vanessa brightened.

'Chanel Number 5,' she said. 'He'll get that one because it's the only scent he's ever heard of.'

'Let's see…'

Tim appeared again. 'That's easy. Vee wears Chanel Number 5 – I got her some for Christmas last year.'

'And every year, actually,' said Vanessa ruefully.

Emily consulted her cards.

'Question three: What is Tim's favourite song?'

Three Lions, thought Sophie immediately. *He loves Three Lions.*

Vanessa seemed less sure.

'Song?' she said, picking at a thread on her dress. 'It's probably one of those Britpop bands. Blur? No – Oasis. What's that one? *Wonderwall.* Yes, I'll go for that.'

'Let's ask Tim,' said Emily, revealing her white teeth.

'The first record I actually went into a shop and bought was Three Lions by Baddiel and Skinner, the greatest football song ever. But Vanessa will probably say "Beautiful" by James Blunt. Spoiler alert – it's what we've picked for our first dance.'

The audience laughed in delight, but Sophie was staring straight forward, trying not to react. It was getting hotter in that closed room. Sophie pulled at the neck of her dress, trying to concentrate as the questions kept coming: guilty pleasure, the name of a first pet. They all washed over Sophie; the words didn't matter, she was watching Tim's mouth move, that lop-sided smile, the crinkle at the corner of his eyes. It was like being catapulted back through time, back to when he'd looked at her, their heads side-by-side on the pillow, nowhere to be but with each other.

There was another round of questions about his relationship with Vanessa – Tim's life now. Sophie tuned back in, morbidly fascinated. She had often wondered what Tim and Vanessa had in common; they had barely seemed to speak in Bristol. She found out that they went to a James Bond movie on their first date and that they'd another two dates before they first "did the bad thing". The naughtiest place they'd ever done it was in the loos at the Tower of London. Vanessa had first said "I love you" first on a sailing trip to Salcombe, and Tim wanted three children – two boys and a girl.

Sophie was still trying to work out when *Quantum of Solace* was released and therefore how long they had been together, when Emily's microphone squawked with feedback, demanding everyone's full attention.

'Question number nine. What is Tim's favourite restaurant?'

Vanessa tossed back her hair with confidence.

'He's probably going to say the Four Seasons in Bali. We went over New Year and it was amazing. Apparently, Kim and Kanye were there at the same time but we didn't see them.' Then she smiled. 'Actually no, Tim will say the time we had a romantic sunset dinner at Oia, a little village in Santorini in Greece.'

Emily turned to the screen and Tim started speaking again.

'My favourite place to eat?' mused Tim thoughtfully. 'Well, there's this amazing little taverna right on the harbour in Mykonos. You could see the shoals of fish come right up to the dock and I remember Vee said the sea was so blue it matched the little checked tablecloth.'

Emily paused the film with a click of her fingers.

'Sorry Vee...' she began, but Vanessa interrupted her.

'It *was* Santorini actually,' said Vanessa, her voice tight. 'Tim's got it muddled up. We went to see the sunset in Oia for my 30th. Unless it's somewhere he's been to with some other girl.'

There was more laughter, but Sophie wasn't laughing. Sophie was remembering. It had been the summer after graduation and she and Tim had pooled their funds to go island-hopping around the Cyclades. She remembered the windmills and the heat, the smell of pine trees and lemons, and the colours – the whites, pinks and blues that were the palette of the island. They'd partied in Ios, hiked around the dry, desolate hills in Iraklia and dived off the cliffs into the teal waters of Donoussa, and at the end of it all, they'd had one perfect night in Mykonos Town. They'd arrived when the water still twinkled aquamarine in the lazy, late afternoon sun, and they'd found a perfect little taverna by the harbour, with blue gingham cloths on the little bistro tables, exactly as Tim had described it.

She looked up at his face, frozen on the big screen, and felt a wave of longing so strong she felt as if a giant hand was squeezing her heart.

'Okay, last question,' said Emily. 'And it's the big one. Who – or what – has been the greatest love of Tim's life?'

There was a low hum from the audience and Sophie's eyes locked on the screen.

'I'm hoping he's going to say me,' smiled Vanessa. 'Obviously.'

She looked down and picked at that thread again.

'Although I'm supposed to guess what Tim's response will be, aren't I? So, I think he might say his mum.' She looked over at Jennifer, tapping a thoughtful finger against her lips.

'No, I'm going to say me,' she said decisively. 'It is our wedding weekend, after all.'

They all turned towards the screen as Annabelle clicked the button cueing Tim's answer. Tim looked at the camera, a flicker of a smile, then suddenly his face was still. 'The love of my life,' he said, looking straight at Sophie. Or that was how it seemed to her.

'My greatest ever love is…' he began. And then he stopped. A clear hesitation. An intake of breath. He *is* looking at me, Sophie thought. He is.

'Vanessa knows me very well,' said Tim finally. 'So I'm guessing she won't mind me saying this.'

There was another pause, then that smile again.

'Sheffield United,' he said. 'Sheffield United, the mighty Blades are the greatest love of my life.'

The room erupted. Shouts of 'no!' and 'Jilt him!'

Vanessa's friends jumped up, crowding in, hugging her and commiserating, offering their thoughts on men. Sophie stood up too, moving on autopilot, blindly bumping into a chair. All she could see was Tim's face, his eyes. Looking at her. At *her*.

Sophie slipped out of the screening room and down a corridor, into the ladies. Safely inside a cubicle, Sophie slumped onto the seat.

What the *hell* was all that about? Sophie didn't know; didn't know anything. She actually had to reach out and hold onto the paper dispenser for fear she might fly off into space. The ground didn't feel solid, nothing felt real.

'Pull yourself together,' she whispered. Just because Sophie had imagined that Tim was looking at her when he said 'the love of my life' didn't make it so. He had been looking at a camera in another room, maybe even in another town, no thought for who would be watching. It was crazy to think he was speaking to her alone. And yet, still, it felt as if he had been sending her a secret message.

She bit down on the fleshy inside of her cheek. Was that even what Sophie wanted? Did she really want Tim to still be in love with her? Over the past few years, Sophie had watched a lot of romantic comedies. And in a surprising number: *Four Weddings and a Funeral*, *Sweet Home Alabama* and *Made of Honour*, to name just three, the stories climaxed with vow interruption moments – when the bride or groom realised they were about to marry the wrong person.

Sophie knew it was nonsense. Things like that never happened in real life. But deep down, was it what she wanted to happen at this wedding? Did she still want Tim to be in love with her, and was that – truly – why she had accepted the invitation and was here?

Sophie tensed as she heard another group of women push into the loos, laughing and gossiping. Gently she reached over and made sure that the cubicle door was properly locked, then held her breath as they excitedly began to discuss the quiz.

'You heard it, right?' asked one woman, stopping right outside Sophie's cubicle door. 'That mix up about Mykonos and Santorini? He totally wasn't talking about the same restaurant as Vee, was he?'

'I bet it *was* another woman.'

'For sure.'

'And did you hear the hesitation?'

'What hesitation?'

'You must have heard it. When he was asked about the greatest love of his life and all he had to say was 'Vanessa of course', but he hesitated. I looked at Hannah and she was like 'OMG'! It's someone else.'

'Do you think it was someone he was at the Mykonos taverna with? That was totally another faux pas.'

'But he's been going out with Vee forever. Who else has there been? You don't think he's been unfaithful, do you?'

'If anyone would…' A giggle. 'But I don't suppose we're allowed to say that on his wedding weekend, are we?'

A third girl had joined in the conversation now.

'Charlie's always said that Tim has been holding a candle for some old girlfriend.'

'The ski girl?'

Sophie's eyes opened wide and she held her breath so she wouldn't make a sound.

'Is that the girlfriend who died?'

'Tim's girlfriend died?' said one of the women.

'No, I don't think she died. But she was left, you know, *a cripple*.'

'It was before we knew him but there was some

scandal attached to it. Maybe Jonty knows something about it. He was in with the Bristol lot…'

The voices faded as the girls left the bathroom still talking, the door swinging closed, leaving Sophie alone. And she stayed sitting there for a very long time.

Chapter Seven

THE BAR ON the ground floor of The Swan was heaving. Tim raised a hand to wave at a dark-haired woman sitting at a table.

'That's Cherie,' he whispered, nudging Adam. 'She's single. You could do a lot worse – she's a doctor.'

Adam turned, trying to check out the woman without looking too obvious. She was attractive, around thirty, but in a split second he saw their relationship spiral out before him: she'd want to buy a sofa together, then it would be box-set nights-in, babies, nappies, parents' evenings, Disneyland, dementia and…'

'You alright Ads?' asked Tim.

'Busy, isn't it?' said Adam, raising his voice. 'Is everyone here for the wedding?'

Tim nodded and waved to someone else at the bar.

'Yeah, we'd have loved to have had everyone up at the big house obviously, but given the numbers…'

'I get it – we're the rejects,' smiled Adam. 'So how come you're here?'

Tim rolled his eyes.

'Because I'm not allowed to see the bride tomorrow morning, *obviously*. Vee is being very traditional about everything.'

'About everything?' asked Adam, but before Tim could answer, he jumped in the air. Someone had pinched his backside. Whirling around, he saw slim man with his hands held out like David Copperfield revealing a magic trick.

'Ali?' gasped Adam. 'No way! It *is* you.'

Ali Malik, their school friend. Like the ghost of Christmas past in Cuban heels. Before Adam could react, Ali grabbed him, and slapped him vigorously on the back.

'You're looking well, Al,' said Adam, wiggling free.

Which, against all odds, was true. The last time Adam had seen Ali, he'd still been pocked with acne, hunched and awkward in the catalogue clothes his mother had chosen for him. Now he was groomed and styled, his black, wavy hair slicked back, wearing a sharp suit and heavy-framed designer glasses. It was a cosmetic transformation, but Adam thought there was the same gleam coming from behind those lenses.

'What's it been, like, almost twenty years?' asked Ali.

Adam winced, realising that his old friend was right.

Adam and Ali hadn't seen each other since the day they'd gone back to Ranmoor Sixth Form College to collect their 'A' Level results.

Adam had done even better than he had hoped – flying colours, as they said back then. Ali had performed much worse – not that it had mattered as neither of them intended to go anywhere near a university. Adam's fanzine had translated into summer work experience at *Cream*, which had converted into a junior staff job and, despite having just scored the best set of grades of any Ranmoor College student in fifteen years, he'd taken it without a second thought. Ali Malik, meanwhile, was already halfway through setting up a software company from a room above his uncle's restaurant.

In the intervening years, Ali had moved to Palo Alto in California. Adam had last seen him in *Wired* magazine which talked about him as if he was a tech rock star with the Midas touch, thanks to some sort of digital investment vehicle that the tech press said was going to 'revolutionise cryptocurrency trading'. Either way, it all meant that Ali was rich and successful. And it looked good on him.

'Been far too long, man,' smiled Adam. 'Seriously, it's good to see you.'

Ali had always been a wild card, a catalyst for things to fly off in odd directions, and it wasn't until he was standing in front of him that Adam realised just how much he missed that sort of dice-rolling craziness.

'My mum sends her love,' said Ali, waving a fifty-pound note at the barman. 'She always liked you, Ads. After parents' evenings she'd always crack me round the back of the head and say, 'Why can't you be more like that nice, clever boy Adam?'

'I think you did okay, Al. And you showed your Mum too.'

Ali shook his head.

'You're joking. She's still disappointed I never became a doctor.'

'But you're a Silicon Valley bazillionaire.'

'Asian parents, man,' he shrugged. 'Doctor, lawyer or prime minister, anything else brings shame on the family.'

'Well *I'm* impressed.'

'What, are you going to kiss me now?'

Adam laughed and clapped his friend on the shoulder, wondering why he had allowed their friendship to lapse, why he had let so many of his old friendships go. He looked across at Tim shaking the hand of a tall, ruggedly handsome man. The man was wearing a washed-out rugby shirt and looked slightly confused, like he'd just been woken up and been told he was the only one who could land the plane.

'Adam Stowe,' said Tim, dragging him over, 'Meet Hugo Crabb, Vee's cousin. Hugo's an explorer. I think you're all on the same table tomorrow.'

Adam shook his hand, feeling the bones crush.

'You're an actual explorer?'

'Genuine article, I'm afraid,' said Hugo, beaming and pumping Adam's hand.

Tim reappeared, shaking Adam by his shoulders.

'I'm a genius. I've just booked the last taxi in a ten-mile radius.'

'Why no cabs?'

'Friday night in the countryside. But the barman called his brother-in-law, who said he'd take us to Malvern Castle.'

Adam grinned. He could feel the night beginning to pick up speed and right on cue, Ali arrived with a tray of glasses.

'Tequila shots for everyone!' he announced.

'Aren't you Muslim?' said Tim.

'Only on the Sabbath,' said Ali, handing them around.

'To Tim's last night of freedom,' said Adam, raising his glass.

'Hey, hey! Listen!' shouted Ali, lifting a finger to indicate the music swelling from the jukebox. Adam recognised it immediately: The Kaiser Chiefs.

Their eyes met each other, smiles spreading, bouncing on the balls of their feet, then jumping as one, arm in arm.

'I PREDICT A RIOT!'

They collapsed in laughter.

'Here's to Tim's stag!' shouted Ali, raising his glass.

'To going mental!' added Tim.

'Na zdravi!' shouted Hugo, knocking back his tequila and throwing his glass into the fireplace, smashing it into a thousand pieces.

Adam jumped back to avoid the shards. He looked around: the entire bar had stopped what they were doing to glare at them.

'Don't you do that here?' whispered Hugo.

Adam slowly shook his head.

They jumped as a loud car horn blared at the front of The Swan. Adam exchanged a grin with Tim. This was more like it.

‘Taxi!’ he shouted. And they sprinted for the door.

THE TAXI WASN’T big enough for four of them; they should have known. Hugo’s Yeti-like proportions didn’t help, with his knees practically touching the roof, but even so, things were uncomfortably cramped with five grown men squeezed into a tiny hatchback. Ali leant towards the taxi driver.

‘No offence mate, but what’s with the Fiat Panda?’ he said. ‘Shouldn’t you have a Prius or something?’

‘It’s me mum’s car,’ said the cabbie, fingers drumming restlessly at the wheel. He was mid-twenties and painfully thin, his cheeks dark hollows beneath the peak of his ‘Adidoff’ baseball cap. ‘If you don’t like it, I can always take you back,’ he said.

‘No, no, it’s fine,’ they all said at once.

‘That’s good, because I’m the only taxi left in the area. Well, when I say taxi…’

He trailed off and Adam and Tim exchanged a look.

‘You were called by the barman at The Swan weren’t you?’

‘Don? Oh yeah. I mean I’m not a taxi-*taxi*. Not officially. I’m not licensed, strictly speaking. Still on probation, you see.’

Adam glanced at the plastic fake-looking ID stuck to the car’s dashboard with yellowing Sellotape. The driver caught the look and grinned, revealing a missing incisor. Adam’s gaze drifted over to the door locks, then out at the dark road, wondering how dangerous it would be to jump from a moving vehicle.

'Listen, do you mind if I stop off on the way?' said the driver.

'We are in a bit of a hurry,' said Adam carefully. 'There's a band on you see…'

Before he could finish, the driver jerked the wheel to the left and swung the cab into a near-deserted car park next to a grey stone pub.

'Two secs, gents,' he said, opening the door and running up the path.

They sat in stunned silence for a full minute before finally Tim let out a long breath.

'This is great. Not.'

'How long do you think he's going to be?' asked Ali.

'He'd better not be much longer,' said Adam, grabbing Ali's wrist and peering at his chunky watch. 'The band are on in… less than an hour.'

'I could do with stretching my legs,' said Hugo, which no one could really dispute.

'Why don't we do it walking to the bar?' said Tim. 'Might as well have a quick G&T whilst we wait?'

The others were already walking towards the pub before Adam could stop them. Swearing under his breath, Adam followed.

He pushed inside, the noise swelling around him like dry ice. If The Swan Inn was an interior designer's idea of the perfect English pub with its limewash and distressed baskets, The Hare and Hounds was a through-the-looking-glass version where asking for a white wine might get you stabbed. Plus someone *was* being murdered: Elton John.

A day-glo green sign over the bar announced the reason: 'KARAOKE NIGHT at the HARE'. Craning his neck, Adam could see the noise was coming from a red-faced man swaying on a small stage, his half-full pint raised aloft, his eyes closed in ecstasy as he sang.

'*Tie me* down with *sheeeets of lemon*,' cried the man into the microphone.

Linen, thought Adam as he threaded his way towards Tim who was standing at the bar. *It's 'sheets of linen'*.

'I love this song, don't you?' said Tim, raising his voice over the music. Adam just nodded. He wanted to say that he had loved 'Tiny Dancer' since he was twelve, when he'd discovered the *Madman Across the Water* album in a stash of his Dad's vinyl under the stairs, dumped there with the rest of his father's possessions, abandoned the day he had walked out.

'Look, I don't think we should stay,' said Adam, cupping his hand around Tim's ear.

'What?'

'I said, 'I think we're going to get our heads kicked in.'

Tim shook him off.

'Don't be such a bigot. Just because it's the country doesn't mean they're violent yokels.'

'What do you want?' said the young barmaid, her words dripping with disinterest.

Tim ducked his head to read the titles on the front of the beer pumps. 'Pint of Hamhock, please.'

‘’Hock’s off,’ said the girl, making no move towards the glasses. ‘So’s the Bishop.’

‘What *do* you have?’ asked Adam.

‘Lager.’

Adam held up four fingers just as Ali appeared.

‘The cab driver’s gone,’ he said cheerfully.

‘What?’

‘Fella in the loos just told me. Saw him drive off in the other direction, “Like Lewis Hamilton.”’

Tim looked at Adam with sympathy. ‘Not sure we’ll be going to the festival, Ads. Sorry mate.’

But Adam wasn’t ready to give up. Not yet. He leant across to the barmaid, cranking up his smile to full power.

‘We’re trying to get down to Malvern Castle,’ he said. ‘Do you know any cab firms I could call?’

‘Dave!’ she shouted, without taking her eyes from Adam. ‘What’s the number for that limousine company? The one with the solid gold seats?’

Adam’s smile froze.

‘No cabs then?’

She shook her head and held out her hand.

‘£14.80 for the lager.’

Adam felt in his pocket just as his phone buzzed. He fumbled it out and looked at the screen. Lauren.

‘Hey Lauren, how’s things?’ he said, clamping the phone to his ear.

‘How’s things?’ she said. ‘Not brilliant, as you might have heard.’

The karaoke seemed to be getting louder, so he knocked back his beer and pushed through the pub and out of the rear exit. After the fug of the bar, it was cold, so Adam zipped his flimsy London jacket up to the neck.

'Adam?' Lauren's voice, irritated. 'Are you still there?'

'Lauren, sorry about that,' he said, perching on an edge of a picnic table.

'Yes, I'm hearing that a lot from you lately.'

He closed his eyes, rubbing his forehead. He'd met Lauren at the office Christmas party. She was pretty, bubbly and despite dressing like one of the contestants from *The Apprentice*, she had three piercings in her left ear, so Adam had guessed she might have hidden depths. Lately, however, Adam couldn't help feeling there was something missing, some essential incompatibility, so over the past two weeks he had been repeatedly ducking her like a boxer on the ropes.

'So, what do you know about *Cream* folding?' he said, pressing on.

Another pause, then a resigned sigh.

'Ollie, the publisher, came in just before lunch and made the announcement. Apparently, he'd already told editorial, because they were already in the pub when we got there.'

Adam felt a strange pang of jealousy, imagining himself there with the team, united for once in their misery.

'Pretty bleak, I imagine, eh?' he said. 'Everyone in the same boat.'

Another of those pauses. Ominous this time.

'Well… not everyone,' said Lauren. 'A lot of us

are staying on.'

'What do you mean, "staying on"?'

'Haven't you seen the press release?' asked Lauren. 'They've folded the print magazine, but there'll be a re-branded digital version of *Cream* online. Ellie Simmons and most of the others are being shifted across to that. The Ad team are being moved cross-platform.'

Re-branded digital. Cross-platform. Adam shivered and it wasn't just the cold this time.

'Adam, I'm really sorry you're not being kept on. Ellie told me.'

Which was more than she had bothered telling him.

'It's fine,' said Adam, wishing he'd ordered something stronger to drink. 'Maybe I can do some freelance or a column or something.'

'Yes,' said Lauren, a little too quickly. 'I'm sure that's the plan.'

He shook his head, the distant thump of the music inside the bar feeling like a cruel parallel to his life.

'Are you okay?' she asked. There was kindness in her voice. She meant well, Adam knew, but it made him feel embarrassed.

'Sure, I'm great.'

He didn't feel great, but if they set off for Malvern Castle now there was a good chance he'd feel better before the end of the night.

'You've been talking about doing something else for ages, haven't you?' she added. 'You've had a good innings.'

He had to laugh at that one. Lauren left another one

of her pauses.

'So maybe we can do something,' she said finally. 'Tomorrow night, maybe? You can come round. I'll cook…'

Right now, it didn't seem like a bad option. Someone taking care of him, someone to stroke his bruised ego. And with the talk of a meal, Adam realised he hadn't eaten anything all day, which might explain why he was feeling a little skittish.

'I'd love to, Lauren, but I'm at a wedding all weekend.'

A proper boyfriend, he realised, would have told his girlfriend that already.

'Ah,' said Lauren, perhaps thinking the same thing. 'Maybe another time then,' she said more stiffly.

Down the line, he heard someone call Lauren's name, then a swell of laughter and Adam finally twigged: she was still out with the editorial 'team', his ex-colleagues, celebrating their change in direction. And once again, Adam had been left out in the cold.

'I'd better go,' said Lauren.

'I've got to go too. We're off to see Belasco at Malvern Castle.'

As Adam hung up, he was struck by the sense that this was the last time they would talk, but before he had time to think about how he felt about that, he heard a cough and looked up to see Tim standing in front of him, holding a pint in one hand and a cigarette in the other.

'Want one?'

'I thought you'd never ask.'

Chapter Eight

SOPHIE HAD BARELY touched her lychee parfait. It looked nice enough, sitting spot-lit like a giant pearl on a saucer-sized plate, overlaid with petals and a drizzle of something purple that looked suspiciously like beetroot juice.

She hadn't touched her nettle velouté or the roasted carrot either. Sophie just wasn't hungry; in fact the thought of eating made her want to throw up. She glanced around, nervy and paranoid. Did everyone know that she was the 'ski-girl'? Had Vanessa seen the hesitation during the *Mr and Mrs* quiz? And most of all, how could Jennifer have been so cruel as to trick her into coming here in the first place?

'Are you not going to eat that?'

Sophie jumped. Tensed for the worst, she was almost surprised to see the woman sitting next to her – Zara was it? – pointing at her with a spoon.

'Please. Be my guest,' said Sophie, pushing the dessert across. 'I'm full.'

The woman had the slightly flushed face and unfocused eyes of someone who had started on the cocktails mid-afternoon. She seemed friendly enough, which was more than could be said for the hen Sophie had sat next to for the main course: Jenna, a 'mummy blogger' who seemed genuinely distraught that she couldn't quite break through 10,000 followers on Instagram.

'You're full? On this?' laughed Zara, sticking her spoon into the parfait. 'The last time I was this hungry was when I tried the caraway fast. Have you tried it? Nothing but caraway seeds and only during daylight hours.'

Sophie watched as Zara took a mouthful.

'How is it?'

'Tastes like compost, but if I don't get some calories soon I'm going to pass out.'

Sophie smiled for the first time since the quiz. At least someone had a sense of humour.

'So, are you staying here?' asked Zara.

'No, I'm at The Swan.'

Sophie didn't add that it was highly unlikely she would be spending the night at the pub. As soon as she could get some reception on her mobile, she fully intended to call Christa and arrange an evacuation first thing in the morning, if not sooner.

'Me too,' said Zara, leaning forward. 'Vanessa says there's some cute guys up at The Swan. Have you seen any?'

Sophie thought of the naked guy in the bathroom and found herself blushing.

'So it *is* true!' said Zara triumphantly. 'Vee said there's a tech billionaire and some hot journalist who's mates with Beyoncé. Have you seen Vee's cousin? He's just like Indiana Jones apparently, that would suit me nicely. I wouldn't mind a boyfriend that's hardly ever there.'

Sophie began wondering who the billionaire might be. She still subscribed to the *Harvard Business Review*, *Forbes*, *Fast Company* and *Wired.* It was a shame that she had no intention of staying for the rest of the weekend as she would quite like to have met him.

'So, what's your connection to the bride and groom?'

'I'm a stylist. Vanessa works with lots of celebrities, so we've spent a fair bit of time together on shoots. I pointed her in the direction of a couple of designers for her wedding dress and she invited me here. When you're my age and single, you don't pass up a swanky party.'

They both looked up to see Annabelle hitting the gong.

'And switch, everyone,' she shouted. 'Let's keep this moving, ladies. Let's mingle!'

Zara grumbled to herself, but duly picked up her half-eaten dessert and moved down the table. Sophie looked up to see who was coming her way and felt a flutter of panic as Jennifer slung her bag over the back of the chair next to Sophie and sat down.

'Finally,' she beamed. 'So sorry for abandoning you – I've been commandeered by Elspeth all evening. Can you believe she's already bagsied Tim and Vanessa for Christmas? Apparently, they'll be taking it in turns to switch between the families but it's already been decided they'll be in Surrey this year. Awful.'

'You'll survive,' said Sophie crisply.

Sophie had been wondering how to play it with Jennifer from the moment that Emily had told her that Tim's mother had invited Sophie to the wedding, not Tim and Vanessa. She supposed that Jennifer was only trying to be kind, but still, surely she had to realise how stupid it would make Sophie look?

'How are you enjoying it?' said Jennifer, taking a coffee from Anton the waiter. 'Met any fun people?'

Sophie couldn't hold it in any longer.

'I met Emily, the bridesmaid,' she said, her voice tight. 'She told me that it wasn't Tim who invited me to the wedding.'

Jennifer took a sip from her cup. It was a few moments before the older woman spoke.

'Strictly speaking, she's right. I did ask to have you added to the guest list. But Tim agreed and that's because he wanted you to come.'

Because she's disabled, thought Sophie, remembering Emily's words. *Because he couldn't say no.*

'But Tim hadn't desperately been trying to track me down, had he?' said Sophie, lowering her voice for fear of shouting. 'I mean, before I met you in South Kensington, had he even mentioned me?'

Jennifer shifted in her seat.

'Just because you weren't on the original guest list doesn't mean to say he didn't want you here,' said Jennifer carefully, her eyes flitting up to check no one was listening to their conversation. 'When I said I'd seen you and suggested you come along, Tim was absolutely on board from the moment I mentioned it.

He wanted as many old friends here to celebrate with him as possible.'

'But I'm not an old friend, am I, Jenny? I'm an old flame. It's different.'

'You were an important part of his life.'

Jenny was painting a convincing picture of what might have happened, but Emily's version of events was more believable. Sophie could image the fractious phone call between Tim and his mother, Jennifer suggesting it would be a 'nice gesture' to invite Sophie to the wedding, Tim in his big, glass corner office, objecting, then hassled and busy from his important job, finally sighing reluctantly, saying he'd 'see what he could do'. And then she could imagine Vanessa throwing the hissy fit Emily had mentioned – an entirely understandable hissy fit. Which bride wants their boyfriend's ex-lover in the room when they are saying their vows? But in the end they'd all agreed to it. To do 'the decent thing', given everything that's happened, *poor thing*.

Before she could reply, music started blaring. Clearly it was time for the disco. Sophie cocked her head as she realised the track blaring out was Beyonce's 'Single Ladies'.

'Perfect,' Sophie whispered to herself. 'Just perfect.'

Shaking her head, Sophie pushed her chair back.

'Where are you going?' asked Jennifer.

'I need to go and make a call.'

'Sophie, you're upset, I can tell. Let me explain.'

'Jenny, I'm fine. I just need to speak to my sister.'

Sophie grabbed her bag and walked towards the hotel entrance. She was determined to find a signal somewhere so she could call Christa, even if she had to break into one of the guest bedrooms and ring out on a landline. And if Christa couldn't fetch her, she'd call an Uber or a minicab or a bloody donkey, anything that would get her out of here.

Screw Jennifer, screw Vanessa, screw all of them. She wasn't going to stay here another minute. As she walked into the lobby, Sophie was looking down at her phone, so didn't see the man and walked straight into him.

'Sorry,' she stuttered, stepping back. It was only then she noticed the man was wearing a police uniform.

'I'm looking for a Vanessa Louise Farringdon?' said the policeman.

'Oh,' said Sophie, feeling a wave of panic. 'Vanessa's in the dining room. Is everything alright?'

The policeman was already moving towards the music, but Sophie tried to block him. Whatever was wrong, it didn't have to be dealt with in public.

'This is a private event,' she said quickly. 'It might be better if she steps outside. I can go and get her for you if you'd like?'

The policeman shook his head and side-stepped, walking straight into the party room.

'Please officer…'

But the policeman was already scanning the faces of the women dancing on the makeshift dancefloor in the middle of the bar.

'If you could just point out which one she is?'

Sophie was about to object again, but she saw that Vanessa had spotted the uniform. Even from across the room, Sophie could tell she had gone pale.

'Miss Farringdon?' said the policeman as Beyoncé faded and stopped. 'Miss Vanessa Farringdon?'

'Yes,' said Vanessa. 'Is there a problem?'

'I'm afraid there have been some complaints, madam,' said the policeman, taking a notebook from his jacket pocket and flipping it open. 'Rowdiness and whooping,' he said, referring to his notes.

Vanessa shook her head, looking towards her mother with panic. It was hard not to feel sympathy for her.

'But we booked these rooms months ago,' stuttered Vanessa. 'And we have exclusive use of the hotel. I don't see how anyone would complain.'

The policeman focused all his attention on Vanessa.

'Has there been rowdiness?' he asked.

'I suppose someone might have called it that, but…'

'Well in that case, I'll have to take down your particulars.'

He paused, winked, then added: 'But not until I've taken down mine.'

'I'm *sorry*?' began Vanessa, but the policeman turned to point at Annabelle who was standing behind the record decks. Music jumped from the speakers: Joe Cocker's version of 'You Can Leave Your Hat On'. It wasn't until the policeman began to unbutton his tunic that the penny finally dropped for Sophie.

He wasn't a policeman at all. He was a stripper. And from the look of glee on Emily's face, this was clearly her idea of a bridal shower gift for Vanessa. Sophie looked around the room: not everyone was quite so pleased. Mostly they looked appalled. And most appalled of all was Vanessa, who looked like she wanted to summon a real policeman.

The song was filled with instructions that the faux-officer was only too pleased to echo in his own dance routine, shrugging off his shirt one shoulder at a time, advancing towards Vanessa with a lascivious look on his face. Joe Cocker's voice was so loud, Sophie could barely hear what she was saying to him, but she could tell from her body language that she just wanted him to put his kit back on. The stripper seemed undeterred and shimmied up close, undoing his trousers one button at a time; he obviously took the horror on Vanessa's face to be a come-on. Or maybe strippers always got that kind of reaction.

Despite it all, Sophie actually felt sorry for Vanessa; clearly her idea of a good time didn't involve a complete stranger in fancy dress rubbing up close to her. And Sophie could also see that no one was going to do anything to help her. Vanessa's friends either had their hands clasped to their mouths in horror or were whispering urgently to each other, their eyes wide.

He turned towards Sophie and rotated his hips. Sophie suddenly felt quite light-headed. She hadn't seen a naked man for fifteen years and now she had seen two in one day. Vanessa meanwhile was backed up against the wall, her head down, and a memory jogged. The quieter, more timid Vanessa who once had a panic attack at the Students' Union. Sophie remembered seeing her in the corner of the disco, unable to breathe. She'd run over immediately to help her, got her out of the close confines of the room, and out onto the street, holding her hand, and putting her palm on her back, warm and damp from sweat, until she calmed down.

'Off! Off! Off!' shouted the prosecco-fuelled crowd.

Sophie couldn't move very quickly, but she slipped around the gyrating stripper as fast as she could towards the decks where Annabelle was grinning and laughing, jabbing her finger in the air in time to the music.

'Turn it off!' shouted Sophie.

'Can't hear you,' yelled Annabelle, over the music.

'I said turn it *off*,' repeated Sophie, leaning in to Annabelle's ear. 'Look at Vanessa! She's hating every minute of this.'

'Get out of the way will you. This is hilarious.'

'Annabelle, she's on the verge of tears. This is her hen night. It's supposed to be fun.'

'This *is* fun! Look at her!'

There was a shriek from across the room, two words running together.

'It's Gucci!' cried Vanessa, as the baby-oil slick stripper shimmied against her, dancing back to reveal a greasy hand-print on the pale green silk.

'That's it!' snapped Sophie, leaning over the decks,

looking for the stop button. As she stretched out her hand to press it, she heard a sudden whoop from the other side of the room. Happy whoops, delighted whoops. Sophie turned and was amazed to see Jennifer standing on top of a table.

'Check *her* out!' said Annabelle as Jennifer beckoned to the stripper, then flapped her skirts around like a flamenco dancer.

The fake cop – now only identifiable as an officer of the law by the peaked cap on his head – grinned wolfishly and turned away from Vanessa, who almost sank to the floor in relief.

The stripper danced over to the table and made a playful grab for Jennifer, but she planted a foot on his chest and pushed him away to more shrieks of laughter.

Sophie watched in wonder as Jennifer began to dance. The stripper, to his credit, did the only thing he could in the circumstances; he played along. Even Vanessa seemed to relax, her traumatic personal assault over – for now at least. Annabelle switched the music to the disco groove of Shake Your Booty and everyone was up their feet.

'This is brilliant!' shouted Annabelle to Sophie.

Sophie laughed despite herself. Somehow, Jennifer had flipped a switch that allowed these image-conscious women to loosen up and let go a little. Vanessa's red face was losing its colour. Elspeth, the bride's mother, looked less thunderous. Even the faux-bobby seemed to be enjoying himself. Freed from his act, he had pulled his jacket back on and was just dancing for the hell of it, straight white teeth shining. Even Anton and Matt, the waiters, were dancing.

'So what do I know?' murmured Sophie, shaking her head in wonder.

She turned as Jennifer walked over, pink spots at the centre of her cheeks.

'Time to go,' she said, panting. 'And I'm driving.'

Chapter Nine

ADAM FELT DIZZY.

'Christ, no wonder I gave these up,' he said, looking down at his cigarette, the tip glowing orange in the dark.

'Lightweight,' smiled Tim, blowing a thin stream of smoke up into the blue-black sky. They were standing by the pub's back door, hunched against the cold, a curious mirror image of their younger selves. All those break-times they'd shared behind the science block, cupping a sneaky B&H and trying to look tough, partners in crime, just like they had been since their first week at Harling Comprehensive. To this day, Adam didn't know what had made him take Tim under his wing; after all, Adam Stowe had plenty of friends, knowing at least half the year from primary school, football and scouts. But by the end of the week, they were best friends and it had stayed that way until the day Adam had left for London.

'What were you doing out here, anyway?' said Tim, flipping up his collar.

'I had to take a call.'

'It wasn't Vee checking up on me, was it?'

He said it like a joke, but Adam knew it was exactly the sort of thing Vanessa would do.

He shook his head. 'Just someone from work…'

'Lauren from advertising?'

Adam looked at him in surprise, then remembered that he'd used Lauren as an excuse to bail out of a drink with Tim a couple of months previously.

'You still seeing her?'

Adam avoided his gaze.

'No.'

'Don't be shy, lover boy,' teased Tim, nudging him. 'There's nothing wrong with settling down like the rest of us. You should have told me when I asked about a plus one. Seriously, you can still invite her if you want and I can squeeze you onto table five.'

Adam gave a non-committal grunt and tapped his cigarette moodily, watching the sparks die. Lauren was nice enough, but whoever put 'nice' on their list of wants for an ideal partner? Adam wanted 'spectacular', he wanted 'heart-stopping', he wanted his soulmate. He hadn't left it this long to accept second best.

Inside, they could hear a mangled version of 'We are the Champions'.

'So you know your dad's coming tomorrow?' said Tim.

Adam looked up, startled.

'Graham's coming to your wedding?'

'Just the reception. My dad still sees him at Aston Park – you know for the fishing? He invited him then.'

'Jesus.' Adam hadn't anticipated this. His father had worked abroad for many years ever since he walked out on them, and although Mr Stowe had recently retired and returned to the Sheffield area, Adam hadn't known Graham still kept in touch with the Jamesons.

'Surely he's not coming all the way from Sheffield for a buffet?'

'Actually we've spent a lot of money on the evening do,' said Tim, his chin rising. 'There's a hog roast, the fireworks….'

'I didn't mean that,' said Adam. 'I meant my Dad's not one to do anything unless there's something in it for him.'

Adam hadn't seen his father very often in the past few years and when they had managed to get together, Graham had always seemed in a hurry to leave – some appointment or prior engagement.

'When was the last time you spoke to him?' asked Tim gently.

'A few weeks ago.'

It was over six months. Adam had received multiple texts and emails from his father, asking when he was next up in Sheffield, but he had deflected all of them. His mum Susan spent most of her time in Lanzarote with her second husband, Richard, so Adam was in no rush to go back, but in the end, they'd met up at the Oxo Tower when his father had come to London for a meeting – 'a bit of consultancy work to tide me over,' he'd explained – and Graham had ordered oysters, the Chateaubriand and a good bottle of red – the sort of media lunch that Adam enjoyed on a regular basis in the Noughties but which didn't happen so much these days. Adam had felt guilty accepting his largesse – he was still bitter – and they hadn't spoken since.

'Don't you think this might be a chance to bury the hatchet?' said Tim. 'I mean, you don't have to be best mates or anything, but resenting him for running off when you were a kid hasn't done you much good, has it?'

'When did you get so wise, Judge Judy?' he said, glancing across.

'Seriously Ads, families are tricky enough at the best of times – you wouldn't believe how clingy my mum's been over the past few weeks – but Graham? I mean he might have been a prick, but he's still your dad.'

Adam grunted again, not wanting to admit how keenly he had felt the estrangement of his father lately. The previous Christmas had been the first one that Susan and Richard had spent in the Canaries – something to do with the sunshine being good for Richard's arthritis. They'd invited Adam to come out to join them, but their two bedroom apartment was tiny and the flights had been expensive and so Adam had declined, convincing himself that Christmas Day alone with Netflix and a Marks and Spencer meal for one would be the peaceful recharge he needed. Instead he had never felt more lonely.

'I'll think about it, okay?'

He very much wanted to change the subject.

'So how are you feeling? About tomorrow?'

Tim screwed one eye up against the smoke and shrugged.

'Can't wait for the honeymoon if I'm honest.'

Adam looked at him meaningfully.

'You do know you can talk to me.'

'About what?'

'Stuff. The wedding. In case you had any worries or anything.'

Tim looked at him.

'You think I'm worried?'

'No, *just in case* you were. I'm here if you are. I know you're supposed to have this discussion with your best man, but I'm here too.'

Tim had chosen his younger brother Rich as his best man, which had hit Adam harder than he'd expected. He and Tim had grown apart, but even so…

'You know I had to ask him, right?' said Tim. 'I mean, Rich is my brother and you haven't been around much over the past few years.'

'It's fine,' said Adam, but it wasn't fine.

'So you're sure? About getting married.'

'Taken me ten years to get here,' said Tim with an exasperated laugh. 'You can't accuse me of making a snap decision.'

Adam took a long drag of his cigarette.

'Have you been with Vanessa that long?'

Tim counted on his fingers.

'Hell, no, it's twelve years.'

'I thought she'd have got you down the aisle sooner. She seems a very persuasive woman.'

Tim shrugged.

'Had stuff on.'

Adam grinned. 'Climbing up that corporate ladder?'

Tim raised one eyebrow. 'Takes more brainpower than you'd think. Office politics are a full-time headache.'

'So where are you going on honeymoon?'

'Maldives.'

Adam gave a good-natured snort.

'And there I was, almost feeling sorry for you.'

'Just for a week, all I could swing. The corporate world's like a gangster movie, you know? Take your eye off the ball for a moment and someone will step in and take your turf. Vanessa wanted to do three weeks, adding in Dubai and Sri Lanka, but I had to say no.'

Adam smiled to himself, wondering what saying 'no' to Vanessa sounded like.

'So, what does it feel like, committing yourself to one woman forever?'

'You say it like it's a bad thing.'

Adam laughed, but he found he was genuinely interested to know.

'Seriously. I've never met anyone I thought "I want to spend the rest of my life with you". It must be pretty awesome to feel that way.'

There was a pause, a soft crackle of burning paper, then the whoosh of smoke.

'It is,' said Tim softly, then pointed at Adam with a lop-sided smile. 'But you love the music, right? You've been working for the same magazine for how long?'

Adam grimaced, smoke wreathing his face.

'Too long.'

'What do you make there, these days?'

He was a good enough friend to ask the question, so Adam told him his salary, rounding it up to the nearest ten thousand.

'Really?' Tim didn't look impressed. 'How long do you think you're going to carry on doing it for?'

'You mean am I too old to be running around on Metallica's tour bus?'

Tim shrugged.

Adam had been asking himself the same question recently. Lately, he felt as if he was at a party where everyone else was having fun, everyone except him. But since his whole career had fallen through a trapdoor, that old life of tour buses and glamour suddenly seemed magical again.

'Luckily it's been taken out of my hands.'

'What has?'

'The decision. *Cream* is folding – *has* folded. I found out this afternoon, that's why I was talking to Lauren. I'm unemployed.'

There was genuine concern on his friend's face.

'I'm sorry, man. Are you okay?'

'It's fine,' he said trying to keep his voice light. 'I think it's about time I made a change anyway.'

Adam felt Tim's gaze on him. 'What are you going to do?'

Adam took a last drag and dropped the cigarette onto the floor, watching the sparks, wondering whether to tell Tim the truth, to tell his oldest friend about his dream. When they had been fifteen, that was all they'd done: sat in Adam's bedroom jabbering about their big plans. They were going to be rock stars, poets, film-makers, they were going to live in LA or Paris or briefly, when their English teacher had forced them to read *Call of the Wild*, in a snowy cabin in the Yukon, shooting grizzlies. Then one day Adam had picked up a music magazine and his dream had changed – and against all odds, he'd flown off and lived it. But dreams had a way of shifting, didn't they? Over the past few years Adam had been working on a new dream: he was going to open a record shop. QT Records, that was what he was going to call it. It would be a bricks-and-mortar vinyl specialist, with wooden racks and rare picture discs on the walls, but it would have an events arm too, hosting intimate acoustic gigs and one-off record launches. Adam had the knowledge: he was enough of a geek he could tell you the serial number on a Japanese pressing of "The White Album". And he had the contacts to pull it off: PRs, managers, label big-wigs. The one thing he didn't have was money. He glanced at Tim. Could – would – his friend help in that department, did his empathy stretch that far? He was sure he had the funds: Adam had felt the weight of Tim's credit card, seen him order from the expensive outer reaches of a wine menu without flinching. But would he understand that Adam still had a dream? Would he *get* it?

'What am I going to do?' he said, flicking the wheel of the lighter.

'I'm going to meet the perfect woman. Here, at the wedding. Some hot heiress. With a really nice car.'

Tim hooted with laughter.

‘That’s your plan?’

‘Why not?’ said Adam, slightly annoyed. Why couldn’t he pull a model-grade rich girl? Whenever he went to Ibiza on holiday he was always popular enough. ‘Weddings are hotbeds of romance, aren’t they? I could meet my perfect woman and live happily ever after. Just like you.’

Tim gave a weak smile.

‘So, what’s she like, this perfect woman?’

Adam smiled. This had been another of their favourite games as teenagers: build the perfect woman. So you’d get the body of Kelly Brook, the brains of Cat Deeley, Nigella’s way with a pie and Marty McFly’s car in the garage. Like the dream-exchange, it had been a way of two boys working out who they were and what they wanted from life. Tim might have narrowed it down to one woman, but Adam had never stopped playing the game. He wasn’t sure he ever would.

‘Pretty, smart. Kind, obviously. Brunette probably…And she has to be a great dancer. That’s an important one.’

‘A dancer? Why?’

‘It means she’ll be into music, she’ll probably be good in the sack too, and most of all, she’ll be good fun.’

‘Fun?’ said Tim, frowning.

‘Isn’t that important?’ asked Adam, but Tim never got to answer. They both looked up to see Hugo looming over them. His face was grave.

‘Chaps, I think we might have trouble.’

‘What’s up?’ asked Adam.

Hugo raised a finger in the air. The muffled sound of music and off-key singing floated out from the bar. Adam’s eyes met Tim’s.

Ali.

Adam quickly followed the others back into the pub. As they turned into the main room, Adam could immediately feel that the atmosphere had changed from raucous fun to something more menacing. In front of them on the little stage, surrounded by a crowd, was Ali, jacket off, his shirt unbuttoned to the navel. One arm was extended, holding a microphone out to the audience and the other arm was around the waist of a pretty young woman. Adam didn’t know who she was, but from the blazing looks of fury on the faces of a group of men by the side of the stage, he guessed she was a girlfriend or younger sister of one of them.

‘Oi, Ali!’ shouted Tim, making a desperate cutting motion across his throat, but the music was too loud and anyway, Ali was oblivious, evidently loving his time in the spotlight, singing of all things, ‘I’m Too Sexy’ by Right Said Fred.

‘Come on! You know the words…’ Ali shouted, mistaking the glares of the gang for adoration. He pulled the giggling girl closer and began to sing. ‘I’m too sexy for my cat…’

Adam pushed his way to the front. Ali was now pawing at the girl’s face.

‘Poor pussy,’ he growled. ‘I’m too sexy for my love… Adam! Adam Stowe,’ he said, noticing his friends. 'Come and join me up here.'

Adam had almost made it to the stage, when a man-mountain in a Megadeth T-shirt got to Ali first.

The music cut off, there was a scream, the sound of breaking glass and Adam was shoved sideways, going down painfully on one knee. As the lights clicked back on, he watched Hugo throw Ali over his shoulder like a rolled carpet as he made for the door. An angry patron loomed up in front of them, blocking their exit, but Hugo's arm shot out to fend him off. Adam began to back away, but bumped into a table, sending glasses crashing to the ground. A dozen faces swivelled his way.

'He's one of them!' shouted one.

Adam didn't hesitate. He turned and ran, ducking into a narrow corridor, hoping that it was an exit. He hurdled a metal mop bucket, then slammed a shoulder into a wooden door with a push-bar and was relieved to feel it give, his feet slipping but staying beneath him, the cold air in his lungs. He sprinted across the same patch of concrete he and Tim had just been standing on, swerving around the mossy picnic bench. His jacket caught on a bush, but hearing shouting behind him, he kept going, expecting, at any moment, a hand to fall on his shoulder like a brick.

Adam didn't stop running. Many men his age were doing triathlons or Tough Mudder; Adam hadn't even set foot in a gym since the early Noughties and even then it had only been after reading a piece in *The New Yorker*, which claimed gyms were the hot new place to meet girls. This was a bald-faced lie: Adam had only met sweaty men in baggy vests and he hadn't been back. Now, he was regretting it as he heard more shouts behind him.

A hedge filled his vision and Adam plunged in, twigs and thorns raking his face and arms, not daring to stop, forcing himself through. On the other side was a dark country lane and Adam dropped to his knees, smelling the cowpat ground into the tarmac. He couldn't get up, couldn't run any more.

Then there was a screech, right next to his ear.

Adam turned his head towards the sound, screwing up his eyes as he was washed with stinging white light. He heard the growl of an engine, felt its heat. And the logo, inches from his face. A silver Zafira. There was a pause, then the buzz of a window.

'I almost hit you! Are you alright?'

'Fine, fine,' he said, trying to regulate his breath as he ran around to the driver's side. A middle-aged man with a friendly red face peered out.

'Listen, are you going anywhere near The Swan pub? It's my friend's stag do and...'

'The Swan? You're not with the Farringdon-Jameson wedding party by any chance, are you?'

'I am,' said Adam with relief.

'I'm Tim's uncle. Dennis.'

'We've met, many years ago. It's Adam. Adam Stowe.'

'The famous writer! Well, jump in, lad and you can tell me about the time you met Pink Floyd.'

Chapter Ten

THE ROAD IN front of the Mini was black. Out here in the countryside, away from the lights of the Big House – or any other building for that matter – the darkness seemed thicker and more complete, pressing in around the car. Sophie looked through the windscreen at the grey strip of road lit by the pale yellow cones of the Mini's headlights, but beyond that, it was just a tunnel of nothingness.

Yet inside the car, it was beginning to feel like a nightclub. Closed in by the cloying heat from the vents, hot breath fogged the windows, music blasted from the speakers and as Jennifer sang along to Kylie at the top of her voice, the car swerved ever so slightly as her hands on the steering wheel moved in time to the beat.

'Are you sure you're okay to drive?' asked Sophie, raising her voice over the music.

'Just had the virgin mojitos all night,' said Jennifer, banging the flat of her hand on the gearstick. 'Must have had about half a dozen of them. They were absolutely delicious.'

Sophie gripped the door handle, sincerely hoping that Matt had got his orders right.

'Do you think the stripper would have got naked if you hadn't stepped in?' asked Sophie. 'I mean – is that even allowed these days?'

'The pouch was traumatic enough for poor Vanessa,' said Jennifer, raising her voice over the music. 'Those bridesmaids are absolute cows. What were they thinking?'

They came to a T-junction and Jennifer looked left and right, as if weighing up her options. After a moment, she signalled left, then as Sophie watched, she seemed to mutter something to herself and turned right, gunning the engine. Before Sophie could query it, Jennifer began talking.

'The thing is, you're all so uptight,' she said. 'So bloody stiff.'

'Who? Me?'

'All of you, your whole generation,' said Jennifer. 'Millennials, Generation Y or whatever you are. None of you seem to know how to have fun anymore. It's all this social media tying you all up in knots. You're terrified you're missing out and you're terrified you're getting it wrong. Everything's "must have" or "must do", you're constantly comparing your lives with everyone else.'

Sophie actually liked to think of herself as Cusp Generation X. Certainly the idea of being a 'snowflake' – of complaining about anything after all she had been through – was anathema to her.

'Not everyone is like that, Jennifer,' she said.

'Oh yes? I saw you in there at dinner, Sophie, worrying about what those hens were saying, worrying about whether you fitted in with those girls and their empty bloody lives. None of it matters, none of it. Certainly not fretting about which hashtag to put next to a picture of a latte.'

Sophie opened her mouth, then closed it again.

'All I'm saying is that life is too short to sit back,' said Jennifer, her tone softer now. 'Life's bigger than an Instagram photo. Live life, don't just document it. Because it all goes by so fast.'

Sophie wasn't sure about that last part. She felt as if her life had been limping along at a snail's pace, her inch-by-inch progress from horizontal to upright a visible metaphor for her personal development. Meanwhile, every time she came to a party such as tonight's she would see what she had missed – the big milestones like marriage and children, promotions and moving up the property ladder, but the small things too – the chatter about spa treatments and restaurants, mini-breaks with new lovers and college reunions with old friends – all the things that Sophie hadn't experienced, might seem insignificant to some, but which felt desperately important to Sophie. She felt tears begin to well and she turned away, concentrating on the dark road outside. Open fields, black woods, no buildings, no lights. The car's speed seemed to be picking up.

'Are you sure we're going the right way?' she said, desperate to get to bed.

'We'll see the village any second.'

Almost in slow motion, Sophie turned back towards the road, just as another black bend loomed ahead of them.

'Jenny! Look out!'

She made a grab for the steering wheel, too late. The hedge filled the windscreen, jagged claws of a tree smashed against the wing mirror and with a sickening thud, the wheels bounced over a rut, lifting them out of their seats. And then they were flying into the darkness, Sophie's mouth open, her scream lost in the night.

'ARE YOU OKAY?'

Sophie blinked twice, just to make sure she was still alive.

Yes, she was fairly sure she could still feel everything. Toes, fingers, neck moved. No obvious pain radiated from her back. It seemed they'd been lucky. The car's offside tyre had bounced them off the raised embankment like a tennis ball, spinning them 180 degrees through the air and ping-ponging back onto the tarmac, finally skidding to a halt facing back the way they'd come. It wasn't elegant, but it had done the job: they were still on the road and they were – as far as Sophie could tell – unhurt. Jennifer drove them into a lay-by, safe at least from any juggernauts tearing around the bend. Jennifer killed the engine and they sat in the silence, both staring straight ahead.

'I don't know what just happened,' stammered Jennifer.

'You were going too fast,' said Sophie fiercely, her whole body shaking.

‘I’m sorry,’ said Jennifer. ‘Sophie, I’m so sorry.’

Her hands were still on the steering wheel and Sophie could see they were trembling. Sophie took a moment to calm down and then reached across to Jennifer.

‘It’s fine. We’re fine. Just maybe go a bit lighter on the accelerator next time.’ She’d said it kindly, but still, Jennifer was crying, a trail of tears leaving a silvery ribbon down her soft cheek.

Sophie put an arm across her shoulder. ‘Jenny, we’re okay. No harm done,’ she said, but Jennifer was now sobbing.

‘Don’t take it so badly. Is it Tim? Is it because you’re giving him away tomorrow?’

Jennifer shook her head sadly.

‘Not really, no. Well, a little.’

Sophie handed her a tissue from a box in the central console and Jennifer dabbed at her face, then turned to look at Sophie.

‘I’ve got cancer,’ she said flatly. Sophie blinked, feeling the darkness press in again.

‘It’s in my stomach,’ said Jennifer. ‘Well, stomach and liver now. Lymph nodes too probably. The tests aren’t all back yet.’

‘Oh Jen,’ whispered Sophie.

‘That’s why I saw you that day in South Kensington,’ said Jennifer. ‘I was on my way to the Marsden.’

Sophie didn’t know what to say. The Royal Marsden was a cancer specialist hospital. If Jennifer was under their care, it told its own tale. Jennifer’s face was bleak.

‘I haven’t told anyone else,’ she said quickly.

‘Not even Bill?’

She drew her mouth into a thin line.

‘Obviously, Bill knows I’m sick, but he doesn’t know the full extent. I told him there’s a tumour in my stomach, but he thinks it’s still operable.’

Sophie swallowed.

‘Isn’t it?’

Jennifer took a long breath and let it out. ‘No. Not really.’

Sophie pressed her lips together and nodded, feeling terrible for her earlier outburst.

‘Are you getting treatment?’

‘They’ve started saying words like palliative care. Given that they probably can’t make it go away, I think I should just enjoy my life. What’s left of it anyway, without going through all sorts of side-effects.’

Sophie still felt shell-shocked. She had seen far too much of this in hospital. People wheeled away never to return, shambling round-shouldered family groups broken by diagnosis. The mundane weight of death filling corridors like unseen fog.

‘What about clinical trials?’ she asked. ‘Or immunotherapy? You can’t give up. Jennifer, you can’t.’

‘It’s not giving up,’ said Jennifer with feeling. ‘It’s facing the truth. There’s a big difference.’

She turned, her shining eyes towards Sophie.

‘Tim and Richard don’t know,’ she said firmly. ‘Please don’t breathe a word of this tomorrow.’

Sophie blinked and nodded. It was her choice. Sophie understood that it was the sufferer’s right to make those sorts of decisions: they were the ones standing on the cliff-edge. But it was still a heavy thing to bear, especially when it affected so many other people.

'Don't you think you should at least tell Bill?'

'I will,' said Jennifer wearily. 'I only got these latest results a couple of days ago. But it's going to hit him hard and I'm not ready to see that yet.'

Sophie didn't know Bill that well, but he'd always seemed jolly and kind – he was a teacher too, the cool sort that the kids always loved – and Sophie could easily imagine how he might be the softer half of the partnership. And she understood Jenny's logic too; she had seen first-hand how illness affected her mum and dad and how it was often harder for loved ones and carers. Doomed to watch helplessly, powerless to cure. And yet Sophie also knew how the support of others could lift you up, make things lighter, easier.

'I think Bill might surprise you,' said Sophie firmly. 'You can't go through this alone.'

'I can't say anything, Sophie. Not for the next couple of weeks, at least until Tim's back from honeymoon. It won't make any difference and it will just make the boys miserable. And you know, I'm grateful that I'm getting to see the wedding at least. I get to send my eldest son off into the world. So many people don't even get that, do they?' Her voice cracked. 'Because I know Tim will try and save me. He'll insist on me taking the drugs and I'll spend my last weeks feeling like death.'

The word hung in the air between them. Jennifer

finally turned and looked at Sophie.

'That's why I invited you to the wedding,' she said quietly. 'I just wanted things to go back to how they were. They were such happy days, weren't they?'

'Oh, Jennifer…'

'I'm sorry if I made you feel embarrassed or uncomfortable. I truly didn't mean to.'

Sophie gripped Jennifer's hand, all thoughts of phoning Christa forgotten.

'We're going to have an amazing day tomorrow,' she said, with a spike of resolve. 'We're going to laugh and sing and…'

'And dance?'

Sophie laughed.

'I haven't danced since I was 22.'

'I think it's about time you started again, young lady,' she said, reaching forward and firing the engine. It coughed, then caught. 'Because when you stop dancing, you might as well be dead.'

And she swung the Mini back onto the lane, the cracked headlights cutting through the gloom.

Chapter Eleven

ADAM STOOD ON the path up to The Swan, his face turned up towards the sky. It wasn't black, not quite. More of the darkest purple of a damson, if you really opened your eyes. For some reason, that made Adam think of Mr Berry, their art teacher at Harling Comprehensive. He had always claimed that using black paint was cheating, because there was 'always colour somewhere'. Adam had spent most of his time in art class doing pencil portraits of Kate Moss and doodling band logos. He hadn't been Mr Berry's favourite. He hadn't felt anyone's favourite for a very long time.

Closing his eyes tight, Adam took a deep pull of the cold night air, imagining himself floating in the limitless black void. Weightless, rootless, just drifting up towards the stars. Then he spread his arms and looked up again, marvelling again how brilliantly clear the sky could be away from the city, the rash of distant pinpoints twinkling like an infinite glitter ball.

'What are you doing, you weirdo?'

Adam's heart jumped and he stepped backwards into a puddle, soaking his only pair of shoes.

'*Tim?*'

To his left, a tiny white gate opened and Tim stepped out, beckoning furiously. Adam followed him through an arch and onto the garden terrace of Tim's room.

'Where the hell have you been? I've been calling you since the pub, you selfish cock. We've been worried sick. We thought you'd been beaten to death.'

Adam held up his hands in a calming motion.

'Relax, I'm here. Where are the others?'

Tim nodded back towards The Swan.

'Safely back in their cages, no thanks to you.'

'Hang on, how is this my fault?'

Tim put on a mocking version of Adam's voice. 'Let's go out on a *proper* stag. It'll be *fun*.'

Tim looked at him, face stony.

'Ads, I could have been killed tonight.'

Adam bit his tongue, deciding not to point out that it was Tim who had booked the crazy taxi driver, Tim who had unilaterally decided to go into the scary pub and, crucially, it had been Tim who had invited Ali to his wedding knowing how much of a loose cannon he was.

'So how did you get back before me?'

Tim frowned, as if it was obvious.

'The taxi driver picked us up.'

'The same guy? In the Fiat Panda?'

'He pulled up in front of the pub, Hugo threw Ali in the back and we tore off before any of those inbreds could catch us. It was like *The Fast and the Furious*.'

'Thanks for waiting for me.'

'If we hadn't shot off, our heads would have been

on spikes outside that pub. And we were chased by the police.'

'The *police*?'

Tim nodded, a tight look on his face.

'Turns out our cabbie friend's main career is in dealing weed. That's why he disappeared from the pub at high speed. Apparently, he'd spotted a couple of plain clothes coppers waiting for him, so he bolted then came back when he thought the heat was off. It was pure luck he arrived just when we were legging it from the pub.'

'And the police followed you?'

Tim shook his head.

'No, thank goodness. The last thing I want is trouble before my wedding day. So how did you get back?'

'Uncle Dennis gave me a lift.'

Tim managed a smile at that.

'So you've met your number one fan then? Did he bend your ear about Dire Straits?'

'Pink Floyd.'

They laughed and the tension diffused. Adam wallowed in the moment.

In a few hours, Tim would be married – and nothing would be the same again. He looked at his old friend, glad that they had spent that last night together, realising far too late that he had missed him.

'At least it *was* a proper stag,' said Adam.

'It was fun. At least, if I wasn't in fear for my life most of the time.'

'How about some midnight flaming Sambucas to round it off?'

'With our luck, we'd probably burn this place to the ground.'

'Sure?'

Tim nodded. 'But thanks anyway,' he said, holding up a fist. Adam bumped his against Tim's. 'You're welcome.'

Tim walked back through the French doors and closed them behind him. Adam thrust his hands into his pockets to warm them up. Evening dew was settling on the lawn and it glittered under the full moon. He walked round to The Swan's front entrance and rattled the door. Locked. Had there been some sort of instructions about how to get in after dark? It was just then that he saw movement inside the window to the left. Cupping his hands to the glass, he saw a woman in the bar and tapped urgently on the glass. There was scuffling, then the pub's door yanked open and the receptionist with the Cubist haircut scowled out at him.

'Can I help you?' she asked.

'Adam Stowe. Room… the one in the eaves. I've forgotten my…'

He tapped his pockets, then with an 'oh', pulled out his key.

With a snort, the woman let him inside.

'Listen, I don't suppose the bar is still…'

The receptionist was already striding back to her office. 'On the left,' she snapped. 'And you have twigs in your hair.'

Adam ran his hand over his scalp as he peered into the darkened bar. The lights were off, towels draped over the pumps. Clearly it was closed.

'You do seem to have a problem with doors,' said a voice in the gloom.

It took a moment before Adam realised it was the girl from the shower sitting on the sofa by the window.

'Are they still serving?' he said hopefully.

'No. But there's an honesty bar just over there.'

Her accent spoke of money and class. Fully dressed, she looked elegant too, certainly not the type to be sitting alone knocking back whisky in a hotel bar.

'Do you mind if I join you?'

There was a hesitation, then a shrug. 'Free country,' she said.

He'd met plenty of women like this before, spiky and difficult to impress. Adam generally found he could win them over, but tonight he wasn't in the mood, no matter how pretty she was.

'So are you here for the wedding?' said Adam, walking across to a table laden with bottles. He poured an expensive-looking gin, then sat down opposite his neighbour.

'I think everyone is,' she replied crisply.

She sat forward and offered him her hand.

'Seeing as you've already seen me naked, I think it's only polite if we are formally introduced. I'm Sophie Wallis. I was at Uni with Tim.'

Her formality made him smile.

'Adam Stowe,' he said, clasping her palm. 'Tim's friend from school. And I'm really sorry about earlier.'

'Honest mistake.' She gave him a sideways glance. 'At least, I hope it was.'

'It was,' said Adam, with a smile, rubbing his head again, making sure all the leaves were gone. 'We've obviously got connecting rooms and someone didn't lock some door they should have.'

'We're in the family suite. I checked. And to avoid further embarrassment, I've spoken to the manager and you can use the staff bathroom on the second floor. I hope that's okay.'

He nodded. Objection was clearly not an option.

'So how was your night, Sophie?'

'The usual. Stripper, car crash, nothing out of the ordinary. You?'

'Same. Karaoke, chase across the fields. Quite dull, really.'

As they laughed, the mood softened until they were cut off by a sudden hammering on the door.

Adam watched the receptionist stride across to the front door, scowling. Twisting in his seat, Adam peered through the window and his stomach dropped. Two burly men were standing at the front, one holding up an official-looking ID wallet.

'Oh no,' he muttered.

'What?' asked Sophie, craning her neck to look over his shoulder.

'I think it's the police.'

'Not more strippers, surely?' she replied.

'Strippers? No, the real police. I think they may be looking for us.'

'Us? Are we Bonnie and Clyde all of a sudden?'

If Adam hadn't been in so much trouble, he would have smiled. He certainly liked the way she took it in her stride. But he was worried for Tim – and for himself. If the coppers had seen him get dropped off at The Swan…

Sophie was talking but he wasn't following what she was saying. Something about a quiz and a vegan meal.

His heartbeat quickened as the police came into the bar. One of them looked around for a switch and the room flooded with light.

'Sir?' said the younger of the two men, flipping his ID wallet in Adam's direction. 'Could we have a word?'

'Of course. Is there a problem?'

'This lady says you've just arrived at the pub,' he noted, nodding over to the receptionist who was still lurking in the hallway.

Adam felt heat rise up the collar of his shirt. Reminding himself he hadn't done anything wrong, he took a sip of the gin he hadn't yet paid for.

'Have you been to the Hare and Hounds in Albany by any chance tonight?'

Adam could feel his already over-taxed brain overheating. If he said no, he was lying to the police and for that, he felt sure there could be consequences. If he said yes, there was the very real chance that he – and Tim – could be charged with being the Surrey Hills answer to Pablo Escobar.

'We've been here all night, haven't we darling?' said Sophie cutting in. 'Except when we gave Mrs Jameson a lift back from Haslop Hall.'

Adam tried not to betray his shock. He'd known

this woman for two minutes. What was she *doing*?

The older policeman looked at them. 'So you two are *together*?'

'Sometimes I wonder, officer,' said Sophie, with a tone of mild despair. 'But yes.'

Both policemen frowned suspiciously and the elder one turned to the receptionist who was still hovering.

'They are upstairs. In the eaves,' she scowled, blowing her lips out like an angry horse.

'Can I ask what the problem is, officer?' asked Sophie.

It wasn't just her accent that was classy. She had the quiet confidence of rich, smart people, that commanded attention and gave her instant authority.

'We've had reports of an incident at the pub,' said the younger officer. 'Someone was assaulted. A drug deal gone wrong, we think.'

'Assault? Drugs? I had no idea that sort of thing happened around here.'

'Keeps us on our toes, Madam,' smiled the young copper, standing up a little bit straighter. Adam could tell he was loving every minute of it. He could also tell that the copper was distracted by Sophie's legs, which annoyed him more than it should have done.

The older policeman seemed slightly more focused. 'So, can you tell me why this lady on the front desk said you've just arrived at The Swan?'

'My fault I'm afraid,' said Sophie. 'My dress was in the car. I didn't want it all screwed up for the Big Day tomorrow, so I sent him out to get it. But you only bloody forgot your key, didn't you darling?'

Adam nodded, shooting Sophie a grateful look.

'Big day?' asked the older policeman.

Sophie gave a tinkling laugh.

'Oh, sorry. It's the wedding tomorrow, up at St Mary's Church and then Haslop Hall. It's a very big day for both of us.'

She took Adam's hand and he felt a tingle of electricity fire to every nerve ending.

'To think, we were supposed to get an early night,' he said, squeezing her fingers.

'Now if that's all, officers, do you mind awfully if we head on up to our room?' She said it with such charm, it was impossible for them to say no. The policemen exchanged shrugs.

'Of course. I think we're done here.'

'You both have a good night,' said the younger copper, with an envious glance at Adam.

'And congratulations on the wedding.'

'Thanks,' said Adam, looking across at Sophie. 'I'm a very lucky man.'

Chapter Twelve

SOPHIE WAITED UNTIL they were standing at the bottom of the stairs before she dropped Adam's hand.

'There was an *assault*?' she said turning to him. 'You didn't mention that when you sneaked in ten minutes ago.'

She was pretty sure he wasn't the violent sort and besides, she had strangely enjoyed the whole performance in front of the policemen. Sophie had never considered herself to be a good actress. At school, the big parts in the plays had always gone to Julia Townsend and Anita Patel, so that by the sixth form she didn't even bother auditioning. But she'd certainly enjoyed her impromptu role as the soon-to-be Mrs Adam Stowe, even if her fiancé had been something of a dead loss as a straight man.

'It wasn't an *assault* assault,' said Adam quickly. 'Although it might have been if they'd caught us. My friend Ali – Tim's friend – got a little carried away on the karaoke and the locals didn't seem to share his sense of the dramatic. All the others ran off and the locals came after me. Of course, my natural athleticism meant I could out-run them….'

‘I see,’ she said sceptically, but she was still winding him up. Sophie had helped Adam out because she already knew who he was. Returning to The Swan after their car-crash revelations, Sophie had hung back when Jennifer had gone up to her room, pretending she had a call to make. In truth, she had simply dreaded returning to the eaves alone where she knew she would spend hours staring at the ceiling going over and over everything that had happened that night, so she had detoured to the bar, hoping to find some noise and frivolity to distract her, but seeing it was deserted, a G&T in the dark seemed equally appealing.

That was when she heard voices, or rather one voice in particular: Tim’s voice. She froze, hidden in the shadows, listening as Tim and his friends fell through the door, jabbering about The Hare and the karaoke and their missing mate Adam.

‘Thanks for what you did back there,’ he said, shaking her from her thoughts. ‘My room’s tiny but at least it’s better than a jail cell for the night. You saved my skin. I appreciate it.’

She nodded in acknowledgement, not wanting to admit that Tim was the real reason she had lied to the officers. Despite everything, she hadn’t wanted trouble on the eve of his wedding, hadn’t wanted the situation to escalate, and if that meant an entire charade about being engaged to Adam Stowe, then that was the way it had to be.

They took the stairs to their rooms slowly. She could tell Adam was drunk, but he didn’t seem to mind or notice the glacial speed of their ascent. When they got to the landing, he loitered outside the door to his room.

'For the record, I'm not a drug dealer either,' he said fishing his key out of his pocket. 'Although I will plead guilty to liking the odd bit of karaoke.'

'Adam, I've heard all about your reputation,' she said, wishing they were standing a bit further apart, wishing the corridor wasn't quite so narrow.

'My reputation?' Even in the low light, she could tell he was shocked.

'I went out with Tim for three years,' she said, with a half-smile. 'Don't you think I heard about all your crazy partying and brushes with the wild side of rock.'

He looked as if it was dawning on him, just as she realised who Adam was the moment she'd heard Tim talking about his friend outside The Swan.

'Sophie. You're *that* Sophie?'

She felt herself colour, wondering what he'd heard about her.

'Can you believe we never met? Tim said you were always off somewhere glamorous. I don't blame you, Bristol University's Student Union doesn't quite compare to Madison Square Gardens.'

The rock star. That's what Tim used to call his old friend from Sheffield. She remembered a pinboard in his student room – a patchwork of photos, phone numbers scribbled on crumpled receipts and tickets stubs for gigs and festivals. Even now she could picture a polaroid in the middle of it – a faded shot of two old friends punching the air with their fists. Tim and Adam – brothers from another mother, or so he once described him. She could still remember the way her boyfriend used to talk about his best friend. Tim looked up to Adam, admired him, although she had quickly realised that he was glad to be out from under his shadow.

'Well, we've met now, so how about another drink to celebrate, seeing as the drugs bust meant we had to abandon our gin.'

'I'm not sure I want to take my chances with the receptionist again. Our copy book is definitely marked.'

'Luckily, I have some brandy,' he smiled, nodding toward his room.

Sophie flinched. Here was some man she barely knew and he was inviting her into his room as if he wanted to have *sex* with her.

'I'm safe in taxis,' he said, as if he had detected her reticence.

Breathe, just breathe, she told herself, willing herself to relax. Adam seemed fun, she did need a drink and besides, she was intrigued to chat more to Tim's oldest friend.

'Come to my room, if you'd like,' she said, deciding she would feel more comfortable there. 'I think I saw a mini-bar under the desk.'

'Only madmen and millionaires drink from the mini-bar,' smiled Adam. Sophie inhaled sharply, willing herself to live a little. Isn't that what Jennifer Jameson had told her that evening?

'Brandy it is then. It's what we're supposed to have at the end of the night, isn't it?'

She started to panic as Adam went to get the drink and she went to her room, closing the door behind her. Sophie was not used to inviting men back to her place. There had been a few dates over the years but no one had ever made it back to the converted garage. At least her room was tidy. Sophie always liked everything to have their place. The case was stowed away in the corner, her dress for the wedding hung up, her wash bag and towels were on the ancient chest of drawers by the tiny window.

Taking off her jacket, she walked straight across to the fridge and opened it, lining the miniature cans of soda along the top. Coke, lemonade, tonic.

A minute later there was a gentle rap on the door.

She smoothed down her skirt and let him in. He was holding a bottle of Cognac and she noticed some of it was gone already.

'Glasses?'

She looked around the room. There was a kettle, cups, tea-bags, nothing to drink brandy out of without looking like a student.

'There'll be some in our bathroom,' he said, disappearing through the connecting door.

When he returned, he poured the brandy into two small tumblers.

'Coke or lemonade?'

'Either,' she said quickly, perching on the end of one of her twin beds, and pulling her skirt over her knees.

'There.'

Adam gave her a drink and went to sit in the armchair in the corner of the room.

There was a short silence.

'I see your place is as spacious as mine, then. They say it's a family suite but families from where? Lilliput?'

He leaned forward, cradling his glass.

'So tell me about the strippers…'

She looked down, bashful and warm. 'It was a hen night thing. Vanessa hated it. But Mrs Jameson saved the day. And then we left.'

'Mrs J saved the day? That sounds about right. What did she do? Or what goes on tour, stays on tour?'

'Something like that,' said Sophie, taking a big gulp of brandy.

He nodded towards the twin beds.

'Sharing a room?'

She shook her head. 'I'm here on my own.'

'Me too.'

'We'll probably be on the same table, then.'

Adam gave a soft snort. 'The Singles Table. By the way, when I said I'm safe in taxis… Back in the day, when debutantes were being ferried around London by eligible young men, the respectable ones were said to be safe in taxis…'

'I know what it means,' she said, looking away from him.

'Just so you know. In case it comes up tomorrow.'

'Are you thinking you might try it on with the bridesmaids? I've met them, they will eat you alive.'

He gave a low, slow laugh and his eyes twinkled. She couldn't deny that Adam Stowe was good looking, just as Tim had always said he was, with a cool that none of her university friends had ever even halfway possessed. In the soft beam of the moonlight, holding his drink like a rock star, his dark hair tousled as if he had recently got out of bed, she didn't doubt he could have his pick of anyone at tomorrow's wedding – single or otherwise – bridesmaid or possibly even bride, if he really put his mind to it.

'So, if you didn't go to Bristol, where did you go?' she asked, sipping her drink.

'I didn't go to uni,' he shrugged. 'I had a place but I didn't take it. In fact, I turned it down two weeks before Freshers.'

'Bold,' said Sophie. 'Where were you going to go?'

'Cambridge.'

Sophie almost coughed up her brandy. 'You had a place at *Cambridge* and you didn't go?'

Adam gave another modest shrug.

'It sounds mad, but I just knew what I wanted. I suppose it would have given me bragging rights, and yes, Cambridge is plenty of people's dream – but it just wasn't mine, so I reckoned someone should have the place who really wanted it. When you know what you want, you go out and you take it.'

Sophie looked at him with different eyes. She'd always imagined Adam Stowe as some sort of crazed hedonist sleeping on the floors of airports and tour buses. She didn't have him down as the single-minded type. Or clever enough for Oxbridge either, if she was honest.

'So what happened with you and Tim?' asked Adam. He said it playfully but there was an edge to it. Or was that just Sophie reading yet more subtext into everything? Adam might be bright, but he didn't seem like the subtext type.

'I mean, why did you finish?' he added. 'Was it the snoring? I spent four nights in a tent with him at Glastonbury. The sleep deprivation was so bad I'd have been better off going to Guantanamo Bay.'

Suddenly Sophie felt as if she was floating free of the conversation, of the room itself. He didn't know about her, about the accident. It was strange, feeling cut adrift from history.

'I had an accident. I was out of the loop for a very long time. A lot of people disappeared from my life, Tim included.'

'An accident? What happened?'

Very few people asked about it so directly. It was refreshing not to have to beat around the bush.

'The year after we left Bristol, we went on a skiing trip to Verbier,' she said slowly. 'My godfather had given me a week in his chalet as a graduation present. In my head I wanted it to be like the "Last Christmas" video, you know: friends, fondue, twinkling lights. Tim came, obviously, and a bunch of other people you might know – Charlie K, Karen. Vanessa was there too. Sixteen of us, I think, all billeted up in this Alpine cabin.'

'Cosy,' he said.

She found it easy to talk to Adam – another surprise. She had expected preening, name-dropping and me-me-me. Instead he just sat and listened and it felt good.

'I was a good skier. I adored it,' she said honestly. 'I still love the mountains and the blue skies behind those big white peaks. That clear air. I was always the first one out on the piste in the morning and the last one back after dark.'

For a long time, all Sophie ever talked about was her accident. To doctors, therapists, support groups. But now she thought about it, she hadn't told this story for years – and now, for the first time, she didn't feel the dread.

Sophie had been told many times that people with her injuries could often not remember the events surrounding their accidents, but Sophie didn't have that problem. As she spoke, Sophie felt herself transported back to those slopes. There had been no fresh snowfall for the entire trip and by the end of the week, the pistes were icy. They'd had lunch at a café on the mountain, they'd been laughing – something to do with Tim's meatballs. Sophie could clearly recall kicking into her skis and pushing off, swooping down, turning, picking up speed. She could feel the wind in her face, the bite of the cold on her teeth.

She looked at Adam.

'And suddenly I was just falling,' she said quietly. 'It turns out someone had run over the back of my skis.'

She took another sip of her drink, feeling her hands shake just a little. Jittery.

'I fell badly and hit my head,' she said. 'I can't

remember all that much, but I do remember looking up at the sky and knowing – *just knowing* – that it was really bad. I had to be airlifted off the mountain.'

'Was it your back?'

Sophie shook her head.

'My brain,' she said quietly.

'Isn't that what happened to Michael Schumacher?'

'I believe so,' she replied. 'It's called a TBI, or traumatic brain injury, and it can alter neurological function. I was put in a medical coma, they kept me there for a week, then I was in a Swiss hospital for two months in critical care. The doctors told my parents that I probably wouldn't walk again, maybe not talk again, or ever be able to look after myself.'

She felt less brave now. She turned her head, pressed her fingers against her lips, fighting back the emotion as she thought about her past.

'Sorry,' she said. 'I thought I was over this.'

She took another breath. 'Eventually I came back to England, another hospital, then a rehabilitation centre. My mum gave up her career to look after me. She'd been a barrister, a very successful one, and all the things that made her a brilliant lawyer, all that grit and drive and determination, they helped me get better. And slowly, I did.'

She gave him a weak smile, trying to lighten the mood. '*Really* slowly. I spent most of the next few years in bed'.

Adam looked at her, willing her to continue.

'So yes, a lot of people disappeared in those years.

And to be honest, I wanted them to. I wanted everyone to remember me as the girl I was, not the one I had become.'

Sophie forced herself to meet his gaze. She wondered whether she should have said anything. They'd been having fun, and now the mood had changed. No-one wanted to hear about misfortune and near-death experiences.

'But you recovered,' he said simply, without any of the pity she usually got. 'And I don't think it was just your mum's grit that made it happen. No doubt she helped, but you're walking today because you decided to do it. And that's pretty incredible.'

It was kind of him to say, but it made Sophie feel strangely uncomfortable. She took a nervous belt of her drink, sucking cool air through her teeth.

'So come on, tell me,' she said, trying to perk up. 'What's Vanessa like?'

'I should ask you that. You were mates at Uni.'

'It was a long time ago. She was a quiet thing, back then. Not a close friend. She only came on the Verbier trip because someone dropped out at the last minute.'

'A dormouse went into a chrysalis and came out a peacock.'

That made Sophie laugh. 'Nicely put. You should be a writer.'

She hesitated, then asked the question she'd been dying to ask Adam.

'So, when did Tim start dating Vanessa?'

'I see where this is going.'

He seemed to think it over. 'Truthfully, I don't

know. Tonight he told me they'd been together for twelve years. But how they got together or exactly when, I'm not sure. Does it really matter now?'

Sophie was surprised to find that it still did. She took a moment to calculate whether that dozen years tallied with Vanessa's Bond-movie detail from the quiz earlier that night.

'Are they happy?'

She didn't want him to say the one thing that she feared. That Tim *was* happy. That he was better off without her. But Adam Stowe just shrugged.

'I'm not the man to ask. You know, I don't see Tim much anymore. I always thought I'd be his best man, but I'm starting to think I barely scraped onto the guest-list at all. When we do get together, we never really talk about our love lives, so I don't have that kind of insight.'

'So what *do* men talk about?'

He laughed. 'Sport, music, kung fu movies, who'd win in a fight between the Yeti and the Loch Ness monster, whether it's possible to eat your own weight in Scotch eggs…'

Adam finished off his drink and put down the glass.

'Look, if what you're really asking here is whether Vanessa's the right woman for Tim… honestly, I don't think it matters.'

She gaped at him.

'Surely that's the *most* important thing.'

Adam leant forward.

'They've been together for twelve years. That

means he knows what she's like.'

'Selfish,' said Sophie: it came out before she could stop it, but Adam just nodded.

'She is. Vee's more interested in her wedding dress and the worktops in their new house in Wandsworth than she is in Tim right now. And Tim knows it.'

Sophie was stunned. 'And yet he's still going to marry her? It sounds like a decree nisi waiting to happen.'

'No, it's…' She watched him struggling to find the right word. 'It's romantic.'

'*Romantic?*'

Adam nodded. 'They've seen each other's faults and yet they're sticking with it. Tim and Vanessa made that decision and tomorrow we're going to watch them stand up and declare it in front of the world. If that isn't love, I don't know what is.'

She closed her eyes, and rubbed her forehead. She felt she was losing some sort of important argument, but wasn't sure exactly what it was. She didn't know what she was really saying, what she was asking. And yet Adam seemed to understand her, seemed to understand how Tim…

'Bathroom,' said Adam.

Her eyes flicked up.

'What?'

'Bathroom,' he repeated, one hand over his mouth. He jumped to his feet, launched himself at the adjoining door, scrabbling it open, pushing through.

'Adam!' cried Sophie, 'What the hell are you doing?'

But she didn't really need to ask. The distinctive sound of retching echoed off the tile walls.

'Great,' she sighed. 'Just bloody *great*.'

Chapter Thirteen

ADAM WOKE FEELING terrible. He lay on his bed, eyes closed against the needle-sharp light, wondering if he'd actually slipped and cracked his skull last night. That, surely, was the only thing which would explain a headache this horrific, not to mention the vicious buzzing in his ears and the flashes across his vision like someone was flicking the lights on and off. Slowly he sat up, letting out a hissing groan.

'What *on earth* did I drink?' he muttered. Lager, certainly. And the tequila Hugo had hurled into the fireplace. He pulled his tongue from the roof of his mouth with a sucking noise. Brandy? Whatever it had been, it was still sloshing about in his stomach like petrol.

Adam caught sight of himself in the mirror. His hair was sticking up at the back and there was a ripple-pattern across his cheek due to the fact he had slept on his jeans. *On* his jeans? He looked down and was partly relieved to see that he was still wearing some clothes. At least he hadn't repeated his shower streak in front of Sophie.

He groaned again at the thought of his neighbour, feeling a sheen of perspiration popping on his skin.

Adam couldn't remember everything about the night, but he certainly recalled throwing up in their shared bathroom. He also remembered Sophie making him scrub the bowl before he was allowed to go to bed. Which, he had to admit, was fair enough.

He slumped forward, breathing through his nose, trying not to give in to the sinking feeling. Sophie had been lovely. The way she'd helped him out with the cops, given him an alibi, but still seemed... what? Interested in him? Not in a sexual way, but actually wanting to know what he thought. Even if she was really only interested in Tim. He'd been drunk, but he hadn't missed that.

BANG BANG BANG!

It took a moment before Adam realised the thudding was coming from the door, not from inside his head.

'Get up!'

Adam crossed the room, sighing with relief that it wasn't Sophie here to give him another telling off.

Tim pushed inside as soon as Adam unlocked the door.

'What's that smell?' said Tim, sniffing the air.

'The drains, I think. Old pub. What's up?'

'The band have cancelled,' said Tim.

'Band?'

Tim turned to face him, his cheeks pink.

'The band, the *wedding* band. They've bloody pulled out, meaning Vee is having a nervous breakdown, meaning I need a replacement.'

Adam tried to focus. No wedding band, meaning

no entertainment at the reception. He didn't have much experience with planning weddings but he could see, yes, that could be a problem.

'I can start spinning the discs earlier if you like,' said Adam. 'I've got the entire Pixies back-catalogue.'

'No, no, no,' said Tim, pacing up and down. 'I need a band. Or a circus act or even a dance troupe at a push. Anything, but it needs to be big. This was the *one thing* I had to arrange for the wedding', he said, holding up his fingers in double quotes. 'And Vee is spitting feathers. I haven't heard her this angry, not since… well, ever. Apparently because we don't have someone droning out "I'm A Believer", our wedding is a hideous failure.'

He shook his head.

'I need to fix this double quick, or my life won't be worth living.'

Adam briefly considered pointing out that this was exactly the sort of thing his best man was supposed to help him with, then thought better of it. He was secretly pleased that Tim had come to him rather than Rich.

'Is the band definitely a "no"?' he asked, running his hand over his stubble. 'I mean, can't you get Jonty to threaten them with legal action or something?'

'No,' snapped Tim.

'It's got to be worth a phone-call, hasn't it?' pressed Adam.

Tim's expression looked more wounded.

'Look, it turns out I hadn't *actually* booked them.'

Adam gave a surprised laugh. 'You're kidding?'

'Do I look as if I'm joking?'

'Ah, no.'

'So… can you get someone, Ads?'

Adam looked at his friend, the implication sinking in.

'Me?'

'This is your world, isn't it? You're always going on about how you've been out drinking with Madonna or him out of the Arctic Monkeys. There must be someone you can call? Vee really likes James Blunt, if you know him. Yeah, he would be perfect.'

Adam started to feel clammy again.

'I know some musicians, obviously, but not well enough to pull in that kind of favour.'

'Ads, come on.'

There was a desperate, pleading tone to Tim's voice and Adam guessed it was taking Tim quite a lot to ask. Tim was proud; he liked to be seen as highly capable, always in charge. To Tim, asking for a favour was a sign of weakness. And of course, Adam wanted to help; he would love to get ABBA to reform or air-lift in Chris Martin, but the truth was, Adam didn't know ABBA or Chris Martin. He didn't know anyone really, not well enough to call them the day of a wedding and ask them to drop everything and come and play there.

Adam believed he had a good reason for this after twenty years at the coal-face of rock. He had always believed there were two types of music journalists: those who made friends with their subjects and those who kept their distance. People like Adam's nemesis

Tony Robb were in the first category, sucking up to every vaguely famous face, giving their unlistenable experimental solo albums five stars. And then there were writers with integrity, a group Adam was proud to be part of. Those journos kept aloof, they didn't play the game. How could you give an unbiased review of Sting's new record if you were hanging out doing yoga at his Sussex estate? It was about *honesty*. That's what Adam told himself anyway.

'Look Tim, I'd love to help, but it's festival season. Everyone's on tour, they're not going to be able to drop everything and traipse over to some crappy hotel in the middle of nowhere...'

'Oh cheers.'

'I didn't mean it like that. But see it from the band's point of view. Cancel Glastonbury or play a wedding reception for some guy they don't even know?'

Tim glared at him.

'Glastonbury isn't on this year. Even I know that.'

Tim ran his hand through his hair.

'What about Declan Thingy out of Belasco? He's your mate isn't he?'

'Yes, I *know* him...'

'Well enough for him to put us on the guest list for that gig last night, right? Which means he's taking your calls *and* he's probably still in the area. Can't you ring him again? I'm desperate here.'

Adam looked at his phone sitting on the dresser, remembering the toe-curling message he'd left the night before. Guest-list places were one thing, but asking a pop star to cancel his plans to take the place of a third-rate covers band? There were world-class egos in play here.

Besides, Tim didn't know that Declan wasn't exactly an inner confidante. Adam had interviewed him a few times over the years, hung out with the band on the tour bus at festivals. On one memorable occasion, he'd flown out to Vegas to interview the band, and afterwards had invited Dec to a poker tournament being held at the Bellagio later that day. Incredibly, Declan had turned up and it had been one of the very few genuinely brilliant assignments Adam had had as a writer, a near perfect night of glamour and fun, drinking cocktails, talking crap, eating nuts, fending off women. For one glorious evening, he'd felt like he was in the band, or at least a genuine friend of the band, instead of some irritant waiting at the stage door.

'Please,' pressed Tim.

'All right,' sighed Adam. He knew his friend well enough to know he wouldn't leave the room until he agreed. 'I'll call him. But no promises, alright.'

Tim grabbed him into a rough hug, slapping his back and making Adam's ears ring.

'There's one other thing,' said Tim, pulling a crumpled piece of paper out of his pocket. 'The speech.'

'What speech?'

'*My* speech. You know, the one the groom has to make at the reception?'

Can you have a quick look at it? Being writer of the year and everything.'

Adam raised an eyebrow.

'Ten years ago.'

'I just need you to put some jokes in. And maybe some feelings.'

Reluctantly Adam took the paper, unfolded it and began reading.

> *Thank you, Larry, for that wonderful speech. I hope today does not feel like you are losing your daughter, more as if you have gained a son. In fact you have gained a son, as we are moving in with you.*

Adam looked up.

'You're moving in with Vee's parents?'

'It's a joke. Like they can't get rid of us.'

He read on.

> *As I look forward to my life with Vanessa, I'm reminded of the man who had his credit card stolen, then refused to report it to the police as the thief was spending less than his wife (pause for laughter).*

'Did you just copy this off the internet?' said Adam.

'Some of it.'

'Tim, you're the creative director of an advertising agency.'

'Glasshouse is a *marketing* agency,' he said loftily. 'Besides, I've never been good at the heartfelt personal stuff.'

Adam tried to imagine what he would say to the woman he had just committed to spending the rest of his life with.

'Just say, "thank you, Vanessa, for making me the happiest man in the world."'

'Come on. Can't you just spruce it up a little?'

He supposed Tim had a lot of people doing his bidding these days; staff, cleaners, builders, financial advisors, personal trainers. There had even been reference to a travel concierge the previous evening, someone who sorted out their mini-breaks and flights. Was Adam just another one to add to the list?

Adam rubbed a hand over his face and let out a long breath. Tim was his best mate, and it was his wedding. 'I suppose.'

'Excellent. I knew you wouldn't let me down.'

'Listen, it's still early,' said Adam, putting the speech in his pocket. 'Shall we go for a hair of the dog or a fry-up or something?'

Tim shook his head.

'I'm in enough trouble as it is. I'm going for a run. Last chance for alone time, eh?' He clapped Adam on the shoulder. 'But thanks man, I knew I could count on you.'

Adam watched Tim close the door. It was nice that someone had faith in him. But Adam wasn't so sure. He wasn't sure at all.

Chapter Fourteen

SOPHIE HOVERED AT the door of The Swan's country kitchen-themed dining room, where the receptionist from the night before was guarding the entrance with a clipboard. The place was packed, the noise loud with the clank and conversation of a hundred guests chowing down on their complimentary Full English breakfasts. Sophie was nervous about eating alone, but she was also hungry. She had barely eaten a bite at the bridal shower, and she knew she should probably throw down some tea and toast. It was going to be a long day.

'Table for one, please,' she said, walking up to the podium where the receptionist was examining her seating plan.

She looked up. 'Is your husband not joining you this morning?'

'No. It's just me today, thank you,' replied Sophie.

The receptionist ran a fingernail down the list, looked around the room and then back at Sophie.

'It's going to be about twenty minutes for a table for one. Not unless you want to share the communal table,' she said, jabbing a pen towards the far side of the room. 'The bride encourages mixing.'

It was not an appealing offer.

'Actually, it's fine. Maybe I'll pop back later.'

'Suit yourself. We close the kitchens at ten sharp.'

Sophie wandered through into the bar area – she couldn't face going back to her room, far too many stairs – but the front door was open and sunlight was streaming in. Playborough village had looked pretty when she and Christa had driven through it the afternoon before, and her physio was always telling her a gentle stroll never hurt anyone – now was as good a time as any to test it out. She walked slowly out onto the wide village street of honey stone cottages, purple wisteria winding around bay windows and bright-coloured doors dotted with polished brass. She passed a shuttered cheese shop, a half-timbered off-licence and a bakery still maddeningly closed – the smell of just-baked buns was heavenly.

Ever since she had set off from Wimbledon the day before, Sophie had felt on edge. Her week usually had a set routine. She worked at Warwick Travel on Tuesdays, Wednesdays and Thursdays. On a Monday she would attend a Tai Chi class at the local leisure centre, on Friday night she would treat herself to a take-away, and she would spend all-day Saturday with her parents. Some people might call her life predictable, but it suited her just fine. Coming to Tim's wedding was far out of her comfort zone, but as she inhaled the soft summer air, she could admit that it was agreeable being out of the city.

Sophie turned away from the main street, following a lane at right angles, the road dappled with soft sunlight, flashes of gold dancing between the dense leaves overhead. It was warm already, bees and dragonflies humming through the feverfew as the path sloped down to the river, fringed with green grasses and willows swooning like spinsters, their branches dipping in and out of the waters, stark against the sky. Sophie stood and watched a group of children cross the river on stepping stones, shouting and laughing, then disappearing into the woods on the far side. She thought back to her own childhood, a blur of clambered trees, frogspawn and conkers. She would come home from trips to Wimbledon Common with burrs in her jumper, pockets stuffed with acorns and pretty pebbles for her mum. Happy days.

She walked down to the stepping stones and stood looking across. Long, long years of rehab had drummed one idea into her head: it's not worth the risk. One impulsive jump, one careless slip and all that hard work of learning to walk again, it could be undone in a snap.

Instead she lowered herself onto a bench, closed her eyes and listened.

Moving slowly had a few small advantages: Sophie had developed the habit of opening her senses, taking in the smell of wildflowers and woodsmoke, the feel of the flaking paint under her fingers, the chirp of a robin and the soft 'bloop' of a fish surfacing.

But despite the calm, she felt simmering emotion.

Tim was getting married in three hours. How did she feel about it exactly? Sophie imagined a TV reporter pointing a microphone towards her, keen to hear her opinion on the upcoming celebrity nuptials. She let out a long breath, thinking it over.

Awkward and out of place, certainly that. Embarrassed. Resentful – no, cheated. And angry. Yes. If she was honest, that was her over-riding emotion. Anger.

Anger at Tim, that he was getting married to Vanessa Farringdon of all people. Angry that he had let her down, that he had messed her about – and angry that he was still doing it, inviting her to the wedding – even if it had been Jennifer's idea. But most of all, Sophie was angry at herself. Angry for coming: if she'd had any self-respect she would have torn that invitation in two. And she was angry that she hadn't moved on years ago.

Sophie had woken up that morning thinking about Nikolaus Vetletz as she often did on big days, and as her thoughts wandered back to him, she felt another spike of emotion. Nikolaus Vetletz, German dentist: the man who had skied into her in Verbier, knocking her sideways and changing her life forever. In the months after her accident, Sophie thought about Nikolaus Vetletz every single day. Less so recently, after years of therapy. She had been taught to accept that it was an accident; Vetletz had just hit a mogul – a bump hidden in the snow – sending him veering sideways. He'd managed to swerve around her, but caught the back of her skis, sending her pin-wheeling down the slope. A mistake. Bad luck. At least for Sophie.

As far as she knew, Nikolaus was unaware of the carnage he'd left behind. She only knew his identity because someone had pointed him out to her friend Juliet, who had shot after him and demanded his name. They'd reported it to the police, of course, but the cops had just shrugged their shoulders. Besides, Sophie had more to worry about right then. Indeed, she was barely conscious.

But later, when she had nothing but time on her hands and a strong internet connection, Sophie had tracked him down. His full name was Nikolaus Vetletz, but everyone called him Klaus. He was six-two – a guess from pictures – and had the classic German blonde hair and blue eyes. He was now a dentist in Stuttgart. Klaus had a blonde wife and two blonde daughters and like a lot of men his age, an interest in cycling. In short, Klaus had the life Sophie wanted. Not the dentist or the cycling part. But a full, normal life.

She felt her toes claw into the soles of her shoes and she closed her eyes.

'Are you going for a swim?'

She turned and froze.

Tim, standing there as real as life, dressed in shorts, running vest, a sardonic smile on his face. Despite herself, Sophie felt her heart thud.

'Actually, I was thinking of throwing myself in,' she said, trying to keep her tone casual.

Tim raised an eyebrow.

'I wouldn't.'

'Why not?'

'Because then I'll have to jump in after you and I'm damp enough as it is.'

He pulled at the sweat-soaked vest, stuck to his firm torso, as if to prove a point.

'I wasn't sure you'd come,' he said after another moment.

She tried to smile brightly. 'And miss the wedding of the century? No chance.'

'I heard you went to Haslop Hall last night with the girls. Was it fun?'

Sophie was hardly going to tell him the truth. That she'd hated every moment of it.

'The *Mr and Mrs* quiz was pretty interesting.'

Tim grimaced.

'That was Emily's idea. She persuaded me it'd be a hoot. Was it?'

Sophie smiled.

'There was laughter, yes. But I'm not sure Vanessa enjoyed it as much as Emily.'

'Another thing I'm in trouble for.'

'You're in trouble? What for?' Now Sophie was looking at him, half-hoping that it would be something major. Something irreparable.

'The wedding band has cancelled,' said Tim. 'Adam's sorting out a replacement, assuming he can get out from under his hangover. We had a big night last night.'

'I heard it got lively. Karaoke I believe.'

Sophie enjoyed the look of surprise on Tim's face.

'How do you know about that?' he asked.

'We're sharing a bathroom.'

'You're sharing a bathroom with Adam?'

Was that a hint of jealousy? Yes. It was there, definitely.

'It's a long story,' said Sophie airily. She tried to look mysterious rather than embarrassed, wanting to elicit a response from him. 'I'm sure Adam's version will be much more dramatic.'

Sophie waited for more questions but instead Tim stepped back, as if he was about to resume his run. She stood up, not ready to let him go just yet.

'So, are you ready?' she asked.

Tim looked away towards the line of plane trees.

'Ah Soph, is anyone ever ready for something like this?'

'That's the idea, isn't it? When the vicar says "do you take her forever and ever?" You do have to say yes.'

A shrug: 'I suppose.'

'Ever the romantic.'

'You know me.'

There was something about the way he said it. She did know him. She always had done. And he'd known her too – that had been part of the magic, even though they had been mismatched from the start. Sophie was cultured, academic, elegant, the girl most-likely-to-succeed at St Paul's Girls' School and Bristol University. Tim was dry and Northern, approaching college as a chance to network and charm his way to better things. But still, it had worked between them. Tim had never been one for hearts and flowers and spontaneous declarations of love, but Sophie had loved how he was endlessly able to prick her pretensions and make her laugh. And, Sophie had to admit that she had loved being welcomed into the warmth of the Jameson clan, being treated as one of the family.

'I do,' she said quietly.

Tension shimmered in the air as Tim's eyes met hers.

'You know, when all this is over, the wedding, the honeymoon, you should come round. We're in Wandsworth now. My mum said you're still in Wimbledon.'

'Yep. Still in Wimbledon.' Still living with her parents, stuck like an old record clicking around and around in the middle, long after the dance had finished.

The moment hung heavy between them.

She looked at him, waiting for him to speak. That was one of Tim's gifts. Always knowing what to say. But it was a skill too, knowing when not to say anything.

'I'd better go,' she said, blinking first.

'Me too.'

Tim tried for a smile.

'Wish me luck?'

'Sure,' said Sophie, her voice suddenly hoarse. She cleared her throat. 'You'll be fine, Tim. You always are.'

'Thanks again, Soph, really. For coming. It means a lot.'

'Go, you don't want to be late' she smiled. He started to run and finally when he was almost at the turn back to the village, he gave her a wave.

Sophie stood motionless, running over the words in her head.

You'll be fine Tim. You always are.

It had sounded so sour. She hadn't meant to, but then none of it had gone how it was supposed to. After all, this was the moment, wasn't it? The moment Sophie had spent years dreaming of, the moment when Sophie and Tim would finally be reunited and Tim would realise his horrible mistake. But instead they had spent all their time talking about Vanessa and Adam, not Sophie and Tim.

They had exchanged pleasantries, spoken in clichés. For all those emotions flaring inside her, Sophie had said nothing at all.

Turning away from the river, she took the little lane back up towards The Swan. The swaying sunlight seemed to have gone now, the warmth and hum in the air replaced by a cool breeze. The door to the little bakery was open as Sophie walked past, but she didn't feel hungry anymore.

'Sophie!'

Startled, she looked up, almost walking into a woman wearing a bright orange jumpsuit.

'Zara?'

'Who else?' she laughed, then Sophie saw the woman's smile fade.

'Gosh. What's the matter?'

Sophie hadn't realised she looked so obviously upset. She hesitated, resisting, aware that Zara was Vanessa's friend. But she couldn't stop the tears from flowing. Zara came over and put her arms around Sophie.

'Tell me. What's wrong?'

'I'm so sorry. It's just that I saw Tim. We used to date, but then I had an accident…'

'I know,' said Zara softly. 'Someone told me about it last night. Tim's university sweetheart who had the skiing accident? I figured it was you.'

'Inspector Clouseau,' said Sophie, through a snotty smile. 'It's just hard.'

'I know it hurts,' said Zara. 'Even if you know you are better off with them out of your life.'

Sophie just nodded, feeling her chest shudder.

Zara took a step away from her and held her shoulders.

'I know just what you need.'

'A full English Breakfast?'

The older woman's eyes twinkled mischievously, then linked her arm through Sophie's.

'Not just that. But it's a start. Come with me, and I'll tell you all about it.'

Chapter Fifteen

ADAM TORE OFF another sheet of hotel notepaper, screwed it up and dropped it on the floor. It was beginning to look like it had been snowing under his desk. Writing a wedding speech was harder than it looked.

'Come on, think,' he muttered to himself. 'What do people want to hear?'

The sad truth was that no one really wanted to hear anything. Wedding speeches were something to be endured with a full glass and a fixed smile. Adam had only seen it done well once – a comedy writer friend who did a stand-up routine full of creaky mother-in-law jokes that had them rolling in the aisles. But that guy was a professional and everyone was in on the joke. Tim was in advertising – or marketing, one of the two – and no one wanted to hear him thanking the bridesmaids; they just wanted to jump straight to the free bar and 'Come on Eileen'.

Still, Adam had to come up with something. He groaned, looking down at the blank page. The truth was he felt completely ill-equipped to talk about love. There had been plenty of girls in his life but no grand love story, no slo-mo sprint down the beach, no violins or trumpets. To be frank, Adam's relationship history was littered with failures, but then wasn't everyone's? In fact, wasn't that kind of the point of a wedding? Standing up in church and saying, 'this is the girl I choose, forever and ever.' All the others were just practice.

Even so, Adam wanted to find love as much as the next man, but he wasn't about to settle for anything less than The Real Thing. Lauren from advertising was sweet and even had a decent vinyl collection, but where was the clap of thunder? Where were the crashing waves?

Adam doodled a stick man surfing a giant swell – it didn't take Sigmund Freud to guess that Adam's perfectionism might stem from his parents' divorce. His mother had drummed into him that compromise was a slow road to misery – although that wasn't much of an uplifting message for a wedding speech.

He crumpled up the doodle, shaking his head. Maybe he should copy something off the internet like Tim. He glanced over at his phone, then looked away. That was the other reason Adam was toiling over this speech. It was a displacement activity: he was really just putting off calling Declan. Adam knew he had no option. He had rung around the few friendly PRs and journo contacts he had – not an easy task early on a Saturday morning when the world of rock was prone to a lie-in – and they had been sympathetic, but facts were facts. Most bands were on tour, in the studio or in rehab. Plus, while everyone had been polite, the subtext of 'are you kidding me?' had been pretty clear.

Adam would hardly have blamed them if they'd laughed in his face.

Taking a deep breath, Adam scrolled to Declan's number and pressed the 'call' button. He held it to his ear, listening to that distant ring-tone.

Don't answer, don't answer.

'Hello?'

Oh crap.

'Dec, hey! It's Adam, Adam from...'

'Adam Stowe! Is that you?'

'Yes! From *Cream. Cream* magazine...'

'I know it's you, you plonker,' said Declan. 'I'm just surprised to hear from you at this time in the morning.'

Adam forced a laugh.

'Last night was a rough one actually. You too, I imagine – sorry to disturb you on tour.'

'I've been up for hours,' said Declan brightly. 'Yoga, meditation, wheatgerm smoothie: here I am.'

'Really?'

'Yeah, it's my body clock. The kids get you up at the crack of dawn and even when you're on the road, you wake up expecting to have to make porridge.'

'I know what you mean.'

Adam had no idea what he meant. The nearest he'd ever come to any kind of proper family life was when he'd crashed on his mate Jimmy's sofa and Jimmy's kids had woken him up by jumping on his back, badgering 'Uncle Adder' to play Xbox.

'I was expecting to see you last night,' said Declan. 'Didn't you get the passes?'

'I couldn't make it in the end,' said Adam. 'My friend got into a bit of a ruck on the way over to Malvern Castle. It was a real mess, police and everything.'

'Really? Is he okay?'

Haltingly, Adam told him the story of the abortive stag night, slightly worried that the newly teetotal Dec would disapprove of such crashing stupidity. Instead, the singer cracked up with delighted laughter.

'Right Said Fred? Adam, that's genius. I'm glad someone's still living the rock and roll lifestyle.'

Adam closed his eyes: time to take the plunge.

'Listen Dec, I know this is a terrible imposition, but I'm in a hole here and you might just be able to help dig me out. I'm best man at my mate Tim's wedding and there's been problems with the band. So I was wondering…' *Say it, say it*, 'Could you turn up with your guitar? Just one song, that's all. Five minutes tops.'

There was a silence. A terrible, terrible, horrific silence. Adam braced himself.

'Sure.'

Adam blinked.

'What?'

'I'll do it,' said Declan. 'If it was anyone else, I'd have given it a swerve, but I owe you one, Ads.'

'You do?'

Declan laughed.

'Adam Stowe, you have tirelessly championed Belasco for fifteen years. You did our first live review, you gave us single of the week and ten out of ten for

Freebase, when it was a six at best. You've been a one-man PR campaign for us, so I don't think I can really say no, do you?'

Adam gave a low chuckle of disbelief.

'Cheers, Dec. It's really, really good of you.'

'Don't get too excited,' said Declan. 'We're playing in Newcastle tomorrow night and the rest of the band like to get there early, so I just need to make sure the timings work.'

'Totally understand,' said Adam, feeling his triumph drain away. 'It was always a long shot.'

'Don't get me wrong, I'll be there if I can. What I'm saying is, it might be a good idea to have a back-up plan.'

'Sure, sure,' said Adam, although he had zero idea what that plan might be.

'I take it you asked Elton first?' Adam almost laughed before realising that Declan was serious.

'No. I wanted to see if you were up for it before I called him,' he said hurriedly, not wanting to point out that he'd never even met Elton John. 'Look, I'll let you go. Will you call me later to confirm?'

'Sure and give the happy couple my best.'

'Really?'

'Definitely, I love weddings. I always cry.'

I think I might cry too, thought Adam as he put down the phone, punching the air with joy. Okay, so Declan might not come, but he would *try*. He hadn't said no, had he? Grinning, he crossed back to the desk, suddenly inspired for the speech. Yes, maybe the weekend would work out after all.

Chapter Sixteen

'YOU LOOK GORGEOUS.'

'Hmm,' said Sophie, looking at herself in the mirror, unconvinced.

She smoothed her dress down and turned sideways, trying to make herself look smaller.

How had Sophie allowed Zara to talk her into this? Her new friend's plan was to make her 'the most incredible looking woman' at the wedding, but Sophie had known it was a mistake the moment she had walked into Zara's suite-cum-dressing-room, a sunny, open space filled with racks of brightly coloured dresses, neat rows of shoes, wheeled cases spilling scarves and shrugs, hats and bags. This just wasn't her world. Sophie didn't like 'look at me' clothing. Her wardrobe was full of sensible, neutral pieces, flat shoes and clothes in soft fabrics that didn't cling or squeeze. She hadn't put a foot into a swanky fashion boutique since, well, before the accident.

Zara on the other hand, was in her element, sliding into action, circling around Sophie, picking and choosing, holding fabrics and patterns against her skin, grunting and nodding to herself until she was satisfied.

The dress she had finally picked was a sheath of

dark scarlet silk. It was sensational, there was no doubt about it, but still, Sophie felt uncomfortable. Right now, Sophie didn't want to be the most incredible looking guest at the wedding because that would mean getting people's attention.

'So what do you think?' grinned Zara. 'Dolce sent it to me for Kate to wear at an Academy awards thing but I know Stefano would be even more thrilled to see you in it. All we need now is to find you some shoes.'

She bent down to rummage around in a suitcase and stood back up holding a pair of five-inch heels. Sophie looked at them as if they were a set of thumb-screws.

'Lovely, but no. I can't stand up for long as it is, I don't think I'd manage thirty seconds in those.'

'Then how about these?'

Zara pulled out a pair of low wedges from another bag, emblazoned with the distinctive double 'C' of Chanel.

'You're lucky I still have these,' said Zara, directing her to the velvet sofa to sit down. 'I offered them to Tess, but she said they were too Milan.'

'Tess?'

'My daughter,' said Zara, slipping them onto Sophie's feet.

They fitted perfectly and Zara gave a sigh of relief.

'You like?' she smiled, putting her hands on her hips.

Sophie was about to say that no one would recognise her, but as she looked at her reflection, her face dewy with well-applied make-up, her hair glossy after

Zara's blow-dry, something struck her.

'You know what? I think I look a little like my old self,' she said.

Zara shook her head.

'This is the *new* you – and the new you is hot. Now let's go and show them all.'

It was a five-minute walk from The Swan to the church, the steeple poking up over the trees like a celestial middle finger. Sophie leaned on Zara's arm, grateful for the support, both physical and emotional. She didn't know why this woman was being so kind to her, but then over the past decade Sophie had found that some people just were more decent, more caring, more happy to help other people *just because*. Nurses, doctors, volunteers, even just passers-by who might stop and ask Sophie if she needed help with the stairs. There was a great unmapped well of kindness deep under the bedrock of the country that she had never known was there.

Up close the church was as beautiful as she had imagined. The bells were ringing, cow parsley fringed the flint walls, a smiling vicar shook the hands of every guest as they filed through the flower-trimmed lychgate to the grounds. Even the mossy tombstones had an eerie beauty. Sophie had never given much thought to her own wedding. At 22, it wasn't the sort of thing you dwelled on, and since the accident, Sophie's love-life had been so uneventful, she'd put all thoughts of getting married to one side. But occasionally, when she had wondered what it might be like, it had been something like this.

'You okay?' asked Zara quietly, as they tottered up the uneven stone-flag path, arm-in-arm.

Sophie nodded. She was glad that Zara had insisted she 'dress up'. Hidden away in The Swan, it was easy to pretend that the Jameson wedding was a modest affair, but the scene before her – a sea of morning suits, crepe de chine, even a couple of top hats – suggested something much more grand.

Two ushers book-ended the door to the church. 'Bride or groom?' asked one of them, handing her an order of service.

'Bride,' said Zara, flashing him a smile, just as Sophie's clutch bag began to vibrate.

She fumbled with the unfamiliar latch and looked down at her phone – *Serena*. Her boss. Damn.

'You go in,' muttered Sophie. 'I'll just be a minute.'

She moved away from the bottleneck and out into the churchyard to take the call. It wasn't the first time Sophie had received urgent work messages from her boss on the weekend – in the travel business, it was an occupational hazard. Strikes, hurricanes, guests falling ill, they all had to be dealt with, whatever the day was. And her boss, Serena White, the owner of Warwick Travel, was the worst sort of micro-manager, panicking at the slightest thing.

'Finally!' snapped Serena down the line. 'Why haven't you replied to my messages?'

‘What messages?’

‘The *messages* I sent *over* twenty minutes ago.’

Sophie took a deep breath.

‘I’m sorry Serena. I’m in the countryside at a wedding and reception is patchy here. What’s happened?’

‘We have a problem with the Bennisons in Africa.’

Sophie frowned.

‘The Bennisons?’

Serena’s irritated snort was like a cymbal crash.

‘The BENN-isons, Sophie. The couple on safari. Don’t you ever read the schedule?’

She could tell that Serena was in one of her moods.

‘Okay. Can you be more specific than “Africa”?’

Serena exhaled loudly. ‘They’re on a guided tour of the Serengeti. This *was* the tour that you arranged…’

Sophie’s short-term memory had improved drastically since the months after her accident, when things would drop out of her mind like the Wi-Fi in her parents’ Cornwall cottage. Her recall was still not as sharp as it had been at university, nor was she sure it would ever be; she had been warned early on that the part of her brain that handled learning and remembering had been damaged, so now, Sophie overcompensated by being super-organised, recording everything in triplicate. So she was absolutely sure that she’d had zero dealings with a Mr and Mrs Bennison, and besides, her colleague Caroline usually dealt with the African trips. Sophie took a breath, reminding herself that she had been lucky to get this job. A travel agent who couldn’t travel? An organiser with a history of brain damage? Serena was a friend of a friend of Sophie's mother and never missed an opportunity to remind her that she had 'taken a risk' in employing Sophie. And for that reason, in the seven years that she had been employed at Warwick Travel, Sophie had never said 'no' to Serena, no matter how exacting or unreasonable her boss might be.

'So where are they exactly?' she asked.

'At the Ngorongoro Crater. Apparently there was no vegan gluten-free option at the lunch. The poor woman is starving and they're about to leave for a supper under the stars experience at the local Maasai village. Someone mentioned the words BBQ buffet so I'm not hopeful that there's anything edible there either.'

Serena paused. *Here it comes*, thought Sophie. 'Can I just leave this with you Sophie? Allegra is in a lacrosse tournament this afternoon and I'm already running late…'

'Serena, as I said, I'm at a wedding. Perhaps if you called Caroline then she can…'

'Sorry, Sophie, you're breaking up. I'll leave it in your capable hands, yes?'

In the distance, Sophie could see a huge ivory car like an over-polished whale glide towards the church. The bride.

'Alright Serena, I'll see what I can do,' she said, trailing off as she realised she was talking to dead air.

'Damn' she hissed, dropping the phone back into her bag and turning back into the church, where she practically collided with a man moving the other way.

'Sophie!'

'Rich?'

Tim's younger brother was wearing a tailored morning suit that flattered everything inside. He seized her by the shoulders and kissed her on both cheeks.

'Wow, Sophie. You look amazing.'

She felt his eyes on her, felt his appraisal. It seemed Zara's makeover had worked, although Sophie wasn't sure what he had been expecting.

'So… you're the best man?' she said awkwardly.

'It has been said.'

His grin was infectious.

'Look, Tim asked me to come and grab a hymn book. Wouldn't look good if he wasn't singing along, would it?'

Her pulse was racing just at the mention of Tim's name.

'Well, the bride's arriving out there. You'd better get back.'

'I better had,' said Rich. 'See you later on?'

'Look forward to it.'

'Bride or groom?' The usher's question was simple, but for a moment it threw Sophie. She looked past him into the church – Zara was on the bride's side, Sophie could see the back of her head in a sea of fascinators.

'Groom. No, Bride…' she said, suddenly feeling panicked. She was Tim's guest after all, but would that look possessive? How would Vanessa react? But then Sophie looked across to the bride's side and even from this distance she could see some of the women from the hen night, some of whom would be the girls from the loos who had called her 'the ski-girl'. She didn't want to spend the next half hour feeling their glances on her.

'Which is it?' said the usher, not unkindly.

'Groom,' said a voice behind her.

She turned to see Adam, wearing a dark blue suit with a skinny tie. His hair was brushed off his face. He looked good, especially for someone who was almost certainly feeling pretty ropey.

'Adam. I wasn't entirely sure you'd surface at all today.'

'Rumours of my demise have been greatly exaggerated,' he said, taking her arm and striding confidently down the aisle. For the first few steps, Sophie was glad of his presence – at least she didn't have to walk down alone. But Adam kept walking, closer and closer to the altar, ducking into the fourth row from the front, which felt about fifteen rows too close.

'Adam, we shouldn't sit up here,' hissed Sophie. 'These seats are for family.'

Adam glanced across. 'I *am* family, practically. And anyway, I want to see the whites of Tim's eyes when he realises that Rich has forgotten the ring.'

'Has he?'

'I'm speculating,' smiled Adam. 'Plus I haven't brought my glasses, so I need to get in close.'

There was nothing wrong with Sophie's eyesight. She could see Tim in full widescreen Technicolor, the back of his head at least, bent in whispered conversation with Rich. What were they saying? Trying to listen in was all Sophie could do to keep herself from kicking off Zara's Chanel mules and bolting for the door.

'Look Sophie, I really wanted to apologise for last night,' said Adam, leaning in close.

'Whatever would you have to be sorry about, Adam?'

He didn't seem to catch the sarcasm in her voice.

He lowered his voice. 'You know, *being sick* and everything…'

He started to tell a story about someone called Belasco, but Sophie wasn't listening. She turned with everyone else as the organ struck up the dramatic first bars of Mendelssohn. Now she was the one who felt as if she was about to vomit. The organ shifted up a notch, and as one, the congregation sighed as Vanessa appeared at the back of the church. Hattie would have loved the dress. It was ivory silk, sleek, with a long train being held by a pair of angelic little girls in Bo-Peep outfits. Sophie had to admit that she looked spectacular.

And Vanessa had the graceful glide mastered. She was a swan on a glass smooth lake, confident and proud. As Vanessa pulled level with her, something made Sophie turn back towards the altar – and there he was. Tim was looking her way. And just for a moment, their eyes met and Sophie stood, lost in those blue eyes, feeling like there was no one else in the room. Just Tim and Sophie, their two hearts beating as one. A frozen moment in time, the second hand suspended in a held breath.

And then – nothing. No smile from Tim, no gentle shrug, no 'well, it could have been us, huh?' No hint of sadness. His gaze simply slid back to his wife-to-be, leaving Sophie alone, cold, like that imagined sunshine had gone behind a cloud. She watched, numb, as Vanessa stepped up next to Tim, side-by-side, faced the priest and the ceremony went on.

'Dearly beloved….'

Sophie stood, barely hearing the words, her fingers gripping her hymn book until her knuckles turned white. What did she think was going to happen? Those rom-coms where the groom realises his terrible mistake might seem romantic, but in reality it would be horrible.

When Sophie managed to force her attention back towards the altar, she realised the priest had reached the part where he asked, 'If anyone knows a reason why these persons may not marry, let them speak now.' There was a palpable silence around the church during which Sophie could barely draw breath.

The vicar stopped, an embarrassed smile on his round face. Then he turned to Tim.

'Tim, will you take Vanessa to be your wife?'

No.

No, I will not.

NO.

Tim turned to smile at Vanessa. He actually smiled.

'Yes. I will.'

And Sophie felt as if she was tumbling end over

end, Alice plunging through the rabbit hole, her heart thumping in her ears, breath caught in her throat. It was over. Done.

For richer, for poorer. In sickness and in health. 'Til death us do part.

And Sophie knew in her heart that it had been over for more than a decade, for most of her adult life.

A life I've wasted, she thought. Wasted obsessing over stupid fantasies and childish wishes that had zero chance of coming true. She felt tears rolling down her cheek. Not because she'd lost Tim, but because she'd lost herself.

She flinched at a touch on her elbow.

'Here,' whispered Adam, handing her the silk handkerchief from his pocket. 'Try not to blow.'

She nodded her thanks as the organ swelled up and the happy couple walked down the aisle hand-in-hand, beaming and just a tiny bit embarrassed by all the attention, neither even glancing in her direction. Sophie stood there, watching, not moving as the guests began to file out, letting Adam go, letting everyone go. Until she was alone. Carefully, Sophie pulled her phone out from the tiny clutch and, fighting back the tears, tapped out a text to Christa.

Help.
You were right about everything.
Can you come ASAP?
I need to go.

Chapter Seventeen

THE SINGLES TABLE was empty. In fact, the whole reception room was empty. That was good. Adam glanced around, but apart from a couple of waiters flitting in and out at the other end of the room, Adam was alone. No big surprise: Adam had been one of the first to hop into the mini-bus bringing the wedding party to Haslop Hall. Everyone else had hung around to throw confetti and get in on the group photos, but Adam had a more pressing mission. This wasn't Adam's first rodeo – he'd been to plenty of weddings down the years, and the last thing he needed today was being stuck next to someone who wanted to talk about their love of cats or even worse, their relationships.

The Singles Table was, as it always was, shoved at the back next to the loos, as far as possible away from the 'top table' where the bride and groom sat. No-one on their big day wanted to be reminded of romantic failure.

Adam paced around the table, squinting down at the little cards with their handwritten names: *Mr. Paul Hobbs... Dr. Cherie Akinowa... Mr. Ali Malik... Miss Sophie Wallis... Mr. Hugo Crabb.... Ms. Zara Stephens... Mr. Adam Stowe.*

Hang on! He'd been shoved between Tim's cousin Lucy and 'Zara Stephens'? Who was *she*? And how come Ali got to sit between Sophie and Cherie, the doctor that Tim had pointed out to him in the bar the night before. *I see what you've done there, Vee*, thought Adam with a shake of the head. Vanessa had put Ali next to Sophie, Tim's ex, presumably in the very real expectation that Ali would do something embarrassing. *Naughty Vee.*

'I'm righting a wrong here,' he said to himself, quickly grabbing the place cards and rearranging them. Plus from his brief time with Sophie Wallis, he'd gathered that she was pretty no-nonsense. If Ali tried any of his so-called 'seduction techniques' on her, Adam guessed Sophie would crush his nuts. So Adam was simultaneously saving Ali's tackle and avoiding embarrassment for the party. That, and giving himself a chance to repair the damage he'd done with Sophie by puking in her bathroom. Win-win.

His mission completed, Adam strode back through the hall out of the grand entrance and onto the striped croquet lawn where the guests were now arriving for a sun-lit reception, each taking a glass of fizz before peering at the chart of seating arrangements, discovering their relative status within the wedding party – how close or otherwise they had been placed to Vanessa's carved golden throne, the focus of the room.

It was glorious out here, Adam had to give Vanessa that. Obviously the woman was a control freak and spending the best part of a year planning one party was deranged, but this had to count as one of the most impressive weddings he'd ever been to. The Hall itself was a white stone palace glowing with dignified elegance and the sun was slanting across the manicured grass at just the right angle to make the fountain sparkle. Even Vee couldn't have guaranteed this perfect weather – but there it was – robin's egg blue sky, with a gentle breeze just ruffling the ladies' up-dos.

'Adam! Thank God you're alive,' said Hugo, thumping a big hand down on his shoulder. 'I was worried you'd be languishing in a Guildford jail cell.'

'No, got away scot-free,' said Adam, glad to see his new friend. He looked around to see a pretty girl about half Hugo's height standing in his shadow. She had angular dyed-black hair, an off-the-shoulder green dress and ox-blood red biker boots. Her kohl-scrawled eyes projected mischief, an elaborate rose tattoo peeked out from the inside of her cleavage.

'Sorry, terrible manners,' said Hugo. 'Have you met Lucy? We've just been catching up on the bus. We're both cousins, would you believe? Different sides of the family, but still.'

'Cousin Lucy?' smiled Adam, the penny finally dropping. 'We *have* met, but you were about this high back then,' he said, holding his hand at waist height.

'I remember you wiped ice-cream all over my Levis.'

'You've grown too, Adam,' said Lucy, raising a suggestive eyebrow. Adam grinned, wondering briefly if he'd made the right decision swopping places with Ali.

‘So how are you Luce? Still mad for chocolate chip?’

‘Every flavour I can get,’ she purred.

Adam laughed and took a glass of Pimm’s from a passing waiter.

‘Well, we can all get reacquainted as we’re all on the Singles Table. Everyone else might feel sorry for us, but we’re going to have the most fun, right?’

‘Right!’ shouted a voice in Adam’s ear as Ali appeared from nowhere and jumped on Adam’s back. ‘Let’s get this party started!’

Adam shook him off and was surprised to see the dark eyes of Dr Cherie looking him up and down.

‘Do you know Cherie?’ asked Ali, taking Adam’s drink from him and swigging it back. ‘We met by the seating chart. We’re table buddies.’

‘Delighted,’ said Adam, shaking a slim hand. Up close, Cherie was even more pretty than she had appeared the night before, but he noted Cherie’s intelligent eyes and her reserved smile: he could tell she was no push-over.

‘So how do you know the bride and groom?’ he asked.

‘I live next door. In Wandsworth.’

‘Is Vanessa always popping round to borrow a cup of poison?’

Cherie suppressed a laugh. ‘She’s not that bad.’

‘Who do you have on the other side? Lucrezia Borgia?’

This time Cherie did giggle.

‘So how long have you been friends?’

'Not long, actually. Me and my flat-mate Henry invited Tim and Vee around for a barbeque when they first bought the place. And, well, I saved Tim's life.'

Adam looked up.

'Really? How?'

'An olive went down the wrong way. Upper airway obstruction leading to apnea, seeing as you're asking.'

'Did you give him the Heimlich manoeuvre?'

'I slapped him on the back and the olive flew out into the dahlias, but Vanessa still believes I'm some sort of magician. Since then she's been coming round regularly to ask about her medical complaints.' She glanced around, then whispered. 'Cystitis. Too much sex apparently.'

Adam laughed.

'So where are the happy couple?' he asked, reaching for a new drink. 'I suppose congratulations are in order.'

'Still at the church apparently,' said Cherie. 'Knowing Vanessa, it'll be a full-on photo shoot. Co-ordinating the swans and the doves might take some time.'

Adam grinned. It seemed that Cherie had the measure of the new Mrs Jameson. Maybe this was going to be fun after all.

'Look, someone's waving.'

A man with neat sandy blonde hair was making his way across the terrace. Adam was immediately reminded of his Action Man toy from his youth. This guy looked capable, wiry, like he could build a shed, then wrestle a tiger, but he was walking with a strange jerky motion.

'That's Paul, he's sitting with us at dinner too,' said Cherie.

As the man cleared the crowd, Adam saw the reason for his odd gait: the lower part of both legs ended in shiny metallic limbs. He couldn't help staring.

'Hey, I'm Paul,' said the man, with a slightly sour look. 'And yes, I have no legs.'

'Pleased to meet you, Paul,' said Adam, putting out his hand to shake. 'I'm Adam and I have commitment issues.'

Paul blinked at him, then burst out laughing. 'That beats me.'

Adam breathed a sigh of relief. Paul might have prosthetics but he still looked like he could gut him with a teaspoon.

'So how do you know Tim?' asked Adam.

'I'm his personal trainer.'

Adam tried not to react.

'You think I can't be a trainer with my disability?' said Paul.

Adam shook his head.

'More that Tim looks like shit.'

Paul laughed.

'I was in the army for fifteen years, so I know more about real-life fitness than most Olympians, but with Tim it's more about motivation, goal visualisation, all that.'

'Be the best you?' said Adam, not at all surprised. That sounded exactly like the sort of thing Tim would do. He imagined him listening to business motivation podcasts in that shiny car on the way into Canary Wharf every morning.

Inspired by the idea, Adam turned to the rest of the group, raised his wine glass then turned his gaze to the rest of the table. 'A toast, ladies and gentlemen of the Singles Table.'

They all raised their glasses and clinked them together.

'Here's to us, the rejects and the screw-ups. We may have failed to find lasting love…'

'So far!' shouted Lucy.

'Well said,' agreed Adam. '…but we're all the more interesting and experienced because of it. We are the Singles, but we are special.'

'Special needs!' cried Ali to much laughter.

'In your case Ali, yes, but let us all raise our glasses and vow here and now that we're going to have the most fun at this wedding. Because we are awesome – and because we travel in hope.'

'To hope!' cried Hugo.

'To hope!' they all repeated, drawing disapproving looks from neighbouring guests.

Adam looked around at his fellow singles, suddenly curious about them all. What was it really that had brought them here, what had stopped them from finding a partner? Did they all have a flaw or was it actually better this way? As for the married couples and long-term commitments gathered here on the croquet lawn, were they luckier, having found their soul-mate in a sea of billions? Or were they more prepared to settle? Crucially, were they any happier?

The statistics were stacked against them: one in three marriages ended in divorce and that invariably brought pain. And yet what he had said was true: Adam did travel in hope, always looking for 'the one'. Was she here today? He wondered, looking around.

Dr Cherie? She was attractive, with a dry wit, but possibly a little young. On the positive side, she was a doctor and Adam did seem to have more aches and pains than he used to lately. Then there was Cousin Lucy who had obviously blossomed into a little firecracker, but the dress looked like hemp, which was always a red flag for Adam, a slippery slope down into vegan hell. Plus she did seem to be hanging on Hugo's every word, not that he could blame her for that. If he was a girl, he'd go for a strapping explorer who could make fire with a handful of twigs. The 'Zara' from the place settings had also joined them. Some sort of fashion stylist, she seemed to be getting on famously with Ali, which said something about her tolerance, but she was on the old side – 55-plus? But then Adam wasn't getting any younger either. And then there was Sophie who seemed to have disappeared. What *was* her problem anyway? Obviously, he hadn't made the best first impression, but she didn't need to act so aloof. Still, Adam didn't need to put all his eggs in one basket. He looked over towards the bridesmaids, evidently just arriving back from the wedding photos. Experience taught Adam that the Singles Table wasn't the only game in town at a wedding: traditionally, the bridesmaids were worth a punt too.

'Nice speech,' said Cherie, clinking her glass

against Adam's. 'I liked what you said about hope.'

Adam shrugged modestly.

He started telling her about his career as a writer and was partway through one of his best anecdotes when he realised that Cherie wasn't really listening. Instead she was looking across to the side of the lawn where a young man was arranging hay bales and deck chairs outside a vintage caravan.

'What's going on over there?'

'That's the photo booth,' she said. 'And that's Henry who runs it. Henry's the flatmate I mentioned.'

Adam caught the shy smile on her face and immediately knew that however great his stories about pop royalty were, he was wasting his time trying to impress Cherie. She only had eyes for Henry.

'Good-looking lad,' he said. 'Henry could be in a boy band.'

'I suppose. Never really thought about it.'

'You and Henry, are you…'

'Together?' She shook her head. 'We're in the Friend Zone.'

Adam was familiar with the term because *Cream* had once shared a floor with a women's magazine called *Glossy*. Whereas *Cream* was full of twentysomething men with an unhealthy obsession with vinyl, *Glossy* was staffed exclusively by young women who seemed to write endless features on the same themes – dating, sex and relationships. He remembered reading a *Glossy* feature about 'the Friend Zone'. It was apparently the place you ended up if you failed to make a move on an attractive acquaintance soon enough in your relationship. Instead of thinking of you as a prospective partner, they started seeing you as an actual friend. Comfortable, great company, someone to share a pizza and a movie with, but not someone to inspire great passion. That was the theory, anyway. Adam could have told them that men always found *all* women attractive. For men, there was no 'friend zone': all women were fair game right up until they were actually married – and not always then.

But clearly Cherie felt she'd missed her chance with Handsome Henry. Adam wondered if he could do anything to shift things in Cherie's favour.

'What are you two up to over here?' said Ali, coming over and throwing an arm across both Adam and Cherie's shoulders.

Adam nodded towards the photo-booth.

'Just considering going across. What do you think, Al?'

'Awesome.' He turned towards the rest of the group. 'Oi! Singles Table massive! Come on, we're going to commemorate this wonderful moment in all our lives. Follow Ali!'

Laughing and chattering, the group ambled across to where Henry was waiting.

'Hello there,' he said with a winning smile. 'You're my first customers of the day.'

He quickly explained that the caravan was the booth: they could all cram in the back and close the doors, while an automatic camera would give them a countdown before taking the shots.

'You'll find hats and wigs and props in the back

there, guys. Have fun.'

'Stag party first!' called Adam, jumping inside first and waiting for Ali and Hugo to follow. Ali immediately put on an orange wig.

'Say cheese,' he called, as a light in front of them flashed.

'You know, I might keep this on,' said Ali, adjusting the wig. 'Do you think it might impress Cherie? She's hot. Plus my mum will be impressed if I bring home a doctor.'

Adam shook his head and lowered his voice.

'Good luck with that one, Ali. I think Dr Cherie likes Henry the photo-booth guy.'

'How do you know?'

'She told me. They're flatmates.'

'Ah.' He watched as Ali considered it. 'Then on this day of romance and revelry, we should get them together.'

'How do you intend to do that?' said Adam cynically.

'The old switcheroo,' said Ali immediately. 'I lure Cherie in here with pure animal magnetism, then just when she thinks she's getting a fine slice of Ali pie, I jump out and we push the blonde geezer in and lock the door.'

Adam looked at him. This man owned a multimillion dollar company.

'That's your plan? Seriously?'

'There is some sense to it,' said Hugo, adjusting his Fez. 'In the jungle when you set a trap, you need to draw the animal in with bait. So what's going to get

Cherie in here on her own?'

Ali snapped his fingers.

'Medical emergency. Paul can tell her he's lost a foot.'

Adam looked at him.

'Paul *has* lost a foot. We need someone who Cherie would immediately believe has done something stupid.'

Hugo and Adam both looked at Ali.

Ali held up both hands. 'Okay fine, tell her what you like. When Cherie comes in, I'll go out the other door.'

Adam knew it was a stupid plan, but the Pimm's was already working its magic and Ali was right: it was a day for love stories. He stumbled outside waving his arms.

'Cherie, quickly! It's Ali. He's trapped his hand in the door.'

Adam grabbed Henry's arm and pushed him towards the booth too. 'They need you, as well.'

Four pairs of hands guided the hapless couple inside the van and closed the door. Ali appeared from around the other side, giving the thumbs-up.

'What's going on?' asked Zara running over.

'We've trapped Cherie and Henry the photo guy in there together,' grinned Ali.

'Why the hell have you done that?'

'Because Cherie likes him.'

Zara threw him an incredulous look. 'What are you, twelve years old?'

Just then, Ali flew backwards as Cherie kicked the

booth door open, her eyes glittering with fury.

'We were just…' began Adam defensively, but Cherie was clearly in no mood for explanations.

'No wonder you're single, Adam. You need to grow the hell up,' she spat, turning on her heel, and striding back towards the Hall.

Chapter Eighteen

SOPHIE STOOD AND looked down the receiving line snaking through Haslop Hall's entrance. She thought it a weird tradition. A drinks reception on the lawn whilst the happy couple were having their photo taken – that was fine. But did the whole wedding have to do a formal meet-and-greet with the bride and groom and their parents? Who did they think they were – the royal family? It didn't seem like much fun either, with everyone saying the exact same thing: *Lovely service…Such a beautiful dress…Thanks so much for inviting us.* Sophie wondered if she should throw in a curveball: 'Who do you fancy in the Derby this year?' But she didn't want to cause a fuss.

She had done her best to dodge this toe-curling horror show by leaving it until the last moment, loitering in the garden with her mobile clamped to her ear, doing some fire-fighting with Serena's safari clients. Apparently the BBQ disaster had been resolved with a 'bespoke salad' and Mr and Mrs Bennison were currently watching a traditional Maasai tribal dance, seemingly placated, for the moment at least. But when Sophie finally came back into the hall, Tim and Vanessa were still there pressing the flesh. Gritting her teeth, Sophie joined the queue, quickly shaking hands with Vanessa's father Larry and his wife Elspeth, grinning at Jennifer and Bill like a mad woman.

'Lovely day, lovely day,' she said to each of them, feeling her palm get warmer and sweatier with each shake. Her throat was dry, her heart thumping by the time she got to Tim.

'So nice,' she said, her voice practically a croak. 'The wedding, I mean.'

She extended her hand and feeling static pass between them, snatched it back.

If Tim had noticed any chemistry, he didn't show it.

'Thanks,' he said simply, giving her the briefest smile before letting his eyes drift to the next guest. Vanessa was more effusive, complimenting Sophie on her dress, while Sophie told Vanessa, honestly, that she looked lovely and then that was it. Perhaps she would get through this ordeal after all.

'Where've you been?' said Zara, swooping in behind her as Sophie walked the full length of ballroom, past all the real guests over to the social gulag of the Singles Table. Somewhere between the church and the reception Zara had lost her fascinator and gained an enormous hair clip. Sophie didn't bother asking; she supposed when you were a stylist, you could make as many costume changes as you liked.

'Had to deal with some work thing. What have I missed?'

'High drama,' said Zara eagerly. 'That bloke you were with in church? He's just really upset Cherie.'

Sophie looked across to the far corner where Adam was standing in a huddle with Hugo and Ali, looking furtive. 'What's he done now?'

Zara filled her in on the photo-booth incident. 'I think he meant well,' she said. 'But Cherie's furious – can't really blame her. Who is he anyway? He *is* very good-looking.'

'Adam Stowe,' said Sophie. 'An old friend of Tim's. I only met him for the first time yesterday, but I already know him well enough to know that's exactly the sort of thing he'd do.'

'Adam was supposed to be sitting next to Cherie, but thankfully Lucy has offered to swap or else I fear someone might get stabbed with a fork.'

Before she could say anything else, a gong clanged at the far end of the room where a master of ceremonies in a red blazer was standing by the door.

'Ladies and gentleman,' he boomed. 'Please be upstanding for the bride and groom.'

Chairs scraped back and applause filled the ballroom as Vanessa swept in like Cleopatra, Tim following in her wake.

'There you are,' said Adam, leaning in as they took their seats. 'I was wondering where you'd disappeared to.'

'Just because we have adjoining rooms, doesn't mean we're joined at the hip, Adam.'

Sophie had intended to tease him but it came out too tartly. She was out of practice at this. Sophie poured herself some sparkling water and forced herself to relax.

'So I heard you caused a stir out on the lawn.'

'I was only trying to help,' Adam muttered, casting a wary glance towards Cherie.

'And now you're Public Enemy Number one.'

Too sharp. Again. She had no idea why she couldn't be just friendly to him, or at least civil. Despite his evident immaturity, Adam had been kind to her in church. She was relieved when the guest on her other side extended a hand.

'Hi, I'm Paul,' he said.

'Sophie. Sophie Wallis.'

Paul's grasp was solid, matching his square, upright build.

'We're at the same hotel,' said Paul. 'In fact, I think I have your room.'

Sophie gave him a double take.

'How do you know?'

'I overheard you checking in yesterday. I offered to swap with you, but the receptionist was very keen to tell me there were frauds who wanted the big accessible rooms.'

Sophie frowned and shook her head. 'I don't understand...'

Paul lifted the tablecloth and raised one silver leg.

'Afghan bomb,' he said simply.

Sophie nodded, immediately realising why they had been put next to each other. Vanessa was not subtle with her matchmaking.

'The stairs aren't too bad.'

'But you do have mobility problems,' he said. A statement, not a question.

‘So you’re telling me I *look disabled*?’

Paul laughed.

‘No, but I can tell you’re favouring your left side because there’s pain there, plus right now you’re in a textbook Alexander Technique “sitting bones” shape, which takes a lot of practice to get right.’

‘Or a lot of very mean physios shouting at you,’ said Sophie.

‘Steady – I’m a personal trainer now. Shouting at people is what I do best.’

Paul told her his story: how he’d been two days from finishing a nine-month tour in Afghanistan, when the blast from a suicide bomber led to injuries that meant he had to have below-the-knee amputations in both legs.

‘For a long time there, I’d wake up thinking that I might put a gun to my head and pull the trigger,’ he said frankly. ‘Until a colonel friend came to see me and told me about the Stoics.’

‘The Ancient Greeks?’ Sophie had studied a little Classics at school, but couldn’t remember much about them.

‘The Stoics believed that you have to focus on what you can change and influence and ignore the things you can’t. No amount of wishing and hoping was going to change the fact that I had lost my legs. So I accepted it, and decided to row the Atlantic.’

Sophie looked at him wide-eyed.

‘You rowed the Atlantic? Just like that?’

‘Not exactly “just like that”. It took two years of training and planning. And then it took fifty-six days –

and more blisters than you can believe.'

'Wow, Paul. You've really got it together,' she said with genuine admiration.

'Not really,' he said with less confidence. 'Recovery cost me my marriage.'

Sophie leaned forward with more interest. Perhaps Vanessa had been right, they did have a lot in common.

'You're divorced?'

She knew it often happened to survivors of traumatic injury. Friends in her support groups had told her how personality changes, depression, unemployment were hard to deal with and she had seen the effects of her accident on her own parents' marriage, first hand. Michael and Vivienne Wallis were tough, capable people, but the strain of dealing with it in those early years, often took its toll. They'd stayed married, but there were times when Sophie had wondered if they would.

'We're separated,' said Paul, taking a sip of his wine. 'For three years. We're at decree nisi. It wasn't easy for Tina, my wife. The hospitals, the rehabilitation – we even moved to Surrey to be closer to the rehab unit. And yes, I achieved big things, but in getting back to being me – or a new version of me – I think I neglected the "us".'

TINGTINGTING

They both looked up.

'Ladies and gentlemen, please be upstanding for the father of the bride'.

There was applause and some semi-ironic whooping.

Sophie felt her heart drop. The speeches. She had planned to get out of there before they started but there was still no message from Christa. Up on the stage, a tall, thin man with white hair stood up and waited for silence. Larry, Vanessa's father.

'Thank you all for coming to my party,' he said. 'I didn't want to go on holiday this year anyway.'

There was polite laughter as Vanessa looked across at him and mouthed 'Daddy!'

Sophie tried to tune out as Mr Farringdon spent twenty minutes telling the crowd that he wanted nothing but the very best for his princess. There was generous applause when he'd finished, and as he bent over and kissed his daughter tenderly on the cheek, as if to say goodbye, Sophie even found herself quite moved. It was another moment before a tense-looking Tim got to his feet. Sophie took a swallow of wine and stared down at the table.

'Thanks Larry,' said Tim. 'That was so moving. In the same way I'll never be able to follow you as the most important man in Vanessa's life, I doubt I'll be able to follow that speech. But, well, according to Vanessa's Big Day planner, apparently I have to.'

There was a big laugh and Tim nodded along.

'All of the guides about making a wedding speech say you should start with a joke.'

'Sheffield United!' shouted Adam.

Sophie shot him a look but the crowd seemed to enjoy their rapport and gave it a cheer.

'Thanks Adam, ever the Rotherham fan,' smiled

Tim, after the noise simmered down… 'All of which shows why no one should listen to the internet. So I have taken the unusual step of writing a wedding speech from the heart.'

The whole room fell silent as Tim described how he and Vanessa had started off as friends before they fell in love. Tim's posting to New York was just the start of their adventures together; adventures that one-by-one, brought them closer and closer.

'We Yorkshire men don't always wear our hearts on our sleeve and so, I don't find this easy. Good job it's my first – and my last groom speech,' he began, haltingly turning to his bride. 'All I can say is this, Vee. If I loved you less, I might be able to talk about it more. As it is, you take my breath away. You're in my heart and wherever you are in the world, that's the place I want to be. Now, next week and forever more, I always want to be with you, at your side. Always.'

The whole room was hushed, holding their collective breath. Gently, Tim took his bride's hand and looking into her eyes said, 'Thank you for choosing me, Vee. I will always love you with all of my heart. I hope that will be enough.'

He smiled softly, then looked up at the crowd. 'Now over to Rich for the knob gags.'

The whole place erupted. It was like Bruce Springsteen had come onstage. Sophie couldn't breathe. It was beautiful, mesmerising, the heartfelt words of a man in love. It felt like someone had punched her in the stomach. As the applause died down, Rich stood up and began reading from a card.

'I asked Tim where they were going on honeymoon and he said Wales.' A pause. 'Well, what he actually said was, 'I'm going to Bangor for a week.'

'TOP UP?' SAID Adam, to her left.

Sophie had barely spoken to him throughout the meal but she was now grateful for the offer.

'Yes, please,' she said quietly, dabbing her face with a napkin.

Adam filled her glass almost to the brim.

'I've got to hand it to Tim. That was a great speech,' she said looking at Adam more directly. 'If I loved you less, I might be able to talk about it more.' She sighed at the sheer romance of it, despite her own misery. Tim had never been backwards with his feelings when they'd been together, but clearly that was the problem – he hadn't liked her *enough*.

'It's Jane Austen. From *Emma*,' said Adam sitting back in his chair. 'The bit where Knightley finally declares his love for her.'

She'd read the book at school and seen every version of the film but hadn't remembered the line. She was surprised Adam had picked up the reference too.

'Bugger,' he said, glancing at his watch and slipping his jacket back on.

'I've got to go.

'You're leaving?'

'My mate is supposed to be singing tonight. I just want to make a few calls and check he's en route.'

Sophie was not surprised that Adam had unreliable friends, but still, she had to shake off the sense of disappointment as he stood up.

As he left, Sophie turned to talk to Paul, but he had also disappeared.

'So what do you think about Paul?' asked Zara, shuffling across to his empty seat.

Sophie looked up towards the top table where Paul was talking enthusiastically to Tim. Paul had told her that he and Tim had worked on public speaking, mostly 'visualising a positive outcome'. It certainly seemed to have worked and from the matey backslaps and Tim's wide grin, it looked as though Paul thought so too.

'Paul's a nice guy,' said Sophie. But he's married.'

'Balls.'

'Well, strictly speaking he's getting divorced.'

Zara looked briefly hopeful, but Sophie shook her head.

'He's still in love with his wife.'

'So why the split?'

'I get the feeling she left him,' she said lowering her voice. 'I don't think she could cope with his disabilities.'

Zara took a slug of wine.

'So let's get them back together.'

Sophie laughed and stuck her spoon into the chocolate bombe pudding she had barely touched.

'We saw how well trying to fix people up went with Adam and Cherie. At this rate, our entire table is going to get blackballed before the bouquet toss.'

'But this is different. Paul and… his wife…'

'...Tina?'

'Right, Tina. Paul and Tina have history. They're committed. Their love is real.'

'*Was* real, Zara. They're almost divorced; decree nisi.'

'Which isn't decree absolute. And until that time, there is hope.'

Sophie drained her wine. She was a bit dizzy now. The room was hot and she wasn't used to drinking. She'd sometimes join her parents for a glass of wine when they gathered to watch Strictly, but otherwise, she was teetotal.

'Come on,' prompted Zara. 'Love is in the air.'

'You're an old romantic,' said Sophie with a reluctant smile. 'Still, I'm not sure Paul would thank us – and we don't even know Tina.'

'That doesn't matter,' said Zara, grabbing the phone left lying by Paul's coffee cup. 'We don't need to know Tina, because Paul is going to text her.'

Zara flipped through Paul's apps until she opened a new message and held it out to Sophie.

'What? You want me to write it? Oh no,' she said firmly. 'I'm not getting involved.'

'You said it yourself. Your accident wrecked your relationship with Tim. Let's not let it happen to Paul's marriage too.'

Sophie looked down at the phone, not quite believing she was considering it.

'But what do I say? "Hi, it's Paul, I love you, let's call off the divorce?"'

'Pretty much. Just a bit more subtle.'

Sophie stared at the screen. Then she looked up at

Paul, who was still talking to Tim. And suddenly she knew exactly what she wanted to say.

I'm at a wedding and I can't help thinking about us.

'That's good,' said Zara, reading over her shoulder. 'More.'

She paused, looking back towards the top table. Adrenaline flooded her system, but she knew she had to do this. For Paul, for everyone who had lost someone because of accident or illness. For herself.

Let's not give up. I still love you and I never stopped. I know I'm putting you on the spot, but let's start over again. I'm at Haslop Hall, table 24. I'll be waiting for you.

'Perfect' said Zara. 'Just perfect.'

Sophie's thumb hovered over the 'send' button, then looked up at Zara.

'Are you sure?'

'Of course – this is love, Sophie. What's more important?'

Sophie closed her eyes and heard the 'whoosh' as the message went.

This was not the sort of thing she did. Not at all.

'Are you sure we should have done that?'

Zara shrugged.

'It's gone. We've done all we can. It's in the lap of the Gods now.'

Looking down at Paul's phone reminded Sophie

that she hadn't checked her own phone. There were three message alerts.

'My sister's here,' she said, gathering up her things. 'She's been outside for ten minutes.'

'You're leaving?' said Zara, open-mouthed. 'But what do I say to Paul?'

She felt guilty leaving Zara to deal with any fall-out, but what could she do? Tell Christa to wait in the car park for hours on the off-chance that Tina Hobbs might arrive?

'You'll think of something,' she grimaced.

'Come here,' said Zara, reaching over for a hug. 'Thanks for being my wing-man.'

Sophie gave her new friend a squeeze.

'Thank you so much for lending me your armour,' she said. 'I'll get it cleaned and returned as quickly as possible.'

'Hold onto it,' said Zara, nodding sagely. 'You never know when a girl will need a sexy red dress.'

'But surely you have to return it?'

'Let me deal with that. I'll put it on my to-do list along with avoiding Paul. Now shoo. Off you go. Before we get emotional and Tim thinks you're crying about him.'

She pulled a face, and despite herself, Sophie laughed hard.

'Goodbye Zara.'

'Goodbye lovely Sophie. Wish me luck.'

'Whatever for?'

'I'm going to have a crack at the father of the bride.'

Chapter Nineteen

ADAM WAS BRICKING it. He stood at the front of Haslop Hall, looking at the empty drive, then down at his phone: no Declan, no Belasco, not even a whisper. *Bricking it.* That was what they used to say at school when they were worried about getting in trouble: 'Tommo's bricking it, he hasn't done his Chemistry.' Adam had never been entirely sure of the etymology of the phrase: derivative of the Anglo-Saxon 'shitting bricks' perhaps? Either way, Adam was doing it right now. The BPM of his heartbeat felt up there with drum'n'bass, thanks to the terrible feeling that Declan Hawley wasn't going to show. He hadn't guaranteed Tim he could deliver Belasco but as far as he was aware, there was no back-up plan and he could only begin to imagine the sort of bridal melt-down with a glaring hole in the schedule. There would be no happy couple at the end of this wedding, a situation which pretty much summed up Adam's day. Despite his speech on the croquet lawn, the Singles Table hadn't been anywhere near the fun he'd envisioned. He'd spent the rest of the meal trying to avoid Cherie's laser-beam glare. As for Sophie – he'd sat next to her for almost two hours and she had barely spoken to him. Paul seemed like a nice bloke and everything, but was he really that fascinating? Adam shook his head sadly. Perhaps he should have invited Lauren after all.

He walked away from the entrance, skirting around the lawns and the mini fairground amusements set up there. Couples were playing croquet and lawn darts, there were queues for the coconut shy and there was a fortune teller in a colourful tent. There was no doubt that Tim and Vanessa had pulled out all the stops to keep the wedding guests amused.

Speak of the devil. He turned and watched as Tim ran down the Hall's steps towards him. *What now?* Wondered Adam, bracing himself for a tirade about the late arrival of the band, but as he got closer, he saw that Tim was smiling.

'Mate, mate,' he said, seizing Adam's hand and pumping it up and down, his other hand gripping Adam's forearm in a gesture of sincerity. Then he glanced around furtively, making sure they weren't overheard.

'Mate, that speech?' he said, in a low voice. 'I've never had so many compliments. And the women? They had tears in their eyes, man! If I hadn't just got married, there isn't a bird here who wouldn't drop her knickers for me.'

Adam laughed.

'Tim, I'm not sure that's a good thing.'

'Oh but it is,' said Tim.

'Well, I'm glad you liked it.'

'Liked it? You've made me look like bloody

Shakespeare. And the main thing: Vanessa's looking at me like I'm Mr Lover-Lover now.'

Adam wasn't sure that was a good thing either. The notion of Vanessa in any state of friskiness brought on an involuntary shiver.

'Talking of which, shouldn't you be with your bride right now? Isn't it time for cutting the cake?'

Tim shook his head.

'All done. Two thousand quid's worth of carbohydrates are being boxed up as we speak.'

Adam felt his mouth drop open.

'Your wedding cake cost *two grand*?'

'Seven tiers, man. They're based in Mayfair. Do a lot of stuff for the Beckhams,' said Tim, as if that explained everything.

Tim held up his left hand, pointing to his shiny wedding ring.

'So, that's it. Done. I'm officially a married man.'

Adam smiled.

'And how do you feel?'

'D'you know what? Pretty good. I mean, I won't lie, part of me has been dreading this, but now it's done, I'm glad I did it. I feel – grown up. Doesn't that sound daft?'

'No mate, not at all. Actually it sounds brilliant.'

Adam shook his head and pulled his old friend into a back-slapping embrace, genuinely pleased to see him so happy.

'We've come a long way, Ads,' he murmured into Adam's shoulder.

'We have that,' agreed Adam, even if the good

fortune was pretty much all Tim's. He wondered what those sneery teenagers back in Tim's bedroom would have made of the champagne fountain and the seven-tiered cakes. He smiled: they'd probably just have been happy to get served at the bar.

'Talking of which,' said Tim, stepping back. 'I know you must be feeling shitty about the mag folding and everything, but have you thought about what you're going to do next?'

'I was thinking of opening a record shop,' said Adam. There was a moment's pause, then Tim laughed.

'Yeah, and maybe start selling hula hoops and pogo sticks too.'

He didn't say it unkindly, but still, it made Adam bristle.

'I'm serious,' said Adam. 'Not just vinyl, more of a base for live events and corporate tie-ins, like sponsored festivals and...' he trailed off, his enthusiasm draining under Tim's steely gaze. For a moment, Adam could see him in the board room, dismissing some project with one withering put-down.

'Okay maybe,' said Tim finally. 'But I've got another idea. I know this is left-field, but how about you come to work for us?'

Adam stared at him.

'For you? For Glasshouse?'

'Why not?' said Tim, like it was the most natural thing in the world. 'We're expanding rapidly into digital, social media, audio, all the platforms. You could be content director, Ads.'

'But I don't know anything about marketing.'

His friend shrugged. 'But you know media. You know how to connect with young people through music and film and celebrities. Listen, you were just talking about hooking up with brands for a festival, right? Seriously Ads, a man with your contacts and experience, you'd be an asset for us. Plus, it never hurts to have people around you who've got your back.'

'Content Director?' he said dubiously.

'Okay, so it won't be a board position or anything, but there will be a good salary, a decent pension and a company car.' Tim grinned. 'Hey, maybe I can pass that shitheap I'm driving on to you when I get the Tesla.'

Adam blinked, unsure exactly how to react. He had to admit he was excited and flattered, but at the same time, he was unsettled by the idea. Adam's self-image had been formed in the crucible of teenage rebellion. People like him weren't corporate executives, that wasn't punk rock. But if Adam was brutally honest, *Cream* going under had shaken him. Adam drove a fifteen-year-old car and had a studio flat in Walthamstow; he hardly lived a life of extravagance. But without the magazine, he knew he'd struggle to afford even that. What would he do? Move into shared accommodation with a load of twentysomethings who secretly referred to him as 'the old man'?

'Come on,' said Tim. 'What do you say? If nothing else, it'll be a laugh working together.'

Adam began to open his mouth just as they both

heard Tim's name called. They turned to see Rich waving from the steps of the hall, beckoning him over.

'Tim, photos!' he yelled.

Tim dropped his head wearily.

'*More* photos?' he sighed. 'I'd better go. Look Ads, think about it. We'll talk about it more when I get back from the Maldives, okay?'

'Sure. And thanks. Seriously.' They embraced again and Adam watched him go, running across the drive.

Content director. Despite his misgivings, Adam couldn't help smiling to himself. Come on, admit it, he thought. You're a little bit excited. Adam still loved the music industry and he loved being a tiny part of that machine. Even so, Adam had done nothing else all his working life. A new challenge, a different direction might be just what he needed. And a car with a walnut dashboard. Now that would be *sweet.*

His phone chirped for an incoming message. It was Declan.

'Just left Guildford. Be there in twenty minutes.'

Adam squeezed his hand into fist.

'Yes,' he grinned. 'Yes!'

Chapter Twenty

CHRISTA WAS FACING away from her, sitting on a fence, looking out towards the valley.

'There you are,' said Sophie, hobbling across the grass. Sophie had been right around the car park, then back to the front entrance of the Hall looking for Christa. She was out of breath, and her calves were throbbing. She knew she'd never get up on the fence, so she leant next to Christa, arms resting on the wood.

'What are you doing here?'

'Just looking. It's beautiful, isn't it?'

Sophie followed her sister's gaze out over the valley, the river glinting between trees, the clouds slight and wispy, like a trail of dandelion seeds against a polar blue sky.

'Sorry for keeping you waiting, I didn't see your text.'

'It's fine. I'm enjoying this – the sun on my face for once.' She tilted her head back and took a deep breath. 'I don't get much me-time these days. I can't remember the last time I didn't have Hattie on my hip.'

Sophie had seen Christa's car but her niece wasn't in it.

'Where is Hattie?'

'With Dan. But I can't leave her for long.'

Sophie looked up at her.

'Dan can manage.'

'Probably. You look great by the way. I thought you were going to wear that blue dress.'

Sophie tugged at her hemline, self-conscious.

'Change of plan. I met a fashion stylist and she lent it to me. Can you believe it's Dolce and Gabbana?'

'Well it suits you,' grinned Christa. 'So how was it?'

Sophie paused, remembering that Christa had been good enough to ferry her all the way out here and had come back to rescue her. She didn't want to make it sound a complete waste of time.

'It wasn't as bad as it could have been. At least I met some nice people.'

'Oh good!'

For ages her sister had been encouraging her to make more friends. Sophie still kept in touch with a handful of pals from Bristol and St Paul's, but everyone seemed so busy with family or jobs these days. Warwick Travel hadn't proved to be a fertile ground for meeting likeminded people either. Serena tended to employ beautiful, professionally unambitious women straight out of university, and as such, Sophie was at least ten years older than her colleagues who never invited her out when they went husband hunting on the Kings Road. There was Mary and Diane, who she had met at Tai Chi, but they were both touching seventy, and as much as Sophie enjoyed going for coffee with them after their class, she knew that her sister was right, and that a social circle her own age might be what she needed.

She took a breath and told Christa about Zara and Paul and Ali, although she kept quiet about Adam and the bathroom incident, thinking Christa might read something into it.

There was a heavy pause as they both listened to the wind ripple through the air.

The air was soft and heavy with the smells of summer, freshly cut grass, wildflowers and sunshine.

'I saw him. I saw Tim,' said Sophie finally.

'And was it how you imagined?'

Sophie exhaled deeply.

'No. I mean, I'd prepared myself. I'd expected to see him changed, living a different life. It was just harder than I thought. He has everything, Chris. A great job, a beautiful wife, hundreds of friends, all in this amazing setting. It didn't even rain.'

'No one's life is perfect, Soph.'

'Except yours and Dan's.'

'Right.'

The hitch in Christa's voice made Sophie turn: she was shocked to see her sister's eyes glistening with tears.

'Hey, hey! What's the matter?' she said.

'Dan's moving out,' said Christa, wiping her face.

'What?'

Christa's life with Dan and Hattie seemed so idyllic. It wasn't as grand or as impressive as Tim and Vanessa Jameson's: Dan was a cameraman for wildlife documentaries and they had a cute terrace tucked away in Raynes Park. It was humdrum, ordinary even. But that house always seemed so full of light and love.

'He's met someone else, Soph. Some tart from his cycling club.'

It didn't compute. Dan had always seemed so decent.

'How do you know?'

'I found a condom in the backpack he takes on a ride. So I followed him one day. He met her at one of those fancy riverside flats by Putney Bridge. When he came home in his sweaty, disgusting Lycra he actually dared to say he'd been so long because he'd cycled all the way to Dorking.'

Christa sighed.

'Soph. I can't compete with a woman in Lycra. See-through Lycra at that.'

'See-through?'

'Have you never followed a cyclist from behind? Their shorts always look sheer. Anyway, her name is Amy. She's a lawyer for some American firm.'

Sophie didn't know what to say. She put her hand over her sister's.

'When I found out, when I told him I knew, he promised me he'd end it. And for a couple of months I believed him. But it was still carrying on and now I feel so bloody foolish.'

Sophie felt awful that all this had been happening to her sister for months, that she had been carrying around all this hidden pain and yet Sophie hadn't even seen or realised it. She pulled Adam's handkerchief from her clutch bag and handed it to Christa.

'Why didn't you tell me?'

Christa didn't reply.

'Do Mum and Dad know?' she pressed.

'You've all got enough on your plate.'

'Christa, you should have told me. You know I'm here for you. I could have helped.'

'You did help me,' said Christa quietly.

'What? How?'

'Soph, without you I'd never have had the strength to tell him he has to leave. I would have muddled on, feeling more and more unhappy, feeling suspicious and betrayed. Instead I just thought about how strong and fierce you've been since your accident.'

'Fierce?' Sophie smiled at that one.

'Yes, fierce. I remember what the doctors said at the Swiss hospital. They said you'd probably never walk again and Mum and Dad told me we had to prepare for the worst. But you didn't let that happen, did you? You fought it all. The chest infections, the breathing problems, the mobility issues. Step by step. It was slow and painful, but you did it. Even coming to Tim's wedding this weekend, going to the hen do. I don't know anyone else who would have done that, Soph. You don't swerve anything. You face it and you fight through it, whatever life throws you. Because you know it will be better on the other side.'

'You said I was an idiot for coming to the wedding.'

Christa's face broke into a grin.

'You are an idiot.'

They both laughed and Sophie reached up to help

Christa down from the fence.

'Come on, let's go and get my things from The Swan and go home,' she said.

Christa sighed deeply. 'I dread going home these days. Dan's still there. I've said he can stay until the tenancy on his new flat starts. I thought he might move straight in with that tart otherwise, so I had to let him stay.'

Sophie nodded. Dan had betrayed her, hurt her, and yet the thought of him moving on was just too painful. She knew exactly how that felt.

'Then stay here. I've got the room at The Swan for another night. And Hattie's safe enough with Dan.'

'He'll feed her cheese puffs and chocolate.'

'She'll survive for one day. And he *is* her dad. Come on, we can watch a crappy movie, drain the mini-bar and order room service.'

Christa hesitated.

'I suppose I could.'

'Then it's settled.'

'But no rom-coms, okay?'

Sophie put an arm around her sister and walked back towards the car park.

She turned as she heard running footsteps and saw Adam pelting towards them, his tie flying behind him like a streamer.

'Sophie…'

He stopped. 'Sorry, I didn't know you were with someone.'

'Adam, this is my sister Christa.'

He flashed his smile. 'Great to meet you. I'm Adam.'

He paused to catch his breath. 'Zara told me you were leaving,' he said, panting.

'Yes. I've got a lift back to London.'

'I thought you were checked into The Swan until tomorrow?'

Sophie shook her head, avoiding Christa's gaze.

'No, got to get back. Christa's daughter is…'

'I thought we *were* staying at The Swan tonight' said Christa innocently. 'I could head over there now, you can stay a bit longer at the wedding. With Adam.'

'I'm not leaving you,' said Sophie, shooting a warning look at her sister who appeared to be deliberately ignoring it.

'Then both stay,' said Adam. 'I'm DJing later, and you don't want to miss my mash-up of Mamma Mia and The Macarena. It's legendary on the party circuit.'

Sophie was about to refuse again, but they all turned as there was a deep rumble from the direction of the drive and in a cloud of dust, a coach with blacked out windows came along the avenue of trees.

'I don't believe it,' said Adam quietly. 'He came.'

'What? Who came?'

He swallowed. 'Declan.'

There was another blast of horn. People were coming to the hall's entrance to see what the disturbance was.

A window slid open in the coach and a man in wraparound sunglasses poked his head out and waved regally at Adam.

'Delivery for Mr Stowe,' he called. 'Did someone

order a crappy wedding band?'

Sophie felt Christa clutching at her arm. 'Is that who I think it is?'

'Who is it?' said Sophie. She had no idea at all.

'It's Declan Hawley,' gasped Christa, her melancholy evaporating. 'I *love* Belasco! Are they playing tonight?'

Adam grinned, then nodded.

'Just put it over here, Dec,' he shouted, beckoning the tour bus towards him like a man directing a 747 at Gatwick.

'Well I'm definitely staying now,' said Christa. 'Screw Dan, he can look after his own daughter for once. And if Declan Hawley's on the loose you'd better get me inside Haslop Hall.'

Sophie laughed. For one lovely moment, she saw the old Christa, the rebellious teenager with dyed hair and a lust for life.

'And you said *I* was fierce.'

Chapter Twenty-One

ADAM FELT LIKE a rock star. He walked through Haslop Hall leading a small entourage of exotic creatures – roadies and a couple of what looked suspiciously like groupies. There was even a photographer running about clicking off frames. Everyone was looking at Adam, whispering about him – and for once, that was a good thing. Okay, so Adam might not actually be a rock star, but today he was friends with a rock star and Declan was playing his part perfectly, smiling, waving, posing for selfies – it was as if Adam were leading royalty through the corridors, and the reflected glow was blinding. Adam even received the ultimate honour, a nod of acknowledgement from Larry, father-of-the-bride, when Declan went over to thank him for the opportunity to play at his party. Such a well-brought up young man. You wouldn't have got that with the Sex Pistols.

Formalities complete, Declan took Adam to one side and explained that Belasco's drummer and bassist had already left for Newcastle, so he was only available to do a small acoustic set.

'I'm just glad you're here,' said Adam, looking at a makeshift stage, where the Belasco sound crew were on their hands and knees, adjusting cables, leads and lights, tens of thousands of pounds of tech required for this low-key, intimate acoustic performance. 'I'm so grateful. We all are.'

Declan winked. 'Any opportunity to get up in front of a crowd and have them clap afterwards is a good time for me. Plus the label's sent a snapper to immortalise the event. It's great PR – makes me look a nice guy who cares about the fans.'

'You *are* a nice guy Dec.'

'Only since the therapy.'

'I thought it was rehab.'

'I'm a singer. Extroverts tend to be bristling with insecurities. The drive that gets you to the top is also your Achilles heel. Tears of a clown, innit?'

'Miracles, 1967. Released in the UK in 1970, b-side of Promise Me.'

Declan shook his head slowly.

'You do know how rare that is?'

'The Tears of a Clown 45? Not very. £20 for a mint one.'

'No, someone working in the music business who actually knows about music. The industry still needs people like you, Ads.'

Adam smiled gratefully, even though he'd felt completely dispensable to the music industry ever since he'd heard about Cream's demise.

Vanessa beckoned him over to the bar and he went to see what she wanted.

'Adam, thanks for helping to set this up,' she said, her face flushed. 'Is it okay if I have a quick word, with him? The singer man?'

'Declan.'

'Yes, yes, Declan. He does know the song, doesn't he?'

'What song?' said Adam. 'Tim didn't tell me there were any specific requests.'

'The song for our first dance.'

Adam glanced up at the stage, a feeling of foreboding stirring in his stomach.

'So what is it?'

Vanessa beamed. 'You're Beautiful', of course. You know. James Blunt. Tim sang it to me the night we got engaged. It's very special.' She glanced up at Declan again. 'He does know it, doesn't he?'

Adam gulped hard.

'I'm sure he's heard of it, Vee. But Declan is expecting to play his own songs. Belasco songs – that's the band he's in. But look, I'm sure he'll do 'Hey Child' or 'Hold My Hand' if you ask.'

Vanessa's face was colouring even more.

'Hey Child?'

'Top three hit about ten years ago. Modern classic.'

'This isn't Glastonbury, Adam. This is my *wedding*.'

'Vee, Declan Hawley is, was, one of the biggest pop stars in the country. This isn't a covers band. Asking him to play James Blunt, it's like asking Lou Reed to play One Direction.

Her face stayed blank.

'You *have* heard of Lou Reed?'

'Not all of us are music journalists, Adam.'

Adam could see tears gathering in her eyes, but they weren't tears of pain, they were tears of frustration, the tears of Veruca Salt, a little girl used to getting her way.

'Listen Vee,' he began, but Vanessa stopped him with a jab of her finger.

'No, you listen, Adam. This is the most important day of my life. Of Tim's life. And Tim is supposed to be your friend. Don't you want him to be happy?'

Adam looked at her. *Yes I do*, he thought. *But my hopes aren't high.*

'Okay, okay,' he said holding up a hand. 'I'll go and speak to him.'

'You are joking?' said Declan, when he explained the situation.

'I'm afraid not.' Adam ran his hand through his hair. 'Look, I know 'You're Beautiful' is actually about drug addiction, so it wouldn't be my choice for a first dance, but Vanessa is pretty highly strung and there could well be a scene.'

'Adam, I'm doing this as a favour,' said Declan, lowering his voice and stepping back into the shadows. 'Blunty's a good bloke and everything, but I've got a snapper here, not to mention five hundred guests all of them with a smart phone. I've already been stopped for about fifty selfies. What happens when someone tweets footage of me. We'll be viral in ten minutes.'

Adam thought that Dec might be overestimating public interest in a band that hadn't been in the top 40 for five years, but he didn't like to point it out.

'It'll be good for your image,' he said. 'By your

own admission, you want to look a nice guy. The worst thing you can look is game for a laugh. Besides, it is a great song.'

To his surprise, Declan actually seemed to be thinking it over, a slow smile forming on his face.

'Alright,' he said. 'I'll play it.'

'Brilliant, thanks so much…'

Declan held up a finger.

'But on one condition.'

Adam frowned. 'What's that?'

'*You* sing it.'

Adam froze. 'What?'

'Come on, with your encyclopaedic pop knowledge,' said Declan, evidently warming to the idea. 'I bet you already know the words off by heart.'

'No Dec, I can't…'

The singer gave a wolfish grin, then nodded towards Sophie, who was at the bar with Christa getting cocktails.

'You might even impress that girl.'

'Girl?'

'The girl you keep looking at. The one in the red dress.'

But Declan was already standing at the microphone.

'Ladies and gentlemen,' he called. 'Please could you all gather in the ballroom for the first dance…'

He turned back and grinned at Adam, then added: 'And a very special musical performance.'

Adam's heart was pounding as he looked down at the dancefloor. It looked as though the entire wedding party was already assembled, every eye trained on them. On *him.*

Closing his eyes, squeezing his hands into fists, Adam gulped in air, then went to the front of the stage, flinching as Dec's lighting engineer lit him up. Was this how it felt for Bowie? He wondered. For Simon Le Bon? It was terrifying, but at the same time, the blood was singing in his ears. He felt alive.

'Ladies, gentlemen,' he said into the microphone, 'Please show your appreciation for... Mr Timothy Jameson and Mrs Vanessa Jameson, the bride and groom!'

There was a cheer as Tim and Vanessa walked onto the dancefloor and the spotlight swung over to bathe them in a white oval. Adam nodded to Declan, who began picking out the familiar opening riff of the James Blunt tune.

Tim and Vanessa turned to face each other, Vee smiling up at him shyly, a Lady Di impression he felt sure she had practised. *This is it*, he thought and took a breath.

'My life is brilliant,' he sang, a waver in his voice, squinting as he was drowned in a spotlight.

There was a pause of disbelief, then a whoop of recognition. Adam could hear Ali's delighted laughter and Hugo shouting 'YES!'

Despite his terror of being on stage in front of such a crowd, Adam still couldn't help smiling.

As Adam sang, he turned to look at Dec, wondering where the percussion had come from, then realised that the crowd were clapping along.

His voice cracked as he went for the chorus, but he hit it – more or less – on the second go. Declan appeared to be laughing as he played the instrumental bridge. Not the review he was hoping for, but he couldn't stop now – and then he saw Sophie, swaying along to the music and as Declan came up beside him to harmonise, Adam began to direct the song towards her. 'You're beautiful…'

Adam's smile faded as he saw that Sophie wasn't watching him at all. Instead, she was staring at Tim slow dancing with Vanessa. *Of course*, he thought, all his triumph fading away, but he managed to hold it together until the song clattered to a close and then he was borne up by a roar of appreciation. Adam did his best to look modest. He suspected they were cheering Declan – or maybe Tim and Vee – but still he took a deep bow.

'Encore!' shouted Hugo.

'Sorry, that's it from me,' said Adam. 'But give it up for… DECLAN HAWLEY!'

Ever the pro, Dec launched straight into 'Hold My Hand', Belasco's biggest hit, and Adam dutifully slunk away. Using the stairs at the side of the stage, Adam moved through the crowd, accepting back-slaps and cries of 'well done', but all the time searching for Sophie's face. If ever there was a time to ask her to dance, this was it. Even the Ice Maiden would find it hard to refuse right now. He spotted Christa standing with Ali on the far side of the stage and began to weave his way through the crowd, before bumping into a blonde woman.

'Sorry,' she said, looking harassed. 'Can you tell me where I'd find table 24?'

'The tables have all been cleared away – they were here where the dancefloor is now.'

She looked crestfallen. 'Oh, thanks,' she said, and turned towards the exit.

'But I was on table 24 – are you looking for someone in particular?'

'Paul, Paul Hobbs.'

Adam wavered. He still wanted to find Sophie, but he couldn't abandon the woman, she looked so lost.

'Come with me. I'll ask some of the others from the table if they know where Paul is.'

He saw Sophie standing by the crowded bar waiting to get served. She grinned when she saw him.

'That was… hilarious.'

'I was hoping for "moving", but I suppose it's better than "horrific",' he replied, then turned to introduce his companion. 'Sophie, this is Tina, Paul's wife. She's looking for him.'

Adam saw all the colour drain from Sophie's face, or perhaps it was because the lights in the ballroom had been dimmed.

'Paul's wife,' she croaked.

'Yes, Hi. I'm Tina,' she said stepping forward. 'Have you seen Paul anywhere?'

Sophie shook her head, then snaked her arm around Adam's waist. For a moment, he was quite excited about the direction things were going until he felt Sophie's fingers dig a warning in his side. He wasn't sure what she was trying to warn him about; was Paul somewhere he shouldn't be? A broom cupboard with the mother of the bride? From his short acquaintance with Paul, that didn't seem like the sort of thing he'd do.

'Tina,' he said, nodding to the bar. 'Why don't you get a drink, we'll go and find Paul and bring him back here? Better than us all roaming about.'

She nodded uncertainly. 'Okay, thanks.'

By the time Adam had pulled Sophie off to the side of the dancefloor, she looked grey.

'What the hell's going on?' he asked.

'Tina is Paul's wife,' she hissed.

'I had grasped that. So what?'

'Zara and I invited her, not Paul. I didn't think she'd actually come.'

Sophie quickly explained what they had done. Adam tried hard not to smile: it wasn't the sort of behaviour he expected from Sophie.

'Do you think Paul will be angry?'

Adam rubbed his face. 'I can't imagine he'll relish the idea of holding a couples therapy session in public, no.'

She looked stricken and Adam knew they had to do something.

'So do you know where Paul is?' he asked.

'He was standing at the back when you were rocking out.'

'Come on,' he said, instinctively taking her hand. 'He can't have got far.'

'Is that a disabled joke?'

He smiled over his shoulder. 'No time for banter.'

They found Paul talking to Hugo by the buffet, a thirty-foot spread of cheese, platters, salad bowls and charcuterie. Adam raised his eyebrows at Hugo, who immediately got the message and stepped away. Adam knew they had to give it to him straight.

'What's up?' asked Paul over the music. He looked from Adam to Sophie and back again, clearly reading something in their expressions.

'Look mate,' said Adam quickly. 'I know you're not going to like this, but I invited your wife to the party.'

Paul looked at him with a slight frown, as if he was trying to decipher what Adam had said. '*My* wife? Tina?'

Paul's face turned red. 'When? How?'

'You left your phone on the table. I heard you were separated and thought it might be a good idea to, you know, get you guys talking again. But now she's here, I realise I might have put you on the spot.'

Paul took an angry step towards Adam, his beer splashing onto the floor, but Sophie put out her hand.

'Paul, no, it was me,' she cried. 'I sent Tina a text from your phone.'

He shook his head, confused, then pulled out his mobile, immediately scrolling to the 'sent messages'.

'Oh God,' he whispered.

Paul looked at them, his anger subsiding. He looked like a teacher irritated by his pupil's idiocy. He held up his phone.

'Why did you write this?'

'Because you said to me "ignore the fear" and

don't miss out on things because you're scared. Something like that, anyway.'

'That's just crap I say to my clients!'

'You don't mean that,' said Sophie, her eyes blazing with passion. 'I know I shouldn't have done it, but now Tina's here, you have to face up to how you really feel.'

Wow, thought Adam, watching Sophie with admiration. In full swing, she was impressive.

'Listen Paul,' he said, stepping forward. '*She came.* That tells its own tale, doesn't it?'

'But I didn't write the bloody message.'

'Tom Cruise didn't write "You complete me" either, but it's still one of the greatest lines in film. And any woman would love to hear their man say it to them.'

Sophie was nodding.

'I lost Tim after my accident,' she said with determination. 'I wasn't in the position to fight for him but I don't blame him for walking away. He didn't know what my future would look like. When you're 22, who wants to commit to the unknown? But you and Tina got through the hard part. You were almost there. Paul, I am in awe of your achievements. The Atlantic Challenge, your business… but you can't abandon your marriage without giving it everything you've got.'

He rubbed his mouth with the palm of his hand.

'She could just have come to yell at me.'

'She's at the bar. Go and have a look at how she's dressed,' said Adam. 'She is not a woman looking for a fight.'

Still Paul wavered.

'Paul, you've been into battle under enemy fire,' said Adam. 'This is a walk in the park.'

'Give me a minefield any day.'

'It's an open goal, mate. Just tell her how you feel.'

'What if that's not enough? What if I'm not enough?'

Adam glanced at Sophie.

'At least you know you tried.'

Paul didn't say anything else. He downed a long slug of beer and went towards the bar. Sophie went to follow him, but Adam held her back.

'He has to do this alone.'

They both craned their necks to watch as Paul approached his wife.

'She's smiling,' said Sophie.

'A smile's better than a slap. Or a drink in the face.'

Sophie looked at him sideways.

'Why do I get the feeling that you have extensive experience of both?'

Adam smiled. 'Not today. Which leads me to my next question.'

Sophie tilted her head and Adam put out a hand.

'Do you want to dance?'

Chapter Twenty-Two

'I THINK WE did well with Paul and Tina,' said Adam, guiding Sophie into the centre of the dance floor. She felt exposed here, but she liked the feeling of his hand on the small of her back as he started to move in time with the music.

In the days when Sophie was in the neuro-rehab unit, when her post-traumatic amnesia had passed, but before she had learnt to walk again, Sophie always dreamt of dancing. She liked to imagine herself at a May Ball, a full moon party in Thailand or a club in the West End, her head tipped back, her arms over her head in abandon, lost in sound. Even though her memories of all of those places were not crystal clear, even though she was in a wheelchair and the thought of ever dancing again seemed so remote, she might have well be wishing to fly to the moon, Sophie enjoyed remembering those times. What it was like to feel alive and free. To be happy.

'Some might say you've redeemed yourself after the Cherie and Henry debacle,' she grinned, glancing across to the bar where Paul and Tina were sitting close together, smiling and talking.

Adam was a good dancer, confident and fluid, and

although Sophie felt awkward and unpractised, she felt herself relax. From above there was a faint pop as confetti fell from the ceiling like pale pink snowflakes and for a moment, Sophie felt like the girl she once was.

'You know what this reminds me of?' shouted Adam over the music, taking her hand and whirling her around. Her left calf was hurting again but she didn't want him to stop.

'What?'

'That Maroon 5 Sugar video.'

She shook her head at him, confused.

'Maroon 5. American band? Did this incredible video for their song Sugar. Gate-crashed a bunch of weddings and surprised the happy couple.'

She didn't mean to look at him blankly but she genuinely didn't know what he was talking about.

'Sorry, I've missed out on a lot of pop culture.'

'Don't worry. I'm happy to give you a musical education,' he smiled, pulling her closer, and as she felt his breath on her cheeks, warm, soft, delicious, she felt her heart speed up.

'Do you always win everyone round?' she said with a soft smile. Sophie had been impressed that he'd tried to take the blame for her text to Tina Hobbs but it wasn't just that; she had originally had Adam down as an egotist, the type who always wants to be centre of attention, but while it was true that Adam could command an audience, she had noticed the thoughtful way he included everyone into the conversation, how he seemed to want the best for everyone. He was someone who made people feel good, and she knew that because it was how she was feeling now.

'I'm hardly Mr. Popular,' he shrugged. 'I've received countless legal letters, and been named on a writ twice. Personally I thought they were my best interviews but the celebrities concerned seemed to think it was libel. Three household names have also threatened to "take me out." So no, I'm not on everyone's Christmas card list.'

'You wrote Tim's speech, didn't you?' she said suddenly.

'Now why would I do that?' he replied, spinning her around again.

'Because Tim's your friend. Because you're a nice guy'

'Have you just paid me a compliment, Wallis?'

She stopped dancing and looked at him directly.

'You didn't answer the question. I saw you hand him something at the church. And that Jane Austen quote… I think we both know that the only thing Tim reads is the *Viz* Annual.'

'Look, he was desperate.'

'So you do have a soft centre, Adam Stowe.'

He looked away, clearly flustered, and Sophie smiled. It was nice to see his vulnerable side, and besides, it meant that perhaps, Tim hadn't truly meant what he said in his speech. When Tim had turned to Vanessa and recited the line from *Emma* – 'If I loved you less, I might be able to talk about it more' – Sophie had thought her heart might break. Now that Sophie knew for sure that Tim hadn't written the line, did it mean it was false? Or had Adam been right when he'd told Paul that even ghost-written lines could still be sincere?

'So how come you've never got married?' she asked.

'I've been married and divorced three times actually.'

'You have?'

'I'm joking. I'm not Jerry Lee Lewis.'

'Was he married three times?'

'Seven. Kenny Rogers had five. Louis Armstrong four, as has Tommy Lee. But Adam Stowe? Never taken the plunge.'

'And here's me thinking you were so rock'n'roll.'

'I guess my parents' divorce just put me off. I want to make sure it's right, when... if, I ever say I Do.'

The music stopped and the whole dancefloor roared.

'I think that's their last song,' said Adam quietly. 'As much as Dec loves a crowd, I'm not sure there'll be an encore. I just need to go and thank them for coming and then, how about we go and check out that Giant Jenga on the croquet lawn?'

'It's a plan,' she said, watching him go.

Sweat trickled down her temple. She opened her bag to get a tissue and saw her phone was vibrating to signal an incoming message. She looked down and her heart sank as she realised it was the fifth message received in the past twenty minutes.

Where the HELL are U? CALL ME!
NOW!! Serena.

Leaving the bar area, Sophie stepped into a quiet alcove and dialled Serena's number, with a sinking feeling.

'Serena?'

'It's a shitshow in Tanzania.'

Sophie swallowed.

'Shitshow?'

'The Bennisons, Sophie! They're having a meltdown. That 'supper under the stars' experience? They were expected to stay in a *mud hut* overnight. Can you believe it?'

Sophie squeezed her eyes tight.

'But Serena, it was supposed to be an authentic Maasai village experience.'

'The Bennisons are paying top dollar for luxury, Sophie,' said Serena with a sneer. 'Understandably our clients did not want to stay. So the guide offered to take them back to the hotel, but they have broken down en route.'

'I'm sure their guide has it under control, Serena.'

'Under control? Their driver has built a bonfire – Mrs Bennison is terrified!'

'Serena. It will be fine.'

'Fine? FINE? Sophie, the Bennisons are connected up the wazoo. If they start bad-mouthing us all over Fulham, we'll lose clients hand over fist. We need to find them!'

Sophie took a deep breath. Only last month Serena had rung Sophie when she was in her doctor's waiting room and demanded she 'magic up' – Serena's actual words – a hotel room in Cannes during the film festival. Sophie was tired of Serena using her as a cure-all for laziness and incompetence, but given the rest of her life seemed to be unravelling right now, Sophie really didn't want to add 'find a new job' to the long list of issues she needed to fix.

'What do you want me to do?' she asked wearily.

'I am going to call the British embassy in Dar es Salaam,' said Serena. '*You* need to locate the Bennisons and arrange the evacuation.'

She hung up and took a deep breath to galvanize herself.

First, she needed to pinpoint the client's location, then hire some transport and get the couple to the closest five-star resort in Tanzania, or ideally, back to their own hotel. That should placate even the most demanding of clients.

She looked up. First she needed a computer with a decent internet connection; there was no way she could manage this on a phone with one bar. Across the other side of the dancefloor she saw the Singles Table gang – Hugo, Lucy, and Zara clapping along as Ali tried to impress Christa with some moonwalking. His dance moves weren't brilliant – he looked more like he was dragging a sack of cement than gliding across the floor – but Ali might just be the man Sophie needed to see. She strode over.

'Hey, here's the other side of the sandwich,' called Ali, dancing over towards her.

'Ali, you're like a tech expert aren't you?' asked Sophie quickly.

'You know it,' he said, biting his lip and pointing

two fingers at her.

When Sophie failed to respond, he nodded. 'Yes, yes I am.'

Sophie led him to the side of the floor and explained her situation.

'I've got a client stranded on the Serengeti. I need to find them, quickly. Is it possible?'

Ali waggled his fingers like he was performing a card trick.

'Piece. Of. Piss.'

He beckoned to Sophie and, sensing some drama, the others followed them out to the lobby area, watching Ali speak to Matt the butler. Nodding, Matt directed Ali behind the reception desk and sat him at the computer.

'This is where the magic happens,' said Ali, his fingers flying across the keys.

'Gimme those digits,' he said and Sophie passed over the cell number Serena had given her. Ali's brow creased as he concentrated, peering at the screen. As he picked up the phone and made a call, Sophie explained the situation to the others.

'Can you actually trace a mobile phone in the middle of nowhere?' asked Lucy.

'Depends,' said Hugo. 'It wouldn't work in the jungle, the canopy would block the signal. The grasslands and plains won't have that problem, obviously, but it doesn't have many phone masts either.'

Ali slapped his hand on the desk and with a whoop of triumph, turned the monitor to face his audience.

'Don't doubt the Ali-man,' he said.

On the screen was a map showing the east coast of Africa, the blue of the Indian ocean and the green island of Madagascar. Ali rapidly tapped a key, zooming in on the yellow of the savannah. In the centre was a pulsing red circle.

'You've found them?' gasped Sophie. 'Ali, you're a genius.'

'It has been said,' he said proudly.

Using the mouse, he zoomed into the satellite picture, until they could see the finer details of the plains. Huts, cars, lodges. In fact, the red circle seemed to be bleeping over what looked like a petrol station.

'Is that their *actual* car we're seeing there?' asked Christa, wide-eyed.

'And those flecks on the screen are the Bennisons,' said Ali, tapping the screen.

'How did you just do that?' asked Sophie.

Ali tapped the side of his nose. 'Friends in high places. Literally in this case.'

I used the satellite technology to trace the car, not the mobile. It's a top-of-the-line Jeep, comes with a proper GPS built in. Would have been harder if they'd been moving.'

He wrote something down and handed it to Sophie.

'They're at a petrol station. There's the address. Now is there anything else I can help you with?'

'Now I need to arrange an airlift.'

'I know some ex-SAS chaps who could probably rustle up a Black Hawk,' said Hugo.

Sophie had to admit that sounded quite exciting, if

a little heavy-handed.

'I'm not sure we need that level of drama yet. Serena has already said that someone was setting fire to things, so we don't want to inflame the situation. No pun intended.'

Ali held out his mobile phone.

'Why don't we just ask them what's going on?'

It couldn't be that simple, could it? Sophie quickly dialled the number Serena had given her. The group gathered around as she put it onto loudspeaker.

It rang, rang, then there was shouting in a strange dialect Sophie couldn't place.

'Hello? Mr Bennison? Are you there?'

More garbled voices. Then the connection went dead. They all looked at the screen, where a cloud of black smoke seemed to be obscuring the car.

'Oh God,' whispered Zara, but Ali was already pressing the redial button on the phone.

'Ben, you're a man of the world. How many languages do you speak?

Hugo see-sawed his hand side-to-side. 'Eleven, twelve perhaps.'

'What language do they speak in the Serengeti?'

'Swahili.'

'Do you speak that?' sked Sophie.

'I spent a little time with the Morani in Ngorongoro. Might be a little rusty.'

'It'll do.'

Sophie pressed the phone into his hand.

'Habari!' said Hugo. 'Habari ya jioni. Ninaweza kuzungumza na Bwana Bennison? Ndio…Kusema kwamba tena? Ah, the choo. Nini wewe ni kusubiri huko?'

He laughed. 'Tu chai? Faini.'

Hugo listened, nodding. 'Asante kwa msaada wako. Goodbye.'

He hung up, smiling to himself.

'What happened?' asked Sophie.

'They're fine. It's not some sinister ritual. They're just on a tea break.'

'Tea break?'

Hugo grinned.

'Apparently it's just a fan-belt problem. Some replacement parts are being driven over but it might take a little while, so the driver lit a fire. They weren't boiling oil, they were brewing up Green Label tea.'

Sophie threw her arms around him.

'Thanks Hugo.'

'Hey!' said Ali. 'Where's the Ali-love?'

Sophie pushed herself across the reception desk and planted a kiss on Ali's cheek. 'Thanks Ali. You *are* a magician.'

Ali pointed at her.

'You owe me a dance,' he said. 'Come on, team. Back to the dancefloor.'

'Thanks again, Hugo,' she said, squeezing his arm affectionately. 'If it had been left to me, I would have been calling in a SWAT team.'

'No problem, I quite enjoyed talking to those fellows.' He got a distant look in his eyes. 'I do love travel, don't you? Doing that has made me feel all twitchy for another trip.'

‘Me too,’ said Sophie quietly. ‘Me too.’

Chapter Twenty-Three

ADAM WATCHED SOPHIE from a distance, saw her kiss Hugo. What was that feeling in his stomach? Jealousy? Jealous of what exactly? Adam could admit that he found Sophie attractive; she was smart and funny and beautiful, the fact she seemed not to know it simply made her more lovely. But while he found women mystifying in many ways – who didn't? – Sophie was particularly hard to work out. One moment it was like she wanted to kiss him, the next she seemed to loathe him. It was possibly just as well, he told himself, watching her cross the dancefloor. She was Tim's ex and there were rules. Guy rules. You didn't date your mate's girlfriends, it was just the way it was, like the rules against marrying a second cousin.

'Here he is, the new Joe Strummer.'

Adam smiled as Declan emerged from the back of the stage, carrying his guitar case. 'You never told me you had those pipes!'

'Very funny.'

'Anyway, we're off mate, all packed up and hitting the road in five.'

'Not hanging around?' said Adam, unable to hide his disappointment. 'There's a five-foot cheese cake made of twenty-three types of cheddar that's about to be sliced.'

'Tempting, but I'm vegan now, aren't I?'

'At least let me buy you a drink. I say, buy. It's a free bar.'

Dec shook his head.

'I'm off the sauce, have been for years.'

'You're joking.'

'Remember that night we had out in Vegas? That was pretty much my last big one. You ruined me, Adam Stowe.'

Adam made a note to store that information. Dec was being kind of course, but still, Adam knew he could tell this story for years to come: 'yeah, I was so rock 'n' roll, I pushed him into rehab…'

'Look, it's tempting to stay and I'd love to hang around and catch up but I want to swing home and drop the girls off before we head up to Newcastle.'

He motioned towards the two young women wearing crop tops and skinny jeans.

'You're taking the groupies home? That is a one understanding missus you've got there, Dec.'

'Groupies?' he laughed. 'Molly and Meg are my daughters, Adam. Carrie's girls from her first marriage. Anyway, all that groupie nonsense is all in the past since I met Carrie and got hitched. You should try wedded bliss mate, best thing I ever did.'

'You'll be giving up touring next,' he said.

Declan's expression turned serious and he glanced around.

'Listen, between you and me, Belasco's days are

numbered.'

Adam's eyes opened wide, his journalistic alarm clanging, then remembered that he had no magazine to report the news back to.

'You're splitting up?' whispered Adam.

'More like melting back into obscurity.' He shook his head and sighed. 'Being a rock star, it's just not what it was. There's no edge to it, the best you can hope for is getting a judging spot on one of those TV talent shows. I'll be honest Adam, tonight's gig has been more fun than the whole rest of the tour.'

'So what are you going to do next?'

'I'm retraining as a therapist in September.'

He noted Adam's look of shock and grinned.

'I know, I know, but it's time to move on, do something different. You only get one life, remember? Well, unless you're Elvis.'

Swinging his guitar around, Declan hugged Adam.

'Listen if the therapy thing goes tits-up – entirely possible, by the way – we can always team up as the indie version of the Everly Brothers.'

Adam clapped him on the shoulder.

'Right Said Fred more like.'

He walked Declan out to the tour bus and watched the red brake-lights flash then disappear down the gravel drive. The light was fading, the sun dipping behind the church spire on the other side of the valley. As he turned back towards the house, he saw the wedding car and wandered across. Adam stroked a hand across the paintwork. It was some sort of classic sports car. Adam knew about as much about cars as he did about cricket, but it was beautiful, a forest-green convertible with a cream leather interior, not the kind of thing you'd want to ruin by spraying 'Just Married' across the back. 'Talking of which…'

Adam walked to the back, expecting to see balloons or tin cans tied to the bumper. But there was nothing.

'Bloody Rich,' he whispered, knowing it was one more thing for Vanessa to be furious about. 'Worst best man in history.'

He straightened up to see Hugo standing on the steps of the hall, hands in his pockets, his face turned up towards the stars just beginning to appear in the darkening sky. Adam smiled to himself: Hugo could probably navigate by those pin-pricks. How amazing to be so self-sufficient.

Hugo spotted him and waved.

'What's going on there?' he called. 'Spot of engine trouble?'

'No,' replied Adam, walking across. 'It's Tim and Vee's going-away car. I was just looking to see if Rich had done his duty by adding the traditional cans and whatnot, but no.'

At first Adam had relished the idea of taking up the slack for Tim's useless brother, but now it was getting irritating. Hugo, however, was already working on a practical solution. He disappeared down the side of the house and re-emerged holding a cardboard box. 'Empties from the kitchen,' he said, handing the cans to Adam and digging into his jacket pocket.

'This should do it,' he said, pulling out a Swiss

Army knife and a spool of dental floss from his pocket. 'Come on.'

They sat down next to the bumper and Hugo got to work punching holes into the cans, whilst Adam tied them onto the car.

'Didn't I see you with Sophie earlier?' he said, asking as casually as he could.

Hugo smiled, catching Adam's implication. 'Sophie's lovely, but not really my type if I'm honest.'

'So what is your type?' said Adam, wriggling on the gravel as he hooked the floss around a bracket.

'I haven't really thought about it in a while. There was a someone once. She was – is – an actress.'

That caught Adam's attention and he looked up.

'Actress? As in stage and screen?'

'Hollywood, actually. She'd been in an action film, you see, like a female Indiana Jones, and the producers had the wheeze of having the premiere at the Royal Cartographic Institute and inviting a load of real-life explorers. I burbled along and we kind of hit it off.'

A distant bell was ringing – he was sure he'd read a news piece about this in the mag. 'Hang on, you went out with *Julianne George*? How come I don't know about this?'

J-Gee was Hollywood royalty, a genuine star. Hugo looked embarrassed.

'It's sort of a secret. We were never in the gossip sheets or anything like that.'

'Was it serious?'

Hugo shrugged. 'I suppose. Jules wanted to settle down, have kids, the whole thing. But I'd be useless at all that, an utter disaster. Young Marmaduke would be potty training but I'd be off canoeing up a river in Peru.'

'You'd call your offspring Marmaduke?' smiled Adam, but Hugo was looking more serious.

'You asked us all earlier why we were on the Singles Table? I think I'm there because that's who I am, Adam. I'm happiest in the jungle, just me and the mosquitoes. I suppose love is where and when we feel most alive.'

'To thine own self be true, huh?'

Hugo handed him the last of the cans.

'On a day like today it seems marriage is the ultimate goal. But really, it's not the only way to have a satisfying life. I'm alone, but not lonely. I have a deep love for something. I suppose that something is adventure.'

Adam smiled.

'Good for you, Hugo. Seriously.'

He stood up and dusted off the seat of his trousers, admiring their handiwork.

He only hoped Tim appreciated it; Adam wasn't at all sure he would.

Hugo was looking up at the sky again. In the time they had been rolling about under the car, the sky had darkened to an extraordinary set of colours, like ink dropped into seawater, over-lapping ripples of violet and turquoise. 'You know, I've been to the Sahara and the Russian Steppes – amazing night skies – but there's still something very special about the English countryside at dusk.'

Their quiet contemplation of the heavens was interrupted by a wash of yellow headlights as a taxi pulled up at the entrance.

'Oh no,' muttered Adam, his heart sinking as an older man got out of the car.

'Problem?'

Adam looked at Hugo and sighed. 'Nothing we can fix with dental floss, not this time. That's my dad.'

He nodded diplomatically. 'I'll see you back inside, then shall I?'

'Adam! Wasn't expecting a welcoming party,' said Graham Stowe, walking across to the car. His taxi grumbled away into the twilight, leaving the two men alone.

'Hey Pops,' he said.

People had always commented on how much Adam looked like his father, which had of course irritated him. But Adam could see it now, could see how inevitable it all was. You could wear torn T-shirts or a fancy suit, but there was no escaping your DNA.

'Come here and give your old man a hug, eh?'

Adam stiffly returned the embrace.

'Tim only told me you were coming last night,' said Adam, grinding the sole of his shoe into the gravel.

'Didn't know myself until last week. Bumped into Tim's dad at the fishing.'

When his father had retired back to Sheffield, Adam's mum Susan had spent an hour on the phone complaining about it, although he didn't really know why it bothered her so much. She was in Lanzarote most of the time and besides, Sheffield was a big enough city to avoid anyone you wanted to.

'You still at it then? The fishing?'

'Yeah, you need to get out of the house, don't you?'

'Of course you do,' said Adam. The sarcasm was immediate, ingrained.

To this day, Adam couldn't understand why a man would leave his son behind. Adam wasn't a parent – although he one day hoped to be – and just couldn't get his head round it. The worst thing was that he hadn't seen it coming. Adam had always considered his home life to be ordinary. Not like Ian Shaw from Scouts whose father had a Rolls Royce or Caroline Noakes who boasted her mum had once been a backing singer for the Human League. The Stowe household, on the other hand was mundane, dull. His parents rarely rowed although looking back, they didn't talk much either. Until one day, Adam had come home from school to find his dad in the kitchen and his suitcase in the hall. He was going on a work-trip, his father had explained, pulling him in close, resting his chin on the top of Adam's head. Graham Stowe had left immediately and never come back and even today, Adam could still remember that final click of the door and the house being incredibly quiet and still, even though a grenade had just gone off in all of their lives.

'So, how's things, son? How's the glittering world of the media?'

He wasn't going to lie.

'Not so good, Dad. *Cream*, the mag I work for? It's

closing.'

'About time.'

'About time? Dad, I've worked there *all my life.*'

'Exactly, son. What is it? Twenty years you've been there. Everything's changed, hasn't it? No more CDs, no more record industry and worst of all, no one reads magazines do they? It's all online for free.'

'So you're saying I'm unemployable?'

'No lad, there will always be a place for someone as creative as you. Some company will snap you up.'

'You mean for a proper job? Like yours? Polluting the planet for a living?'

Graham had started his working life, like most of his generation, in the local steelworks. Unlike most of his workmates, Graham had cleverly sidestepped the dwindling industry, using knowledge learned in the foundry to start a waste disposal consultancy. He had spent most of his career analysing the colour of smoke coming from factory chimneys, often to help the business squeak by on the minimum emission standards.

'I think that's a little harsh,' said Graham more gently than Adam had spoken.

'Look, I get it,' said Adam on a roll now. 'I backed the wrong horse. I joined an industry that was going to be dead within the decade. We're not all as forward thinking as you.'

'At least you love what you do.'

'That's right. I don't measure my success by money, or big houses for my wedding.'

'You getting married?' said Graham, his eyes wide.

‘No.’ said Adam, feeling another blow of failure. ‘Good job, isn’t it?’

Adam knew his Dad was trying to be supportive, but it was beginning to needle him.

‘You get to my age, son, you start to think a lot more about the past and what you missed out on. What you wish you’d have done with your life. But to be thinking your life’s washed up at your age? It’s just daft. Maybe this *Cream* thing is a gift, a chance to do something you’ve always wanted.’

Adam could only shrug.

‘So come on,’ pressed Graham. ‘What is your dream? What would you do now if you had a free choice?’

‘A record shop,’ he muttered with little enthusiasm.

‘What would it be like?’

‘It wouldn’t be one of those dusty vinyl ghettos with crammed bins,’ he continued less sulkily. ‘It would be a bright modern place with coffee and books, somewhere you’d look forward to going. A destination place for music lovers.’

Adam pulled up abruptly as he saw Graham was laughing, just like Tim had.

‘You think it’s a stupid idea, too? Flogging another dead horse, another loser idea from your loser son?’

A sadness came over Graham’s face and Adam felt bad again.

‘I don’t think you’re a loser, Adam. I was laughing because it was lovely to see the excitement on your face as you talked about your idea. As it happens, I couldn’t be more proud of you.’

Adam stopped.

'What?'

'D'you know, I think I've read every word you've ever written. Wherever I was living, Brasilia, Dusseldorf, Pittsburgh – I'd have the magazine and the papers sent out. Sometimes I'd laugh so hard people would bang on the wall.'

Adam shook his head. 'You never said anything.'

'No. And I should have. But I'm saying it now, son. I've always been so proud of you. You had a passion and you went out there and you lived it. Your words – your talent – made people happy, you connected your readers to a dream world they could experience through your eyes. But you know what I'm most proud of? The way you always looked after your mother.'

'I don't understand.'

'I know,' he said sadly. 'And I wouldn't expect you to. Look Son, I loved that woman with all my heart and if I can't be there to protect her, then I'm glad you are.'

He looked at his father, astonished.

'Loved her? You left us. I was twelve years old…'

Graham looked away across the valley, the lit-up windows of the church now glowing orange through the trees.

'Adam, I left because she told me she wanted a divorce.'

'What?'

His father looked back, his gaze clear. He paused for a moment, then sighed.

'Because of Bobby Robertshaw.'

'Paul Robertshaw's dad? Who owned the garage on Borough Road?'

Graham gave a grim nod.

'That day, the day I left. I wasn't feeling well at work and came home. I found them together. Your mum – with Robertshaw. Upstairs in the bedroom.'

'Bullshit,' snapped Adam. 'Don't try to rewrite history to make yourself look good.'

'You think this makes me look good, Adam? I left you – you were just a kid.'

'I *know*, Dad. I remember.'

'I didn't have a choice.'

'That's rubbish– there's always a choice.'

Graham's shoulders sagged and he began again quietly, almost as if he was talking to himself. 'I thought your mother would apologise, make excuses, tell me that it was all a stupid mistake. But she didn't. She was unrepentant. She looked me in the eye and told me that she loved him and she wanted a divorce. Adam, there was no going back after that.'

He paused and looked back at his son.

'I couldn't stay, Adam,' he said, his voice shaking. 'I ran out of there, and I kept going. I'd been offered a job in Germany a few weeks before, so I flew out to Hamburg the next day… I guess I never stopped running.'

'Why are you telling me this now?'

Graham looked at him. He looked old and sad, the deep lines of his face emphasised by the dim light.

'Because I'm sick of you hating me, Adam.'

Adam almost laughed. He didn't hate his father, quite the opposite. At twelve, like every other child from a broken family he supposed, Adam had assumed his father had left because he didn't love him anymore. In those months after Graham disappeared, Adam tortured himself at night with the thoughts of what he had done to deserve it. Maturity softened the idea, but the core belief never really went away.

'I never hated you, Dad. I just wanted you there. I just needed my dad.'

Graham opened his mouth to speak, then closed it again.

'But you turned out alright in the end, eh?' Graham's laugh was weak, his face grey.

'Are you sure about that?' he said as he turned and walked back into the house.

Chapter Twenty-Four

SOPHIE SAT AT the bar, sipping another cocktail and watching the chaos on the dancefloor. Messy though it was, everyone seemed to be having a good time out there in discoland. Christa was dancing jerkily with Ali, Zara and Lucy, which Sophie guessed was supposed be some sort of robot dance, but they were all too drunk to be co-ordinated enough. It looked as though they all found it hilarious and Sophie was glad that her sister seemed to have forgotten her troubles, even if it was just for one night.

If Sophie was honest, the evening reception hadn't been as bad as she had been expecting. Yes, it had been difficult watching Tim and Vanessa for the first dance – close, happy, in love – but mercifully she hadn't seen much of them since: one of the advantages of such a big wedding.

'At least someone's enjoying themselves.'

Sophie turned and looked into the blue eyes of Tim's brother Rich. *Wow*, she thought, then scolded herself. She wasn't sure it was appropriate to think about Rich Jameson in that way. When she'd been dating Tim, Rich had been a cute little kid, all freckles and puppy-dog eyes, and on more than one awkward moment, he'd walked in on them kissing. Now? Well, now it seemed Mother Nature had given Rich all of his older brother's best bits and polished up the rest. *Or maybe I've been drinking too much*, thought Sophie, putting down her glass.

'I'm not talking to you,' she said, turning away with a wry smile.

'What? Because of the speech?'

'Yes, because of the speech,' said Sophie. 'You called me a *pig*.'

Rich held up a finger.

'No, I alluded to Tim's *other* girlfriends being of the farmyard variety. And I didn't mention you by name.'

'Is that an apology?'

'An abject and grovelling apology,' he said. 'And anyway…' Rich leant closer. 'What I really wanted to say was that *Vanessa* is a cow. But not even a Best Man's speech can go there.'

'Anyway, what are you doing talking to me? Shouldn't you be cutting a roguish swathe through the bridesmaids right about now?'

'You *have* met the bridesmaids?' said Rich. 'Emily… Brrr…' He mimed a shiver. 'One touch from that woman and it would freeze your heart solid.'

Sophie laughed. 'I couldn't possibly comment.'

She felt relaxed and playful. There was a good chance it was something to do with the half-dozen cocktails she had consumed; she knew the normal sober Sophie would be nervous talking to such a handsome man, especially one that was the image of her ex, but what the hell? She was free, single and if anyone deserved a bit of fun tonight it was her. Dimly she thought of Adam holding her on the dancefloor, but somehow that all seemed a very long time ago.

'Hungry?' he asked.

'Ravenous,' said Sophie, honestly. No breakfast, three canapes, and a knotted stomach at lunch: no wonder the apple martinis were going to her head. 'I could eat a horse.'

'Well I can't quite offer that, but there's a hog roast out on the lawn if you fancy it?'

'Lead on,' said Sophie, letting Rich take her hand and steer her outside.

Sophie gasped when she saw the scene. She had been to several weddings before, but most of them were before the age of twelve, when she was a popular choice as a flower girl. This was something else.

The mini-fairground on the lawns reminded her of a County Fair she had once been to the summer she had worked as a camp counsellor in America. Strings of lights glowed like fireflies and there were guffaws of laughter from the Giant Jenga as the whole thing toppled to the ground, taking a man in a morning suit with it. The ice-cream vendor had switched her trade to candy floss and there was a rival dancefloor inside an open marquee, the disco replaced by a swing band.

With a mock-serious face, Rich bowed formally and offered his hand to Sophie. 'May I have this dance?'

Laughing, Sophie reciprocated with a curtsy. The sophistication was somewhat undermined by the fact that the song playing was a swing version of 'U Can't Touch This' by MC Hammer, but Rich rolled with it and pulled Sophie into a waltz stance, steering her across the dancefloor and out the other side of the tent, both laughing as they went.

'You got some moves girl!' he laughed.

'I've been saving them up.'

'For me?'

'Perhaps,' said Sophie coquettishly. She really was out of character tonight, but she didn't care.

'Ah crap,' said Rich as they arrived at the hog roast stall to find it shuttered with a sign reading, 'Sorry, sold out!'

'Candy floss it is then,' said Sophie, backtracking to the blue and white van next to the fortune teller's tent. Sophie picked at the enormous pink cloud of cotton candy, powder-dry yet sticky to the touch as it dissolved between her fingertips.

'So I heard you've been hanging out with Adam Stowe?' said Rich, reaching over to pinch a mouthful of candyfloss.

'What do you mean? Hanging out?'

'Looking cosy. My spies tell me you were in the bar together last night. After hours.'

'I don't know what you're suggesting here but it's totally off base.'

He gave her a look that said he didn't believe her.

'Everybody at Harling Comp wanted to be Adam Stowe when we were growing up. He was cool.'

'I think Adam still believes his own hype,' she said, unable to resist a smile.

'You sure you haven't got a little thing for him?'

'Adam?' She shook her head a little too enthusiastically.

'Good. Because it's the one thing that would really wind my brother up. You know, at school Adam Stowe always got the girl.'

Rich signalled to the waiter who dutifully came over with two non-specific bright red cocktails. Sophie didn't know what they were, but damn, hers tasted good.

'So what are you up to now?' asked Rich.

'Bespoke travel troubleshooter,' said Sophie, enjoying Rich's attention. 'Just fixed a problem in Swahili.'

'You speak Swahili?'

'I have staff for that sort of thing. And what about you?'

'Investment bank, obviously,' said Rich, rolling his eyes. 'Making pots of cash, bored out of my mind.'

'What there is left of it.'

Rich nudged her shoulder.

'I like them sassy.'

They walked past the carousel, where Tim and Vanessa were astride matching unicorns.

'So can you see it working?'

'The happy couple?' asked Rich. 'Probably. Why not? I mean it's more like an arranged marriage than a grand passion isn't it? Those are the kind that last.'

'It's an arranged marriage?'

'You know Larry was the founder of the Glasshouse Agency.'

Sophie had googled the agency many times over the years, watched Tim ascend through the ranks, until his handsome black-and-white profile picture was there in the 'Our executive team' section. That Larry was anything to do with the agency was news to her.

'He was?'

'Sold a majority stake about fifteen years ago. But he still has shares and it's all his mates on the board. Larry has influence, so Vee-Vee has influence.'

Sophie fell quiet, trying to work out its significance.

Rich took her hand, but feeling nervous and light-headed, she let go of it almost immediately. She had so little experience of this and found it hard to know how to behave.

'I know, why don't we go over to the photo booth?' she said with forced brightness.

'Sure,' said Rich, placing a proprietary hand on her waist. As they walked, Sophie glanced back towards the carousel, but Tim had gone.

They were approaching the caravan photo booth when Sophie saw Cherie and Henry the flatmate leaning against it, heads together, apparently sharing a joke. They looked intimate, happy in the moment. Maybe Adam's ham-fisted match-making had actually worked, just as it had seemed to have worked with Paul and Tina. Maybe the wedding was putting everyone on a new path. Even her. She glanced at Rich, then pulled him back towards the little fairground.

'Second thoughts, not the photo booth,' she said.

'How about the fortune teller's tent?'

'Even better idea,' he replied.

Rich popped his head inside, then beckoned to Sophie. 'Madame Zora has left the building.'

'We can come back later.'

'No, let's go inside,' he said pulling her in. 'It can be our own little VIP area.'

'What if she comes back?'

'Then we'll cross her palm with silver.'

Inside it was sumptuous and cosy, lit only by the glowing coils of warm fairy-lights. The seats were draped with silk quilts, a celestial map, a web of moons and constellations hung from the domed ceiling.

Rich sat on a winged back chair by the crystal ball, Sophie perched on the chaise longue, her stomach a flutter of nerves.

'Are you going to tell my fortune, then?' she said lightly.

'No, but I can tell you a secret.'

Sophie was intrigued. The news about Larry's ownership of the Glasshouse Agency had been a revelation. What else did Rich Jameson know?

'Go on then,' she said.

Rich looked down at the sawdust floor smiling.

'You know back when you were going out with Tim, I really fancied you, Sophie,' said Rich. 'In fact, you were my dream girl.'

Sophie looked away, embarrassed.

'Rich, you were sixteen years old. I bet loads of teenagers have crushes on their big brother's girlfriend.

'But here's the thing: I still do. You are still my dream woman, Sophie.'

She was blushing furiously. She just wasn't good at this. The neurologist had once told her that her sexual appetite might be diminished after the accident, and although she hadn't really had a chance to put that to the test, she knew she felt uncomfortable by Rich's overt attention.

'Rich, maybe I should get back…'

Before she could say any more, Rich made a lunge towards the chaise longue, dipping his head for a kiss, but Sophie recoiled, backing into the cushions.

'Rich, we shouldn't.'

'Why not.'

'Just no.'

'Sophie, come on…'

'No, Rich,' she said, more firmly. 'I don't feel comfortable.'

'Well then, I'll make you comfortable,' he smiled, pushing himself against her, trapping her with his body. He smelled of wine and sour breath, pressing his mouth against her throat. Sophie gasped as his hand snaked up the inside of her thigh and she shoved him back, dodging as he toppled over onto a velvet beanbag.

'What the fuck was that for?' he said looking up. Just then he looked exactly like the lanky teenager she remembered. 'I thought this was what you wanted?'

'We shouldn't be here,' she said, collecting herself. 'It doesn't feel right. Tim's just outside.'

Rich looked up at her, thwarted desire all over his

face.

'So it's still Tim,' he said bitterly. 'After all this time. Unbelievable.'

He flashed a look of spite at her.

'You must know that he was *always* banging Vanessa, or didn't you ever work that out?'

Sophie felt her mouth drop open and saw Rich's satisfaction.

'Oh yeah,' he crowed, wiping some spittle from his chin with the back of his hand. '*Way* before you split up. He boasted about it.'

'That's not true.'

'Oh it's true,' he laughed harshly. 'The Christmas after you'd graduated, Tim got drunk and told me *all* about it. Apparently Vee's a bit stiff in the sack, but hey, her dad owned Glasshouse. I suppose you could say he slept his way to the top.'

As much as she didn't want to believe it, she knew it could be true. The months running up to the accident were the haziest in her memory bank but she did remember how much Tim disliked his first job – a graduate trainee position at one of the big multinationals which he felt was beneath him. He had wanted to jump ship almost as soon as he had got there, but what lengths was he prepared to go to secure something more glamorous?

'But they didn't start going out for two years after my accident.'

'Don't be so naïve. They just waited to go public. It might not have looked too sensitive otherwise. You know it's all about looking good with Tim and

Vanessa.'

'It's not true,' she whispered.

'Move on, Sophie,' he said, flashing her a dark look. 'Everyone else has. Or haven't you noticed that either?'

'Screw you, Rich,' she hissed, shouldering him aside, fleeing the tent and running across the lawn with tears streaming down her face.

Chapter Twenty-Five

ADAM RAISED HIS hands in the air. 'Make some NOIIIISE!' he shouted.

The crowd roared.

Adam made pistol shapes with his fingers. 'Bigitup!' he yelled.

The crowd whooped.

Adam dropped the needle on 'Uptown Funk' and the dancefloor erupted, arms waving, couples whirling. Adam wasn't exactly sure what 'Bigitup!' meant and he wasn't that mad about Bruno Mars either, but the sweaty, smiling faces on the dancefloor clearly didn't care where Bruno was on the Adam's cool-o-meter – they were having a blast.

If he was honest, Adam's DJ slot had come at just the right time. The last thing Adam wanted right now was peace and quiet, because then he would have to think about everything his father had told him. He clamped the headphones to his ears and concentrated on cueing up the next track. Adam looked down at the dancefloor, at the euphoric, grinning mess. Not indie club kids, just ordinary suburban mums and dads, all grown up. It was incredible how music could still move them, make them throw off their inhibitions. He could speed them up with 'Shake It Off' or slow them down with 'Billie Jean', changing the tempo and mood of the party at will. The teenage Adam would have been horrified that he was playing such mainstream pop, but he had dropped Kings of Leon earlier and it had cleared the floor, so he had switched back to the crowd-pleasers. And anyway, right now, Adam was happy to play Dancing Queen, Mambo No.5 or Come On Eileen – right now, up on the stage, Adam Stowe had the wedding party in the palm of his hand and that, at least, felt good.

Track duly cued up, Adam stepped back and surveyed the crowd, looking for Sophie. Ali had mentioned that he'd seen her with Rich Jameson, which had both annoyed and alarmed him. Rich was a prick. As soon as he passed the DJ baton over to Uncle Dennis, Adam decided he was going to find her and make sure she was alright. In the centre of the dancefloor, Ali was frantically pogoing up and down. Even from his eyrie up here behind the decks, Adam could see his friend was becoming a nuisance, bumping into people, shouting gibberish, whirling around like Morrissey after too many gins. As he watched, Ali missed his footing, slid sideways and knocked over a tray of drinks.

'Bollocks,' sighed Adam. Ali was hardly his responsibility, but even so, he knew he had to do something. Shaking his head, he took the steps down the side of stage to the bar where Dennis was waiting, eagerly clutching a record bag. 'Your turn mate,' said Adam, giving him the thumbs-up. 'I think they need some classic rock.'

Adam grabbed two bottles of beer and turned back to the dancefloor.

'Heyyyy! Mr Dee-jay!' shouted Ali, as he caught sight of Adam, dancing over and throwing his arms around him, planting a sweaty kiss on Adam's neck. Adam waved the bottles in Ali's face. 'Let's go and have a breather, eh?' he shouted, gently but firmly steering Ali away from the dancefloor and off out into the corridor.

'Hey, I can't leave Christa,' said Ali, turning back. 'She needs Ali-man's lovin'.'

'I think she can wait a few minutes, Al,' said Adam, keeping a grip on his friends. 'Plus she's married, so maybe best not to get too frisky.'

'You're so conventional, Adam Stowe,' said Ali, 'So upright.' He burst into hysterical laughter.

'Why don't we go in here?' said Adam, half-carrying him into the library. An elegant couple, enjoying a drink by the fire, shot each other a glance and left the room. It was a beautiful space, lined with books, which had the twin benefits of being quiet and had seating: red leather chairs faced each other. Ali's movements were rubbery and slow and his eyes were glazed as Adam guided him into a chair. Finally seated, Ali slid down into a crumpled heap.

'I think you've danced yourself to a standstill there, Kemo Sabe,' said Adam, taking a sip of his beer.

Ali looked at him, his focus wavering. 'Kemo who?'

Adam laughed. 'Kemo Sabe – it's what Tonto

called the Lone Ranger back when we were kids. Don't you remember we came over to yours to watch the TV show once? You were the Lone Ranger. Can't remember who I was. The Sundance Kid, I think.'

'Oh yeah, Lone Ranger,' nodded Ali, taking a swig of beer and spilling a good portion down his front. 'Ali's the masked man.'

Adam wasn't sure Ali remembered that evening, but Adam certainly did. Not just for the frenzied cap-gun battle, but for the insight into Ali's home life. His bedroom had been bookish with few toys or football posters, but there had been a computer, years before that was common in a kid's room, along with piles of maths text books and – this he remembered very clearly – a hand-drawn time table for revision including work scheduled for a *weekend.* He still hadn't forgotten that timetable.

'So how's things?' said Adam. 'We haven't really had a chance to catch up.'

Ali snorted, curling his lip.

'Like you care.'

'Hey, where's that coming from?'

'Sorry, sorry. Bit harsh. A lot harsh, actually, especially after you took one for the team last night. You, Adam Stowe,' said Ali, pointing a wavering finger, 'You're my only real friend, you know that?'

'I think that's the booze talking, mate.'

'Nah, nah, Ads.' Ali leant forward and clasped Adam's knee. 'You always had my back whatever. What-*ever*, man. Everyone else took the piss out of the puny, pint-sized Asian kid, but not you. The most loyal friend I've ever known. And so, so… bloody inspirational. I. WISH. I. WAS. YOU.'

The word 'inspirational' was slurred, but even so, Adam was taken aback.

'Me?'

'Of course *you*,' said Ali. 'You got out of the 'hood soon as you could, went and did what you wanted. Didn't let anyone stop you. You were creative, brave. Going out there and doing it, making it happen. Smartest dude ever. *Ever.*'

Adam looked at him.

'But Al, you're like an actual genius.'

He waved a hand, like he was swatting a fly.

'Bullshit, all of it.'

Adam laughed.

'Al, I read *Wired* and *Business Insider*. I know how exciting your business is. How revolutionary your tech might be.'

'Smoke and mirrors, man. I've been lying to them. To you, to everyone.'

Adam frowned, feeling a shift in the mood. This wasn't modesty, Ali was serious. He sat forward and saw there were tears in Ali's eyes.

'It was a good idea, def-o,' he said, almost to himself. 'I mean, predict the trends in Cryptocurrency, it's a license to print money, right? But…'

'But what, Al?'

'It didn't bloody work, did it? Or rather it could work, but we've run out of time and money and the investors are threatening to pull out. Do you know how much real estate is in Palo Alto, Ads?

He didn't, but he could imagine. It was certainly upsetting Ali.

'So come home.'

'Can't,' said Ali defiantly.

'Why not?'

'Because of my Dad,' said Ali, his expression bleak. 'He's spent the last ten years telling everyone his boy's in Silicon Valley being the new Bill Gates. If I fold the company, leave Palo Alto, come back to Sheffield, even London, he'll be crushed. The shame of failure.'

'I think your dad might be glad to have you home, Ali.'

'You don't know Ads, the weight of expectation in Asian families. And… ah, Christ.' He wiped away the tears. 'Look at me, I'm a total poof.'

Ali snorted, then up-ended his bottle, chugging down the beer.

'Ali, I don't think you're allowed to say "poof" any more,' smiled Adam, hoping to lighten the mood.

'I'm serious. I am.'

'You are what?'

'Gay. Or Bi. Fuck knows, either way, it's not acceptable back home.'

Adam suppressed the urge to laugh. It was like hearing Rod Stewart was gay.

'You're actually gay?'

'As a goose.'

Adam didn't want to point out that particular simile probably wasn't acceptable either. Or maybe it was fine if you actually were gay. He wasn't sure. It was a lexicon minefield these days.

'I know what you're thinking,' said Ali, his dark eyes sad. 'Ali-man cuts through the ladies like Motley Crue. It's all an act,' he said simply. 'Just like the Tech Billionaire thing.'

A single tear trickled down his cheek.

'Ads, what am I going to do?'

'What you're going to do is come here.' Adam crossed to his friend and put his arms around him, hugging him. Ali immediately began to sob. Adam held on, holding him tight.

'Ali, no one cares about who you love. Not anymore.'

'You have met my Dad, right?'

Adam laughed.

'Okay, maybe not your dad. But then you're never going to please him, and you've spent twenty years trying, so why not stop? Please yourself for once. Go and find your real love.'

'Who's going to want *me*?'

Adam pulled away and looked at him.

'You're kidding me, right?'

Ali shook his head, his face a mask of misery.

'Ali, you're a life force. Everybody loves you. Well, maybe everyone apart from the punters at the Hare and Hounds.'

Ali tried to nod, but his head lolled to one side, his eyes rolling up in his head.

Adam gently set him back in the chair. 'Ali, how much have you drunk?'

'Lost count when I started mixing.'

'Mixing what?'

He held up a little pink pill between thumb and forefinger. It slipped and bounced to the floor.

'Oops, plenty more where they came from. Want one?'

'Ali, what is it?'

'Dunno. You know the drug dealer from the pub?'

'The taxi driver?'

Ali raised a hand in a 'there you are then' gesture.

'You bought the lot?'

'Yuh.'

Adam's eyes flew wide.

'How many have you had?'

Ali's head slumped against his chest.

'Ali! ALI!'

He propped Ali up as best he could and ran out into the corridor, looking up and down.

He spotted Christa and Sophie deep in conversation. He ran up and stopped – it looked as if Sophie was upset.

'You OK?'

Christa glared at him. 'She's fine. What do you want, Adam?'

'Ali's sick. Have you seen Cherie?'

Sophie hesitated.

'More matchmaking?'

'I'm serious, Soph. Ali's taken some pills on top of a boatload of vodka. He keeps passing out.'

'I saw her with Henry by the photo-booth,' said Sophie quickly.

Adam was already running.

'He's in the library, go and stay with him,' he shouted back to the sisters.

Cherie was all business when Adam told her what had happened.

'Show me. Henry, come.'

It was like following behind an ambulance with its sirens whirling. Cherie sprinted into the library and knelt down next to Ali.

'Ali, can you look at me?' she said loudly. His eyes fluttered, then rolled.

'Sleepy,' he said.

'No, no sleeping,' said Cherie firmly, then looked up at Adam and Henry. 'Which room is he staying in?'

'We're at The Swan a couple of miles away.'

She put her hand in her pocket and pulled out a key-card.

'Then let's get him upstairs to my room. Room 26.'

Adam and Henry each took an arm and hoisted Ali up, ducking their heads under his armpits.

'No, Ali needs a sleep.'

'Nonsense,' said Adam with forced jollity. 'We need you back dancing Al.'

'No one cares…' said Ali vaguely.

Adam stopped their pacing and looked into Ali's glassy eyes.

'*I* care Ali,' said Adam. 'You know I do.'

Ali gave a hazy smile, then reached out an unsteady hand to touch Adam's face. 'My friend,' he said, then Ali flopped forward and started laughing. 'See? You're the only one who understands. Ads, my only fre-UURGGH.' He jerked forward, vomiting all over Adam's shirt.

'That,' said Sophie. 'Is what they call karma.'

SOPHIE MANAGED TO find Adam a spare shirt. Apparently Matt the butler always kept a few cellophane-wrapped shirts next to the fire extinguisher and the First Aid kit. They didn't want to have to send a waiter home just because someone spilled gazpacho down them. Adam went into the gents' loos to change. He threw his soiled shirt into the bin and scrubbed his hands until they reeked of hand soap instead of vomit, but by the time he got back to the library everyone had gone.

Grateful for a few minutes alone, he grabbed the beer bottle he had left by the fireplace, and opened the door at the far end of the room, a bronze plaque informing him that this was the way to 'The Orangery'.

Adam opened the door and followed his nose, deciding that he should check it out. Perhaps he could grab a couple of cocktails and take Sophie there later.

He walked down a long corridor and through a glass door into a tall greenhouse. It was huge, full of palm trees that stretched from the iron grilled floor right up to the slanted glass roof, the low-lit spaces filled with drooping ferns and vines laden with strange-looking fruit.

Adam took a deep breath of the fragrant air and sat down on a bench hidden in an alcove by another door at the far end. He had wanted a little time alone to think about everything that had happened, but he heard voices at the far end of the glass house. He looked up: Tim and Vanessa were just coming through the door from outside. He stood, about to go to meet them and tell them about Ali's collapse, but as he stepped nearer, he caught the tone of Vanessa's voice. Angry. Very angry.

'Don't give me that crap, Tim!' she hissed. 'I can't believe you actually invited her.'

Sensing he was witnessing their first married domestic, Adam pulled back into the shadows. He could see them through the thick, waxy fern fronds, but in the semi-darkness, he was invisible.

'Vee, please…' said Tim. Adam saw him reach for his new wife, but she pulled away.

'Don't bloody "Vee" me,' she snapped. 'This is my wedding day. How is she still here?'

'I can't exactly kick her out, can I? And I *didn't* invite her, my mum did. She insisted.'

'And did Jennifer insist you spend the whole day making eyes at her too?'

'What are you talking about? I've barely seen Sophie.'

'Yeah *right*,' said Vanessa. 'And I suppose you're going to say you weren't looking at her all through the first dance?'

'The first dance? I was holding onto you!'

'Over my shoulder!' shouted Vanessa. 'You were looking at her over my shoulder! I could *feel* it.'

'Listen to yourself Vee! Don't you know how crazy that sounds?'

Adam flinched as he peered through the foliage and saw Vanessa jabbing her finger towards Tim's face. He quietly slid back towards the door.

'You still love her, don't you?'

'What? No!' Tim tried to pull Vanessa into an embrace. 'I only love you. I married you today, not her.'

'So why?' said Vanessa, her voice choked with sobs now. 'Why is she here?'

'I told you. My Mum insisted. Why else would I invite her?'

'Because you feel guilty, that's why!'

Guilty? Adam stopped, one hand on the exit handle. This should be good.

'What the hell have I got to feel guilty about?' said Tim, clearly irritated and defensive.

'I *know*, Tim!' said Vanessa. 'I've always known!'

Adam saw shock register on his friend's face. Then his eyes turned distant, glassy. Uh-oh. Tim had always been a terrible liar.

'Known what? What do you think you know?'

'I know that it was you, Tim. You were the one who crashed into Sophie Wallis on that mountain.'

What?

'What?' It was almost a squeak.

'I was there, Tim. I was on the ski-lift overhead – I saw it all.'

'Bollocks! It was that German.'

'*I* told her it was the bloody German, you idiot! I got off the lift, skied down to where she was lying, then told Juliet I'd seen who did it.'

From where he was hiding, Adam could see all of the colour had drained from Tim's face.

'Why?' He asked. 'Why would you do that?'

'Because… I love you.'

Adam silently turned the handle and slipped into the corridor. He didn't need to hear any more; he'd understood the moment Vanessa had told Tim what she had seen. She had kept quiet to protect the man she loved. She had carried the burden of Tim's guilt – and her own – because she couldn't do anything else.

Wow, thought Adam, leaning against the wall. *Love could be complicated.*

Tim on the other hand? That just felt so, so wrong. How could he have just left Sophie lying in the snow?

But then, was Adam really surprised? It had always been Tim first and everyone else second. All the scrapes they'd got into down the years, Tim would let others take the blame, duck out at the last minute, back-pedalling for all he was worth if he was caught. Even last night, Tim had left Adam to be torn apart by the locals – and then had the brass neck to berate Adam outside The Swan for 'worrying' him. Tim had always been that way, the consummate politician, an expert at polishing his halo.

Adam could admit that he hadn't exactly behaved honourably towards every woman in his life, that was true. He'd slunk off in the middle of the night and finished relationships by text. He'd once faked a bout of glandular fever to explain why he'd failed to call a girl back. But this… this was something else. This was brutal, sordid. Sophie had lost ten years clawing her way back to some semblance of normality. Yes, it had been an accident, but the lie – that had been calculated.

Following the sound of the disco, Adam circled through the back corridors and down into the bar. His throat felt tight and dry as he slid onto a stool.

'Vodka please,' he said. 'And make it a double.'

Feeling distanced, detached, Adam gulped at the burning liquid and watched the dancefloor. Dr Cherie was slow-dancing with Henry; Jennifer and Bill were wrapped together tightly. He looked around for Paul and Tina, but they were nowhere to be seen – he hoped they were off kissing and making up somewhere. On the far side, lounging in leather armchairs, Graham Stowe was swopping stories with Uncle Dennis. Everyone having a good time, no one even suspecting the truth of what had happened to bring them all here. He could feel himself slipping into a morose mood. There was a time Adam Stowe would score every night; now everyone was paired up except him.

'Hey stranger.'

He looked up to see an attractive woman. Expensive hair, expensive clothes.

'Annabelle, right? The maid of honour?'

She winced.

'Am I that memorable?'

'Sorry, had a lot on my mind today.'

'Haven't we all? So how come you're on your own?' said Annabelle, sliding onto the stool next to Adam, her thigh brushing against his.

'Can't say I've been flooded with offers.'

'You do know that it's a tradition for the maid of honour and the best man to get together?'

She ran a finger down his shirt. His new, waiter's shirt.

'So how about we go up to my suite?' she purred. 'I hear the room service is *very* good.'

'I'm sure the room service would be first class, Annabelle, but I'm going to have to decline.'

Surprise, then anger flitted across Annabelle's face. Clearly she wasn't used to getting turned down.

'What?' growled Annabelle. 'Why?'

Adam slid down off his stool, leaving the rest of his drink.

'Ask around, Annabelle,' he said. 'You might be the maid of honour, but I'm not the best man. Not at all.'

Chapter Twenty-Six

SOPHIE COULDN'T FIND anyone. Christa was no longer in Dr Cherie's room where Ali was sleeping off his over-indulgence, and she hadn't responded to any of the texts Sophie had sent. There was no sign of Zara, Hugo or Adam either, even though she had traversed Haslop Hall twice, but there were now so many people crammed into the wedding – how on earth did Tim and Vanessa know so many people? – that Sophie could easily have passed any of them in the crowd.

She walked out of the front entrance, wandering along the path towards the lawns and the lit-up fairground area, gazing back at the house, where she could see a glow from the ballroom coming through the big, arched windows, the silhouettes of couples dancing cheek-to-cheek or snuggled in corners exchanging secret whispers. She had no desire to go back inside. Besides, she needed to cool down before she saw Rich, Tim or Vanessa again, otherwise there might well be a scene. And that would never do.

Sophie pulled out her phone and tapped out a message.

Chris, where the hell are you? Freezing to death out front. Call me x

Christa, of course, had wanted to chase down Rich with a harpoon, which Sophie agreed was the correct approach. How could she have been so stupid, allowing Rich to lure her into the fortune teller's tent only to try and put his hand up her dress? Why hadn't she laughed off his nasty slurs, or better still, kneed him in the nuts? As for Tim and Vanessa, she didn't want to believe that they had been having an affair behind her back. She'd tried to recall any sign or clue from the Verbier ski trip, any lingering looks over the fondue, or whispers in the hot tub, but she could think of nothing. And yet, she knew how easily it could be true, and that was what hurt most of all. The thought of them laughing behind her back as they sneaked off for sex. The thought of their pity. A pity that began before her accident, not just after it.

There was a hot chocolate bar, a converted tricycle, manned by a jolly-faced chap in a straw boater. He waved her over.

'I'm about to shut up shop. Can I tempt you with the last of the drinks? We've got hot chocolate or warmed apple cyder.'

Sophie's fingers were beginning to feel pinched with the cold.

'The cyder, I think,' said Sophie, pointing at an urn. She knew she should lay off the alcohol but the sweet and spicy smell was so tempting.

She took a long sip, letting the soothing, cinnamon-flavoured drink slide down her throat, and carried on walking, towards a folly half-shrouded in the dark.

It was a clear, cloudless night and the velvet-navy sky was studded with pin-pricks of light. There were millions of stars up there, possibly millions of other worlds, and right now, she wished someone would send down a spaceship to transport her to one of them.

The folly was a small, stone structure with a turreted roof and stone benches outside. She sat down, shivering. Why had she come here, she wondered, looking back at the house. Things were beginning to get a little fuzzy. Had she wanted to win Tim back? Was that it? Well, that certainly hadn't worked. Did she mean to lay some ghosts? Nope, that hadn't worked either, in fact the ghosts were whirling around her head like at the end of a *Scooby Doo* cartoon. Maybe Sophie had nursed some sneaking hope that she'd meet some wonderful man who'd sweep her off her feet and solve all her problems. Instead, she had met Ali, a cute but silly show-off, Rich, a horrible lech and Paul who was lovely, but still in love with his soon-to-be-ex-wife. And then there was Adam, who…she couldn't exactly think why, but somehow he was the biggest disappointment of all. She looked at her phone again to see if Christa had replied to her text, but there was nothing.

'Bloody hell,' she hissed, feeling her anger swell.

Even on the Singles Table, she had been an outlier. Everyone there had something, even if it wasn't someone. Zara had a daughter, Paul a wife. Ali had a successful business, Cherie, a rewarding career. Hugo had had enough excitement and adventure for several lifetimes and Lucy was just a kid who had her whole life in front of her. As for Adam, he had everything, good looks, smarts and popularity. He just didn't realise it.

Sophie looked down at her phone, thinking of the other man in her life who had everything. Klaus. She flipped to Instagram, knowing she shouldn't, but somehow unable to stop herself. The twin dramas of Rich then Ali should have sobered her up, but all that ethanol was still whooshing around her bloodstream: you couldn't argue with science.

She often hopped on to Klaus Vetletz's Instagram account. In fact she had spent the last decade watching him on social media, following all his little victories – marriage, children, opening a brand new dental surgery in the centre of Stuttgart – but always from a distance, torturing herself with his seemingly charmed progress through life while she, Sophie, just sat and watched.

She could hardly blame Klaus. But that was the thing: she did. It was his fault. If Nikolaus Vetletz hadn't gone over the back of her skis that morning in Verbier, Sophie's life would have gone exactly the way it was supposed to. She would have got the boy and the career and the OBE she'd always planned.

Klaus had certainly been busy today, according to his social feed. He had taken his daughter to a climbing wall and then for lunch at a hot new pizza place. Now they were back at home, a beautiful cedar-clad house in the woods, where the Vetletz family were having a barbeque. There they all were, grinning in unison. She could practically hear them saying 'cheese'. Or whatever the German for cheese was.

'Bastard,' she whispered. 'Bastard, bastard, bastard.' Suddenly, from nowhere, Sophie felt herself seized with an overwhelming fury. How dare Klaus post pictures of his perfect life at the exact moment hers was falling apart? Didn't he have the slightest shred of decency or remorse? He had destroyed her entire existence and yet here he was, rubbing his wonderful life in her face.

With blinding clarity, Sophie knew what she had to do – what she had threatened to do for so long, every night she had lurked in the background, peeking into Klaus' golden life. She was going to tell him.

With practised fingers, Sophie scrolled to the WeisseZahne Dental website, the one filled with perfect blonde models and glowing testimonies from satisfied customers. She knew from endless visits that there was a 'contact us' window, which featured email, landline and an emergency personal contact for Dr Vetletz himself. That was the kind of man Klaus was: caring, sharing, prepared to go the extra mile when you were in need.

'Yeah? Well we'll see about that,' muttered Sophie, angrily tapping the number into her keypad. She jabbed her thumb against the green 'call' button and waited, listening to the unfamiliar Euro dialtone.

Brrrrm. Pause. *Brrrrm.*

Sophie felt wide awake now. She was sharp, focused. She was going to…

'Entschuldigung, ich kann Ihren anruf

momentan nicht annehmen...'

'...Bitte hinterlassen Sie eine nachricht und ich rufe Sie sofort zurück.'

'I'll bloody leave you a bloody message you...'

Beeeeeep.

Sophie stopped, the words right on the tip of her tongue. The thought flittered through her mind that this might not be a fabulous idea. Klaus Vetletz probably had no idea who she was and almost certainly didn't remember knocking an English girl over on a distant slope half a lifetime ago. But it was only a fleeting thought.

Sophie had been able to speak three languages before the age of 21, but German was never one of them.

'Klaus, you German shit!' she shouted, holding the phone out in front of her. 'It's me, Sophie Wallis. Yes, that's right, *Sophie*: the girl you crashed into in Verbier fifteen years ago. Okay, so you didn't hit me, you ran over my skis and sent me flying, but the effect was the same. I hit my head and went into a coma and when I came out, I couldn't bloody walk and my whole bloody life went down the pan– what do you think about that, huh? I suppose you're just fine now, a fully qualified dentist, married with children, five star reviews on *Deutschdental.com.* You're sitting pretty aren't you? But what about me, Klaus? For five years I suffered chronic depression, my career was destroyed, my relationships fell apart and…' Sophie was sobbing now. 'Why Klaus? Why did you do it?'

Exhausted, ashamed, Sophie tapped the 'end call' button and hung her head, giving in to the sobs, her shoulders heaving, tears and snot running off her nose onto the folly's stone steps.

She saw a faint red circle in the dark, a pin prick of a cigarette tip.

'Sophie?'

Then something clicked in her head and her eyes flew open. She should have known that voice anywhere. Tim.

'Oh gosh,' she breathed, wiping both hands over her face, then using the crook of her arm. She was utterly sure that it had done nothing to stop her face from looking blotchy and pink, but it didn't matter. He must have been standing there *the whole time*.

'You shouldn't have heard that. I'm a bit drunk.'

'I don't blame you,' he said, taking a step towards her.

'It's just hard for me sometimes,' she said, her voice beginning to crack.

There was a long pause that seemed to go on forever.

'Sophie, I need to tell you something.'

Something about the way he said it made Sophie look up. A strain in his voice, perhaps, or a trace of emotion. What was it he 'needed' to tell her? Sophie was aware that her heart had begun to beat hard.

'I should have said something before,' said Tim, his voice soft and hesitant. Sophie felt as though she were hovering above herself, an out-of-body experience. Was he going to finally declare his love? If he was, Sophie was pretty sure she would be sick, right there on the bench.

'It… it was me,' he said.

'What? What was?' Sophie was completely bewildered now.

'That day in Verbier. On the slopes. It wasn't that German guy who ran over your skis. I did.'

Her hands were shaking.

'You.'

He took a deep breath and looked away. 'I ran over your skis,' he said quietly. 'I just meant to ski close to give you a fright. But I mis-timed it and I clipped you.'

'Clipped me.'

Sophie gaped at him, not entirely sure she had heard him correctly, not entirely sure if this was Tim's idea of a joke. She let out a nervous laugh.

'That's not funny, Tim. Maybe you don't get how serious this has been for me…'

'No, no, I do, I do,' he said, taking a step towards her. 'I do.'

He swallowed, looking utterly sick. 'It's not a joke. I really did it.'

Sophie knew confusion. She had been there, done that, bought the T-shirt. In the weeks after her accident, her thoughts were a jumble of emotions, memories, knowledge, floating in the viscose spaces in her brain, often touching but never connecting. She never knew which memories were real, which she had allowed herself to dream.

But finally Sophie allowed herself to hear what Tim had just said. To make the connection. He had knocked her down. Tim had caused her injury. Tim had ruined her life.

'It wasn't Klaus.' Her voice was barely a whisper as the words sank in. She had wasted all those years wishing that Tim would come along and save her, to reach out a hand to pull her up out of this dark hole, when all along it had been Tim who had pushed her in. The irony almost made her laugh out loud.

Almost.

'How could you…?'

Sophie said it quietly, in genuine disbelief. It just did not compute. Or rather, it did not fit the character of the man she had imagined Fantasy Tim to be. Who this man standing in front of her was, she had no idea.

'Did you know? Did you know I fell?'

'I looked back,' said Tim. 'I saw you'd had a tumble, but I didn't know you were hurt.'

'Then why didn't you stop? Why did you ski away?'

'I thought you were OK,' said Tim. 'Besides, I knew Juliet and Chas would be along any minute, they were right behind me, and it just looked like a tumble.'

'Just a tumble,' said Sophie, her voice on autopilot.

All the emotion and frustration she had directed at poor Klaus were now re-directed at Tim.

'So just to be clear, you thought I'd just winded myself, but even then you ran off and left your girlfriend lying in the snow.'

'Sophie, I didn't…' he began, but Sophie was still talking. 'And then when you'd heard I'd been air-lifted to the hospital, even then you pretended it was nothing to do with you. Am I summarising correctly?'

'Sophie, I panicked. Everything that was happening was so scary, I just decided to stay quiet.'

'What does that make you, Tim?'

He opened his mouth, then closed it, looking down at the ground.

Sophie nodded. It was about all she could expect.

She bit down hard on her lip to stop the tears. She needed to hold it together, just for a little while more.

'Why are you telling me this?'

He looked up.

'Because you deserve to know.'

'And I didn't fifteen years ago.'

How could she ever have believed this hollow shell of a man could have been The One, the answer to all her prayers?

'I get it,' she said, the penny dropping. 'You're telling me now, because it's your big day, a fresh start, you're not telling me now so I can move on with my life. You want to release your guilt, so *you* can move forward. Isn't that it?'

Anger gripped her chest. She wanted to reach out and grab his scrawny, cowardly neck, she wanted to strike out and hurt him like she had been hurt, again and again. And she realised she had the power to do it. She had just the weapon – and the words were on her lips, balanced there, almost said. The one thing she could hurt him with – Jennifer's secret – the only thing that might sink a dagger beneath Tim Jameson's Savile Row-tailored armour and ruin his wedding day. Instead Sophie closed her eyes and took a breath. No. It was Jennifer's choice, Jennifer's pain. Sophie wouldn't become like Tim and take both.

'Sophie, I loved you. I never, ever wanted this to happen.'

For a moment, she just wanted to climb inside his head. Had he loved her, or was that just another lie? After all, he started sleeping with Vanessa to further his career. Or had he truly loved her but the guilt was the reason he had ended their relationship so soon? It didn't matter anymore.

'How do you sleep well at night?' she whispered.

'I don't.'

She closed her eyes, her heart shot through with sadness.

'Congratulations, Tim,' she said softly, turning to walk back out into the dark garden. 'I hope you have a great night.'

'Sophie,' he called after her. 'Sophie!'

But she didn't look back.

Chapter Twenty-Seven

ADAM WAS DYING for a cigarette. He'd never been a big smoker, but he'd grown up watching French movies, primarily because he thought a working knowledge of *Plein Soleil* or *Belle du Jour* might impress girls. Everyone had smoked in those movies, the blue-grey haze wreathing the actors as they planned a heist or rolled over in post-coital sheets, and right now, smoking felt like a comfort blanket, a forbidden link back to his youth when things felt more simple.

Things aren't so simple now, he thought to himself, cadging an Embassy from Uncle Dennis and walking out across the crowded terrace at the back of the house and down some steps into the Hall's formal garden, now given a tasteful glow by soft blue spotlights. He took a drag of the cigarette and immediately started coughing. Stubbing it out on a stone wall, he moved further into the darkness. How could so much flip upside down in such a short time? But that was the nature of change, wasn't it? One person tells you something and – click – everything changes in an instant. His Dad, Ali, Tim. Each one opened their mouths and the world took a handbrake turn and in a screech of burning rubber everyone was facing another direction.

He looked back towards the terrace, to the chattering, laughing partygoers. How many of them had secrets they were dying to share – or were desperate to bury?

Maybe that was the big truth you learned as an adult: everyone was hiding something. Like his dad, like Ali. Even Tim, someone who, up until now, Adam had thought incapable of keeping a secret – even Tim had managed to keep a terrible, ruinous lie close to his chest. How he had done it, Adam didn't know. Perhaps some secrets were just too bad to let out into the light.

He sighed, thinking about Sophie again. What was he going to say to her? Adam barely knew Sophie Wallis, had no idea how she would take the news of what Adam had overheard, or if indeed she would believe him. Adam wasn't even sure what happened in Verbier was his business to share. But he couldn't *not* say anything, even if keeping a secret was done with the best intentions, like he supposed his father had done. She just deserved to know the truth. It was that simple. Some things were too important not to know.

He turned a corner and walked along parallel to the terrace, stopping at the far end. There was a circular pond here, the underwater lighting catching the orange and silver scales of Koi carp as they drifted beneath lily pads. Just behind it was a stone temple and from inside, Adam could just hear the soft sound of crying. He walked closer, squinting at the figure hunched in the darkness.

'Sophie?'

Silence.

'Sophie, it's Adam.'

He approached her carefully; she was sitting alone in the dark and as he got closer he could see she was shivering. Shivering and crying.

'Here, you're freezing,' he said, taking his jacket off to put it around her shoulders. Sophie looked up with red eyes.

'Thank you.'

'Do you want to tell me what's wrong?'

'It was Tim,' she said her voice barely audible. 'It was Tim who knocked me over in Verbier. He just admitted it.'

'Ah.' said Adam quietly. Sophie looked across at him.

'You *knew*?' she hissed, her moist eyes flaring at the thought of another person who had betrayed her.

Adam put up both hands, palms out.

'Hey, hey – I only found out twenty minutes ago. I overheard him talking to Vanessa.'

Sophie held her breath.

'So she knows too?'

Adam nodded. He had to be honest.

'It sounded like Vanessa has always known. Apparently, she was overhead on a ski-lift and saw it happen.'

Sophie pressed both hands to her face, covering her eyes.

'I've been blaming an innocent German dentist all this time,' she whispered.

'I am so, so stupid.'

'No, you're not.'

'Really? Did you know Tim and Vanessa were shagging while I was still going out with him?'

'No.'

'Did you know she got him a job? At Glasshouse. Rich told me.'

Adam shook his head, but he wasn't surprised. In sixth form, Adam had asked Tim why he had applied to Bristol when all their friends were going to the cooler party towns of Leeds or Manchester. *Because of the money*, Tim had said. Bristol had a reputation for attracting rich people, Oxbridge rejects and public school kids. In Bristol, Tim reasoned, he'd meet the right sort of people. And for Tim, the 'right sort of people' meant the people who could give him the most.

'Tim has always done what's best for Tim,' said Adam sadly. 'So yes, if Vanessa could get him something he wanted, that makes sense.'

She wiped her eyes angrily.

'Why did he do it? Lie for so long?'

'He's a coward. Gutless. Psychopathically selfish.'

'And Vanessa?'

'I'm sure she has her reasons. I suppose in some twisted way, it was love.'

It was what his father had tried to tell him. Graham had believed he was doing the best thing for Adam by staying away, sparing him the need to choose between his parents. And in his own way, he was also showing his love for Adam's mother Susan too, giving her what she wanted and keeping her secret from her adoring son. But it didn't make the consequences any less painful or damaging. Sophie's tears were flowing freely again.

'When they flew me back from Switzerland to London, I was in ICU then the rehab unit. Tim came to see me a few weeks after I arrived, stayed half an hour and then I never saw him again. At first, my parents told me they were just limiting my visitors. A few months later they admitted they'd intercepted a letter he'd sent me, finishing our relationship. I read the letter when I was stronger. Turns out Tim can write big speeches after all. He said he just found it too difficult to deal with, that he couldn't stand to see me in pain, and to be honest, I didn't blame him, not then. But now I know the real reason. He would have felt guilty every time he looked at me.'

He reached for her hand. He expected her to recoil but instead she held on tight.

'Tim and Vanessa deserve each other. You, meanwhile, are worth so much more.'

Sophie squeezed his fingers.

'I'm glad we met,' she said finally.

'You are?'

'For a long time, it felt as if I knew you. Those first few months that I knew Tim, it was Adam this, Adam that. We got to hear all your war stories from the frontline of rock. You know, Tim worked hard at college. That was one of the things I liked about him. He was socially ambitious, yes. Aspirational. But I think at the very heart of it all, was some desire to keep up with you. I think Tim is successful because of you.'

'So it's all my fault.'

They looked at each other and both laughed.

'Sticks in the craw, though, doesn't it?' said Adam, finding it hard not to feel bitter. 'The way he behaves, but everything always seems to fall into his lap. I'm not sure it's the message we'd want to tell our kids.'

Adam felt himself flush at the words 'our kids'.

Sophie looked out into the darkness.

'You don't want to envy Tim.'

'Being married to Vanessa?'

'No. Not that. He's got a difficult time coming.'

'What do you mean?'

Sophie paused, then shook her head.

'Doesn't matter. None of it matters, not anymore.'

She got up and slid off his jacket, holding it out to him.

'Keep it,' he said.

Sophie nodded.

'I should go and find my sister.'

'You are going to stick around aren't you?' said Adam, feeling a flutter of panic.

She hesitated. 'Maybe.'

'Come on,' pressed Adam getting to his feet. 'You can't let him win. I say we find Christa and the rest of the Singles Table, and order the most expensive cocktails on the menu and raise hell. Tim wanted a big, splashy wedding? Well it's going to cost him'

'I'll see you at the house,' she said, giving him a soft smile and disappearing into the dark. Adam didn't move for a minute. He watched the red shimmer of her dress disappear into the darkness until he was just looking at a dark void.

Go after her, you idiot, he said to himself. *Before she disappears for good.*

He stood up, heading for the terrace steps.

'Hey, Ads!' Adam immediately recognised Tim's voice coming from behind.

'Adam, wait up.'

Sighing, Adam turned slowly, trying to compose himself.

'Have you seen Sophie?' asked Tim. 'I think she came this way.'

'She just left.'

Tim clearly saw something in Adam's face because he frowned.

'What's got into you?'

'Take a wild guess,' said Adam, his fury too strong to ignore. 'I *know*, Tim. I know what you did in Verbier. I know it was you who knocked her over.'

If he expected Tim to look shocked, contrite, or apologetic, he was mistaken.

'Ah, you've been speaking to Sophie,' he replied with a knowing nod of the head. 'I've spoken to her too. She's so drunk. Got it into her head that I was the one who caused her accident. Started accusing me and being quite rude, to be honest.'

'Then why are you looking for her?'

'I was worried about her, if you must know. Wanted to make sure she gets back to The Swan safely.'

'Very noble.'

Tim narrowed his eyes. 'What exactly did she tell

you, Adam?'

He took a step towards Tim and was gratified to see him flinch.

'It's not what Sophie told me, Tim. It's what Vanessa said. I heard you both in the Orangery. I know what *actually* happened.'

At least that got a reaction. Even in the dark he could see Tim's cheeks flush.

'Tonight's not the night to go into this, Adam.'

'Really? I thought you wanted it all out in the open. Isn't that why you told Sophie?'

Tim looked awkward now, a man, even a confident man, caught out.

'Ads, it was an accident. I didn't know she was hurt, and once everything started to unravel, it just felt too late to admit it was me. I thought it was a broken leg or something. I thought it would heal and we could just get back to where we were.'

'You left her on the slopes. She was put in a coma.'

'I didn't know that. None of us did. She was whisked off the mountain and taken to hospital. For those first two weeks, Mr and Mrs Wallis kept us all in the dark about how bad it was. By the time I did find out, it was too late to go, "Oh, hey. Guess what? It was me that ran over her skis."'

Adam shook his head in disgust.

'You're taking the moral high ground now?' said Tim, more harshly now. 'Put yourself in my shoes and tell me you wouldn't have done the same.'

'I wouldn't.'

'Really? You sure?' he snorted. 'Anyway, it's

done, Adam. We can't change the past. Vanessa knows, Sophie knows. Now we can all move on.'

'You can move on, you mean.'

His old friend looked at him, his eyes narrow.

'Why do you care all of a sudden?'

'I care because you ruined her life.'

'You care because you fancy her.'

His words hit Adam like a punch.

'Tim, this isn't about me, this is about the way you treated Sophie, the way you lied to her and abandoned her in that hospital, presumably because you were terrified that she'd remember and tell everyone.'

'Listen to yourself: "abandoned her"? You've screwed your way through half of London. You're hardly blameless on the "abandoning" front yourself.'

'Just stop, Tim.'

'No, I won't stop. You want some home truths? Adam, look at you. You could have had it all: the girl, Cambridge, the career, the big fucking car. You had everything, man. The looks, the brain, the talent, And you threw it all away.'

'I didn't throw anything away. I've spent twenty years doing what I love.'

'What, lurking around at the back of some piss-scented pub scribbling down notes? That's what you love is it? Getting paid peanuts to get ignored? Your problem is that you could never dream big. You could have won a Booker Prize or written a Hollywood screenplay. But no. You hang on to an industry that is disappearing before your eyes, unable to move on, and instead of settling down, you start hanging out with younger and younger people, in the hope of what Adam? It's going to stop time?'

Adam felt thrown off-kilter. Somehow his defence of Sophie Wallis had morphed into a personal attack on him.

'Don't keep turning this around onto me when you're feeling guilty,' he said.

'You know why we stopped being mates, Adam? Because of that. Because all the craziness, all the fun, that's all you ever wanted to do. There was always another party, always another girl. You weren't hungry. It was always about fun and never about the future.'

For a moment he thought about Tony Robb and a crazy night out they'd had in the days when they were friends. They'd met a film director, Simon Ritchie, at the Groucho Club and he and Adam had bonded over a love of Akira Kurosawa films and Indian beer. Simon had asked him to lunch the week after to discuss Adam doing a script polish on his latest movie. But instead, Adam flew out to the MTV Awards, and let the contact with Ritchie fade away, while Tony Robb, was pictured hanging out with Simon at a premiere six months later.

'Look Adam, if you really like Sophie, go ahead. Ask her out. I won't mind, although you might have to get in line behind Rich.'

'I don't need any more favours, Tim,' Adam snorted. 'They're always loaded.'

'You're such an ungrateful shit, do you know that?' spat Tim. 'I've always looked out for you. Did I have to offer you a job at Glasshouse? Did I have to protect you when we were kids?'

Adam laughed out loud at that one.

'When did you ever protect me, Tim?'

'Back at school, when your mum was being a slag. I stuck up for you, but you must know the real reason why Paul Robertshaw moved away from the estate. Because your mum was shagging his dad and when Mr Robertshaw tried to end it, she wouldn't leave him alone. He had to move to Macclesfield to get away from her.'

Without thinking, Adam drew back his fist.

Adam hadn't thrown many punches in his life, but this one made up for lost time, looping up over the top and landing square on Tim's nose with a dull 'thwack'. Tim fell backwards, blood already streaming between his fingers. He pulled a hand away and looked at it in disbelief.

'You bwoke my blubby nose!' he muttered in a thick voice.

'We all make mistakes, don't we?' said Adam, surprising himself with how calm he was. 'But you know what? The important thing is to stop repeating them.'

'Screw you, Ads! And you can forget that bloody job too! Let's see how far you get with your record shop, eh?'

He walked back inside, Tim's shouted taunts and insults not touching him.

Graham Stowe was standing at the door, watching.

'Nice punch, son,' he said.

‘Thanks Dad.’

Adam squeezed his Dad on the shoulder and walked inside.

Chapter Twenty-Eight

THE PARTY WAS beginning to move onto the terrace for the highlight of the wedding celebrations: the firework display. Sophie had listened to the girls at the bridal shower gushing about it the previous night. It had cost thousands, they'd said; Vee's dad had pulled strings at the council to get the licence, they said. And apparently the fireworks had been specially designed to end in the shape of a love-heart, fifty feet high.

Despite her half-promise to Adam to stay, Sophie just wanted to go home. The thought of being in the same vague area as Tim and Vanessa, let alone watching more overblown declarations of their love, made her feel nauseous. The only reason she was tempted to stay was because of Adam himself, because, well, everything always seemed just that bit more exciting when he was around. But what was she expecting to happen even if she did stay until Last Orders? She guessed that Adam Stowe had little interest in her. He was good looking and glamorous and she was Tim's miserable ex-girlfriend who only seemed to shout or snivel in his company. She knew she was feeling sorry for herself, but then it had been that kind of a day.

Sophie moved against the flow of bodies heading for the terrace, scanning the crowd for any sign of Christa. She saw Hugo talking to an older man near the lobby – Hugo, at least, was easy to spot. He waved and made his way over, his face full of concern.

'Is everything okay with the Bennisons?' he said.

'Yes thanks, back at their luxury lodge, fast asleep now I'm sure. Thanks for your chivalry and your unflappable linguistic skills.'

'And are *you* alright, Sophie?'

She wondered how he could tell she was not alright. Perhaps Hugo was less drunk than most; after all, when you were six feet six, it probably took a lot more. Plus she imagined, being an explorer, he had a more finely tuned sense of people's emotions than most: it was an important skill when people around you had poison-tipped spears.

'I'm fine – will be fine,' said Sophie as convincingly as she could. 'It's been a long day, but I'll outlast it.'

Hugo gently touched Sophie's arm.

'You know there's an African proverb I find useful in life: 'No matter how hot your anger, it can never cook yams'. Whatever that burden is you've been carrying Sophie, put it down. It isn't worth it. Almost nothing is.'

Sophie smiled. It had, by any standards, been a difficult day but meeting people like Hugo Crabb had more than made up for it. Hugo, Zara, Paul – they were all kind, supportive and genuine people. If the Singles Table was the place for the losers, then Sophie would take failure over success every time.

'Hugo, I'm going to go in a minute, but if I don't see you before, goodbye. It's been wonderful to meet you.'

'Perhaps I'll see you at breakfast?' he said. Sophie was grateful that he hadn't tried to push her into staying. She gave him a tight hug, holding him there for a moment.

'Good luck with all your adventures,' she said quietly. 'May the road rise to meet you. Isn't that the saying?'

He nodded.

'And may the wind always be at your back. Oh, and I'm always at the end of a phone if you need any suggestions about interesting places to go.'

She watched him walk to the bar and then got out her phone to tell Christa that she was definitely going back to The Swan, with or without her.

'Sophie!'

As she turned she saw Jennifer Jameson bustling towards her, and felt a pang of guilt.

'Aren't you coming out to watch the display, love?'

'Not my kind of thing, Jenny,' said Sophie. 'Don't like sudden bangs.'

'Get to my age you take any kind of bang you can get.'

Sophie gave a crooked smile.

'Sorry,' said Jennifer, raising her glass. 'I think I might have had too many Bellinis.'

Sophie glanced around to make sure they weren't

overheard.

'Are you sure you should be… I mean, won't it mix with the medication?'

'Oh, live a little, Sophie,' said Jennifer with a hint of impatience. 'It's not like I have that many more Bellinis or firework displays pencilled in on my year planner.'

'Don't talk like that.'

'Why not? You should know better than anyone, Sophie, life can go out like that.' She clicked her fingers with finality. 'Maybe I've got three months. Maybe a year. Perhaps I'll join a miracle trial and get five or ten more years of life. But right now, I've got tonight. This moment.'

'But you had fun today, right?' she asked instead.

'It was fabulous, wasn't it?' said Jennifer, a grin spreading across her face. 'I've loved every minute of it and I'm staying until they throw me out. I want to make today last as long as I can.'

From where they were standing they could see the dancefloor, where Jennifer's husband Bill was dancing with Lucy. Bill caught her eye and waved.

Jennifer sighed a little sigh of happiness.

'Have you told him?'

Jennifer's face darkened and she flashed Sophie a look.

'Sophie please, we talked about this.'

Sophie smiled softly, and touched her friend on the arm.

'I meant have you told him how much you love him tonight?'

Jennifer clasped her hand.

'Lovely Sophie,' she said, a touch of melancholy in her voice. 'I remember the very first time I ever met you. Tim had brought you home for the weekend. I said to Bill after you'd gone, that you were way too good for Tim.'

'What? No!'

Jennifer chuckled.

'Tim's my son, I love him more than anything in the world, but he would never have been happy in someone's shadow and you were always destined to be exceptional, Sophie.'

'But my destiny changed,' she replied, feeling her mood deflate.

'Perhaps, but you can change it once more, because I've got a feeling you're ready to fly again, Sophie Wallis.'

'So, you've got my number,' said Sophie quickly, not wanting to start sobbing again. Jennifer nodded.

'Next time you're in London, I can come with you to any hospital visits, take you for lunch, anything,' she said. 'The V&A museum is fabulous. I'm a member. You know they've got Fred Astaire's suit in the Costume department?'

'Maybe I can borrow it for the next time we go dancing.'

'I'm sure they wouldn't mind,' she laughed.

Jennifer glanced at her watch.

'Bill asked me to find him a brandy half an hour ago, but he's swaying in the wind, so I think a bucket of black coffee is order of the day. And then, how about you watch the fireworks with me? Up on the roof?'

Sophie glanced towards the door: she just wanted to crawl under the covers back at The Swan and forget this day ever happened, but she knew she couldn't really deny Jennifer. Not today.

'Sure, why not?' she said. She would watch the fireworks for five minutes, then she was definitely leaving.

She took one last sweep to find Christa but there was no sign of her.

The party was still busy. Outside Haslop Hall was a long line of taxis. With a lack of demand for rides, the drivers stood on the gravel, chatting, as if they were having their own private party. Everyone was having a good time it appeared – everyone except her.

Sophie stopped a passing waiter.

'How do I get up to the roof?' she asked. 'Is there some sort of terrace or place to watch the fireworks?'

'You must mean the cupola,' he nodded. 'Take the lift to the second floor, go right down the corridor and you'll see a spiral staircase. It's up there.'

It had to be spiral stairs thought Sophie, taking a breath before heading for the lift.

She pressed the call button and watched the art deco dial indicate the lift was coming back to the ground floor. There was a loud ping, and the doors purred open and suddenly she stood face to face with Vanessa. Her face looked flushed; a thick lock of hair had fallen from her updo, her eyes looked as if she had been crying.

'Sophie,' she said. Vanessa tried to smile but she was tight around the lips. 'Still here?'

'Just for a little while longer.'

Sophie paused.

'You looked beautiful, by the way,' she said. 'At the church.'

She was being honest, and despite everything, it felt the right thing to do.

Vanessa looked completely taken aback by the compliment.

'Uh, thank you. And so do you. Look great, that is.'

Sophie tilted her head.

'You really love him, don't you?' she said simply.

Vanessa blinked, clearly wondering if it was a trap of some kind.

'Yes. Yes I do,' she said, raising her chin just a fraction.

And at that moment, Sophie knew it was true – and she felt a terrible pang of sympathy for Vanessa. She did love Tim, she must have done to have carried that burden for so long, but the terrible truth was that Vanessa would have to keep carrying that weight in the certain knowledge that one day her husband would lie again and cause her pain because of his own selfishness. It was love – true love – but what a price to pay.

Sophie saw Vanessa's eyes flicker to the left, over her shoulder. Sophie turned and saw Tim, standing at the bottom of the hotel stairs. He looked different somehow. Or maybe she was just looking at him differently.

‘Van, are you coming?’ he called. ‘The fireworks are beginning.’

Sophie touched Vanessa’s arm and nodded towards him. And then she watched them go.

Chapter Twenty-Nine

IT WAS A sensation Adam Stowe was wholly unaccustomed to: he wanted to leave a party before it was over. Hugo and Zara were at the bar, nosily gathering supplies for the Singles – three bottles of Champagne and a fistful of flutes – and jabbering about the imminent fireworks. In the normal scheme of things, Adam would have been leading from the front, adding a dash of kir or amaretto to the glasses or organising some out-of-season mistletoe, but tonight he just wasn't feeling it. He was drained and gloomy and the last thing he felt like doing was toasting the happy couple.

'Come on Adam,' said Hugo. 'Henry and Cherie are holding a good spot at the front for us all.'

'You go ahead,' said Adam, forcing a smile. 'I've just got something to do.'

Hugo gave a jaunty wave and Adam smiled awkwardly. He felt guilty lying to his new friend, but it was better just to slip off back to The Swan without giving anyone the chance to persuade him otherwise. But it was true that he had something he wanted to do first.

'Adam, there you are!'

Tim's mother stepped out in front of him and before he could respond, had pulled him into an embrace. 'Where have you been? I've hardly had a chance to speak to you all day.'

'You've been busy, Mrs J,' said Adam, giving her a smile, knowing how much she would hate the thought of him wanting to leave. 'It's been a big day for you.'

'And for you too,' said Jennifer. 'I heard you saved Ali Malik's life tonight.'

Adam waved a casual hand.

'Nothing quite so heroic – he is a bit fragile though, he's upstairs sleeping it off.'

'Just as well his parents aren't here. We did invite Naveen and Nazra but they're on a cruise. Caribbean, apparently.'

'Now you mention it, Ali did tell me he paid for some luxury holiday.'

'I don't think the timing is a coincidence,' said Jennifer, raising her eyebrows. 'He's definitely a man off the leash tonight.'

It was funny, Jennifer knowing Ali so well. They had all grown up together, in and out of each other's houses, with Tim's mother watching over them like a benign sheepdog. Adam wondered if she knew her own sons as well.

'Talking of parents, have you had a chat with your dad yet?'

'We did. It went about as well as usual.'

Jennifer put her head on one side. 'Adam, I thought you might be able to move past this.'

Adam glanced around.

'Look, can I ask you something, Mrs J? My dad told me something tonight. That my mum had an affair.'

'With Bobby Robertshaw?'

'You knew?' said Adam simply. Of course she knew. Susan Stowe had been her friend.

'Tim said that's why the Robertshaws left the estate. Why? What happened?'

Jennifer looked away, her face paler now.

'Adam, I don't want to gossip.'

'This isn't gossip, Jenny. This is my childhood. My life. I need to know.'

'I never knew the whole story,' said Jennifer quietly.

She paused, her gaze distant.

'It was going on for some time between Sue and Bobby, although how long I'm not sure: long enough for Susan to fall in love, or at least think she had. Bobby talked a good game, I think he promised her the world. He certainly led her to believe they had a future together.'

'But I never even saw her talk to Mr Robertshaw. Did he even try to leave his wife or was he stringing my mum along?'

'I guess only Bobby and Karen Robertshaw know the truth about that one,' said Jennifer blowing out her cheeks. 'I did hear that Mr Robertshaw told his wife about his affair with Susan but she wouldn't accept it. She convinced him of what he was throwing away. I supposed that fits with them moving away to Macclesfield. For a fresh start.'

Jennifer looked him more directly in the eye. It was as if she knew exactly what Adam was thinking. How could a mother blow up her family for the sake of a fling? Mrs Robertshaw wasn't prepared to give up on her family, why would his mother? And more than that, Adam had spent most of his life resenting his father for abandoning him – hadn't his mum done something even more damaging?

'You know, when you're fifteen years into marriage, when it starts to feel stale and life seems humdrum and someone exciting comes along offering you the life you've dreamt of, sometimes you're tempted to take it,' said Jennifer answering his question.

'We're humans, Adam. We can be selfish. Your mother didn't want to hurt Graham and she certainly didn't want to hurt you. But she found something with Bobby – excitement, passion, hope? I don't know – she thought it was worth it. Of course, in the end she got her own heart broken as well.'

He tried to recall those months after his father left them, tried to remember any signs that Susan Stowe had been in her own private hell. Perhaps she had, and perhaps on some level, Adam had known. That was certainly the time he had begun spending more and more time at the Jamesons' or locked away in his room with his growing record collection.

'I was surprised you didn't have a plus one for the wedding,' said Jennifer, clearly trying to change the direction of the conversation.

'Is that a more diplomatic way of saying, "how's

your love-life?"'

'Adam, you were never short of female attention.'

'Maybe,' he shrugged. 'Doesn't mean to say I ever found the right one though, does it?'

'Maybe. Or maybe you've just been looking for the wrong girl.'

Adam wasn't even sure what kind of girl he had been looking for all these years. He had dated tall girls, short girls, blondes and brunettes, renowned beauties and great laughs: Adam had always prided himself on being 'type neutral' and look where it had got him.

'So how about Sophie?' said Jennifer.

He didn't want to admit that he had been looking for her at the precise moment he had bumped into Jennifer. That she was the only reason for staying at the party.

'Sophie?'

'Why not?'

Adam pulled a face.

'I'm pretty sure she thinks I'm an idiot.'

'Then she's wrong.'

He looked at her in surprise.

'Adam, I've known you since you were eleven years old. You've been like another son to me. You were always such a smart kid – and such a big heart. I'd say you were something of a catch.'

'I can give you a long list of girls who'd dispute that.'

'Oh yes?' Jennifer looked at him meaningfully. 'Remember Paula Sterling?'

It took Adam a moment. 'Paula from school?'

She'd been one of the nerds at Harling Comp, pretty much invisible until puberty came along and sucker-punched Paula with weapons-grade acne. From that moment, she became Pizzaface Paula, the brunt of everyone's jokes, school shorthand for everything ugly and unglamorous. But seating in Chemistry was done alphabetically and while sharing a Bunsen burner, Adam had discovered that Paula was a real laugh. More importantly, she had 'Portishead' written on her pencil case, which to Adam, made Paula Sterling one of the chosen few.

'Paula's my dentist now,' said Jennifer, baring her teeth. 'She always asks after you when I go in for a check-up.'

'I'm amazed she remembers me at all.'

'Paula remembers that you changed her life.'

'Me?'

'Apparently, you got Paula an invitation to some glamorous party for Ian Cameron's sixteenth-birthday party. You chatted to her and danced with her. After that, people lost interest in calling Paula names and she went back to being Plain Paula – although not *that* plain. She dated Ian Cameron for a little while after you all left school.'

Adam didn't know that. In fact, he didn't know what anyone from school had done. Adam had decided to go to London and had left it all behind. Single-minded, just like his mother.

'I'm glad Paula remembers me,' said Adam. 'But I'm not sure I did much to change her life.'

'You did *enough*, Adam. You changed how people

looked at that girl and you changed how she felt about herself. Now she does subsidised orthodontics for teenagers to help them with their self-image. Maybe a little bit of that is because of you, too.'

It was nice to hear he'd had a positive effect on Paula's life, but Adam suspected that if someone interviewed all the women he'd encountered in his life, the feedback might not be quite so glowing.

'Well I think I should thank you too, Mrs. J.'

'What for?'

'For being there. Growing up, when my mum was working all the time, your house was like a second home for me. I'll always be grateful for that.'

Jennifer surprised him by throwing her arms around him and squeezing him tight.

'I'm proud of you, Adam,' she whispered.

She was pulling away when she seemed to remember something.

'Oh Adam – can you do me a big favour?'

'Sure, anything.'

'I was going to watch the fireworks up on the roof. Could you take a chair up there for me? I'd ask one of my sons, but they're both selfish pricks.'

Adam chuckled.

'Sure.'

Jennifer put a hand to her mouth in a stage whisper.

'But keep it to yourself. It's the best spot in the house and we don't want it to get mobbed up there.'

Grabbing a spindly chair, Adam stopped a waiter who directed him to the cupola via the spiral staircase, which was a challenge to climb holding a chair.

Adopting a system of bumping its legs up one step at a time, Adam finally reached the top. The cupola was a dome-shaped structure at the top of the house, with arched windows on all sides, making Adam feel as if he had stepped into a hurricane lantern. As he reached the top of the stairs, he could see there was already somebody out on the balcony.

His heart jumped as he recognised Sophie, still wearing his jacket, her long dark hair flipped over one shoulder. She was leaning on the balustrade, looking out into the darkness, her hand holding her other wrist. She looked so graceful and serene that he didn't want to disturb her.

The chair clattered to the floor.

'Adam,' said Sophie, turning at the sound. 'What are you doing up here?'

'I was about to ask you the same thing.'

'I'm meeting someone,' she said, folding one arm across her chest.

'Oh,' said Adam, his heart sinking. *Rich Jameson?* In his jacket? Surely fate couldn't be that cruel?

'Jennifer,' she said. 'I'm meeting Jennifer.'

Adam tried to hide his relief. 'Makes sense. She asked me to bring up the chair.'

From this viewpoint, they both had a clear view of the terrace down below and Adam could see Jennifer holding hands with Bill, surrounded by friends and family. They were drinking, laughing, looking in no rush to go anywhere, certainly not up to the roof. They'd been set up.

'I'm not sure she's coming, are you?'

'I guess not,' said Adam, suddenly nervous. He usually had all the lines. He was a natural flirt, with a thousand stories at his fingertips, ready to impress or seduce, but out here on the balcony, high above the crowds, he felt as awkward as a teenager at his first disco, plucking up the courage to ask a girl to dance.

'Do you want to sit?' said Adam, offering the chair to Sophie.

She shook her head and looked out across the dark valley.

'I'm sorry, by the way,' she said.

Adam came across to stand next to her.

'What for?'

'You know: what you found out about Tim and my accident. I hope it isn't going to affect your relationship with him.'

'I think we might be past that,' said Adam. 'I punched him in the face about an hour ago.'

Sophie looked at him wide-eyed and Adam couldn't really blame her. Some might think there were no excuses for assaulting a man on his wedding day. Adam shrugged.

'He called my mum a slag.'

Sophie closed her eyes and started to giggle.

'I'm sorry, I shouldn't laugh, but he really is so dreadful.'

Adam smiled sadly.

'Sometimes you consider someone to be a great friend, but then you realise they're not even part of your life anymore. That they're living another life, with other people, without you in it. They're not friends, they're really just a memory and I think that's how it's been with me and Tim for a long time now. He even admitted it. He said he doesn't see me anymore because I'm not ambitious. But the truth is, I didn't call him either. I think I knew what he was like long before this weekend.'

Just then, there was the swell of music – the James Bond theme tune Adam recognised from just the opening notes – a howling sound ripped through the air, and a shower of green and gold light exploded into the air.

'It's starting,' said Sophie. Adam stood closer, their hands just inches apart on the rail, their chins tilted upwards. Adam had to admit it was a spectacular display and he idly wondered how much it was costing them – all this money simply going up in smoke. That weekend, for the first time in his life, listening to Jonty talking about his luxury holidays or Tim describing his new car on order – Sophie's reaction to the fact he'd turned down a place at Cambridge – Adam had found himself wondering if he'd made the right decisions in his life. But as he stood looking out from the cupola, on top of the world, next to a beautiful woman, watching a light display to a medley of John Barry's peerless film scores, Adam Stowe felt as if he was exactly where he was supposed to be. And he had Tim to thank for that.

The last bangs faded away and the crowd below began to cheer and clap. Sophie turned to face him, her smile soft.

'You know, when I was at my lowest, my most

hopeless, in the weeks after my accident, I couldn't see much point in going on. But then I was lying in my hospital bed and I saw fireworks through the window. It wasn't New Year or Bonfire Night, but someone, somewhere was celebrating. I could only see a few stars and sprays because I couldn't move, but I could hear the crackles and booms. And it was then that I swore to myself that I was going to see and feel joy again. The very next day, I took my first step.'

Adam nodded, putting his hand on hers. She didn't pull away.

'Fireworks are definitely one of the good things in this world,' he said.

'Fireworks and sticky toffee pudding,' she said.

'Fireworks, sticky toffee pudding and Monster Munch.'

'Monster Munch?' she repeated with a down-turned mouth.

'All-time greatest snack, bar none.'

They were standing so close now, Adam could feel her warmth.

'What else? What else do you love?' he asked.

'The sunset over Porthmeor Beach in St. Ives,' she said, looking out into the dark.

'Raising the bar I see, OK... alright, then I'm going for martinis on the terrace at the Hotel Belles Rives, French Riviera.'

'Another literary reference? The world's biggest Monster Munch fan is quite the sophisticate.'

'What about skiing?' asked Adam.

Sophie looked up at him, less sure now.

'What about it?'

'Last night, you said you used to love it. Your face lit up when you talked about it. Would you go skiing again?'

'No,' she said instantly.

'Why not?'

'Because the memories are too painful.'

Adam nodded.

'When I was a kid, I used to love Evel Knievel, you know the daredevil fella? I followed all his jumps. You know, every time he crashed, he was straight back on his bike as soon as he recovered, with even bigger, bolder ambitions.'

'Adam, I'm not Evel Knievel,' said Sophie.

'None of us are,' he said, giving her hand a little tug, inching her closer. 'But the point is, you can't let bumps in the road put you off getting back on the bike. Maybe you just need to try a bigger jump.'

They both looked out over the valley, the sky a blue-black, the lights of Playborough glowing through the trees.

'D'you know, this weekend I've lost my job, had both parents let me down and found out that my best friend is an even bigger tool than I first thought. But right now, right this second, I am happy.'

Sophie's eyes met his, then flickered away.

'You've lost your job? I'm sorry.'

'Don't be,' said Adam. 'I was well overdue a change. Even Evel Knievel had to hang up his helmet eventually.'

'Then this is the exciting bit,' said Sophie with

confidence. 'The planning.'

'Like holidays.'

'Or weddings.'

'Or a first kiss,' said Adam. 'That's one of the best feelings of all.'

The atmosphere shifted as if they were on the very edge of something and the air felt too charged for her not be experiencing it too. Adam took a step towards her, his heart pumping hard.

Then there was a sudden bang as the door of the cupola flew open and crashed against the wall.

'What the hell…?'

They spun round to see Graham Stowe stumble in.

'Bloody new shoes,' he muttered. 'Been slipping about all night. Almost did myself a mischief.'

Graham staggered sideways and Adam let go of Sophie's hand to catch him.

'Thanks lad,' he chuckled as Adam lowered his father into the chair he'd brought up for Jennifer. 'Look, I know it's a bit late and everything, but I haven't checked into my hotel yet and apparently, it's too late now. Waiter fella told me you were up here, so I came up to ask…'

He brushed some dust off his trousers and for the first time, seemed to notice that Adam was not alone.

'Not interrupting anything, am I?' he said.

'No, just watching the fireworks,' said Adam, introducing Sophie and his father.

'Where are you supposed to be staying, Graham?' asked Sophie kindly.

'Some pub in Albany. The Hare and Hounds?'

Sophie turned to Adam with a grimace.

'That karaoke place from last night?'

Adam nodded, his heart sinking.

He took a good look at Graham, half-sprawled on the chair. His eyes were glassy, his cheeks were flushed; his father looked in need of some TLC. Adam looked at Sophie and sighed.

'I should get him back to The Swan.'

'Yes, I think you're right.'

She looked disappointed, which Adam took as a good sign.

'Listen, I'll put him in a cab,' he said, already wrapping his father's arm around his neck to help him back down the stairs. 'I'll be back in five minutes. Just wait here.'

He got Graham out to the line of Priuses waiting by the entrance.

'I'm going to give you my key,' said Adam, as he put his father into a cab and handed him the wooden fob. 'I'm in room number 8, on the top floor, okay?'

Graham nodded. 'Room 8. No bother.'

'Great, see you later…'

But just as Adam was about to close the door, Graham stuck out a hand holding a yellow raffle ticket.

'Son, I've forgotten my coat and bag. Can you just run in and get them for me?'

Adam sighed, then sprinted back into the house. He drummed his fingers on the wall as the cloakroom attendant flipped through an endless rack of tulle and cashmere. He was anxious to get back to Sophie but realised that this could play out to his advantage. Now his father had his key, Adam would have to go back to The Swan with Sophie and if his father had fallen straight to sleep, there might be no alternative but to go next door…

'Adders!'

He felt heavy hands landing on his shoulders and turned to find himself face to face with Rich Jameson. His tie hung loose and there were spots of red wine on his shirt. Adam had never liked Rich, even as a skinny pre-teen when he seemed to take great pleasure from snitching on Tim to Jennifer or Bill.

'So where have you been big man? I've hardly seen you all day.'

'You've been busy,' said Adam, accepting a hold-all and tweed jacket from the attendant. 'Big responsibility isn't it, being Best Man?'

Rich didn't seem to catch Adam's sarcasm.

'So why didn't you come out to Marbella?' said Rich, his tone mildly accusatory.

'I took Tim out last night instead.'

'So I hear. Nearly got him killed, too.' He laughed to show stained, pink teeth, then glanced around. 'Hey, you haven't seen Sophie anywhere have you?'

'Sophie?'

'Sophie Wallis.'

'No. Not for a while,' he lied.

Rich lowered his voice. 'I know the best man is supposed to go home with a bridesmaid, yeah?' he said with a chuckle. 'But bloody hell, the second I saw Sophie, I had to change my game plan. And she's fully on-board, if you get my drift.'

Adam couldn't hide his surprise.

'You and Sophie?'

Rich gave a wink that was gleeful, salacious. 'Oh yeah,' he said, drawing the word out. 'In the fortune teller's tent earlier. Still waters run deep with Sophie Wallis, I can tell you. Which is why I'm looking for her now. I want to pick up where we left off at Madame Zora's. We've arranged to go for dinner this week, but we might as well make a start with breakfast in bed at The Swan.'

Adam's stomach knotted as Rich touched him on the arm.

'But don't tell Tim okay? I mean, he's a happily married man now and all that, but still, it's a bit awkward, yeah?'

Rich frowned. 'Hey Ads, are you feeling okay?'

Adam pushed past him. 'I'm fine. I've got to go,' he said quickly. His head was spinning, his heart felt crushed. *Sophie and Rich? Of all people...*

The Prius driver gave an impatient honk on his horn as Adam stumbled outside.

'Are you coming or going?' shouted Graham through the open window.

'I'm coming,' said Adam, balling up his dad's jacket and getting into the back seat besides him.

Chapter Thirty

SOPHIE LAY COCOONED in the bed, the covers wrapped tightly around her, but even from this position she could see the strip of blue sky visible under the curtains, and tell it was going to be another hot, sultry day.

'Morning sleepy, didn't mean to wake you.' She smiled, feeling her hand brush against warm skin.

It wasn't exactly how she'd imagined this weekend would end, but Sophie liked finding herself in bed with someone else – even if it was only her sister.

The night before, she'd waited half an hour on the balcony of the cupola waiting for Adam to return, but when he never showed, she had angrily returned to the lobby where Christa was – finally – waiting for a taxi back to The Swan. It was a huge anti-climax after the tension she'd felt up on the roof, but considering the drama of the rest of the weekend, possibly for the best.

'What time is it?' Christa grabbed her watch, then fell back onto the pillows. Sophie watched a blissful smile spread across her sister's face.

'I've just remembered that I don't have to get up, make three breakfasts, lay out Hattie's clothes, pack her backpack, make sure she remembers to brush her teeth, help Dan find his keys and the phone he uses to call his mid-life crisis fuck-doll.'

Sophie laughed. 'Got it all out?'

Christa squeezed her eyes shut, then let out a long breath.

'For now. Although between you and me, it's just as well Ali passed out last night. If he hadn't, I could well have copped off with him and I guess that doesn't make me much better than Dan, does it?'

Sophie raised a sceptical eyebrow. She didn't think Christa would have done any such thing; despite the rebellious image of her youth, Christa had always been a serial monogamist and although right now she felt betrayed and was in pain, she doubted 'copping off' with Ali Malik had ever really been on the cards, not for someone with Christa's physiology. Sophie slid out of the bed and clicked on the tiny kettle.

'You can't say yesterday was uneventful,' she said with a sigh as she looked out of the window.

'And how do you feel this morning?'

'About what?'

'About Tim.'

Sophie surprised herself by how little she felt about it. The previous night, sitting alone in the folly, Sophie had wondered if she would ever be able to forgive Tim, but the anguish and rage she'd felt had subsided and now she felt like the air after a fierce storm – still and clear.

'Tim Jameson is out of my life, just as he has been for the past fifteen years. The difference this morning is I've accepted it,' she replied, remembering something Paul had told her at the Singles Table before the speeches – about the Stoics believing that acceptance was the key to a happy life. Maybe the ancient Greeks really were onto something.

She took the tea over to her sister, now sitting cross-legged on the bed.

'There's one other positive about it,' said Christa, taking a gulp. 'Tim has made Dan look good.'

'I'm not sure "good" is the correct term. I'd prefer "marginally less of a shit"?'

Christa laughed.

'And what about Adam Stowe?' she asked, with a knowing smile.

'And there's another one,' snorted Sophie, rolling her eyes.

'Don't give me that, Soph. I thought you liked him.'

Sophie pulled a face. *So did I*, she thought. Adam had been sweet, romantic, genuine and yes, more than a little sexy up there on the roof. Sophie had thought he would be able to hear her heart beating when he moved towards her just before Graham had gate-crashed their cosy confessional. But then he had disappeared, leaving Sophie wondering if she had imagined it all.

She sighed.

'Adam Stowe is fun and he's good-looking, I'll give you that. But obviously my first instincts were correct on him. He's flaky, selfish and totally inconsiderate.

Take last night: Zara saw him leave with his dad in

a taxi – okay fine, he had to look after him, but he could have at least sent me a message, not left me standing there in the cold on the roof like a lemon.'

'Soph, at least give him a chance to explain.'

But Sophie was already shaking her head.

'Life is unpredictable,' she said with sudden feeling. 'It throws you curveballs – we both know that – so we need to surround ourselves with reliable people. People who you know are going to be there for you, and quite clearly, Adam Stowe is not one of those people.'

'Funny, I always thought we need to surround ourselves with people who make us feel good about ourselves,' said Christa. 'When I saw you on the dancefloor together, I just thought you both looked so happy.'

'Well, it's all academic isn't it?' said Sophie crisply. 'I doubt I'll ever see Adam Stowe again and that's fine with me.'

There was a long pause.

'You still have his jacket,' said Christa, nodded to the chair it was thrown over.

Sophie felt her heart jump just a little as she remembered him draping it over her shoulders in the garden.

'I'll hand it in to reception when we go down to breakfast.

'Sophie, don't be so stubborn. He's next door! Go and knock!'

'I don't think so. He's probably entertaining some bridesmaid he picked up in the taxi queue.'

Just then her mobile vibrated with an incoming text. Sophie felt a jolt of excitement. Perhaps Adam wanted his jacket back. Perhaps he wanted to apologise for his behaviour last night and explain why he had left the party and not come back. Perhaps…

Lucinda Bennison wants you to arrange transport from Heathrow to Fulham on Tuesday. No people carriers. She likes drivers who wear a suit.

Sophie threw the phone on the bed in disappointment.

'Who's that?'

'Serena bloody White. That woman is a nightmare. Just a list of demands and no "thank you" for anything.'

'So leave,' said Christa with a shrug.

'It's not that simple,' snapped Sophie. She was glad to have moved the conversation on from Adam Stowe, but life at Warwick Travel was not a soothing thought either.

'Isn't it? You took that job to ease yourself back into the job market, remember? Years later and you're still there. And it's not as if you're even enjoying it.'

'No. But what else can I do?'

Christa raised her eyebrows.

'Sophie, I think the question is what *can't* you do?'

Sophie appreciated Christa's confidence, but there were limits. She wasn't exactly going to get a job working at an ice rink or as an instructor at Pineapple Studios. Besides, she did enjoy working in travel.

When she had talked to Adam on the roof, when he asked her what she most loved, almost all the thoughts that popped into her head were travel-related. At the wedding breakfast too, she had felt a ripple of excitement as she talked to Hugo about driving huskies across the Bering Strait or to Paul about rowing the Atlantic. They were people who believed that travel was something you did to enhance your life, not something to impress people at a dinner party in Putney. Christa sat forward, pointing a finger at her.

'I know you, Sophie Wallis. You've had an idea, haven't you? I can see those cogs whirring round in your clever head.'

'What if there was a travel agency for people like me?' said Sophie, thinking out loud. 'People who used to love travel but maybe a disability or a nervous mindset is holding them back. I don't just mean a list of places with accessible facilities. I mean a tour operator who can plan life-changing, inspirational trips – for anyone, to anywhere. So imagine you need ground-floor facilities or you need oxygen or you even need a nurse, it can all be planned ahead.'

'You could do that?'

Sophie nodded. 'It would be more tricky, but it's the same principle as arranging any other itinerary. And we could use people like Paul and Hugo, book them as motivational speakers, so a trip becomes something more than just a holiday.'

Sophie felt the excitement growing as she spoke. If she had used a company like that ten years ago then perhaps her confidence to go out and see the world wouldn't have withered. It was just an idea, but it was already sprouting shoots – and she could see her enthusiasm reflected in Christa's eyes.

'You always used to say you wanted to be a CEO,' she said. 'I remember you being in sixth form and saying you were going to be bigger than Richard Branson.'

'I said a lot of things when I was 18.'

'But that's the point, Soph, don't you see? You used to have that fire, that mad unshakeable self-belief. And I can see it in you again, as you're talking about this. Just do it, Soph. I think mentally you've already taken the first step.'

Sophie laughed.

'Let's not order the Bentley just yet. I live in Mum and Dad's garage and I'm willing to bet Hattie has more savings in her piggy bank than I have to my name.'

'Details,' said Christa airily. 'If anyone can make it work, it's you Sophie Wallis. And talking of piggies,' said Christa, jumping up. 'I can smell bacon – let's get down to breakfast before it all goes.'

She picked up Adam's jacket and threw it at Sophie.

'And we can see if horrible, selfish Adam is around too.'

THE BREAKFAST ROOM was chaos; tables had been pushed together, chairs had been pulled up next to new friends. There were lots of pale, hungover faces, but still the room had a buzz. The Swan might have been the B-list hotel for the wedding guests, but much like the Singles Table, it was the place to have fun. Sophie imagined the scene back at Haslop Hall, more specifically the bridal suite. Had Mr and Mrs Jameson woken up in the four poster bed still surrounded by rose petals, or had the groom slept on the sofa? Sophie thought it could have gone either way. Sophie and Christa were at a corner table and she glanced around, not wanting to admit to herself that she was looking for Adam. Paul and Tina were at a table outside, shaded from the strong morning heat by a white parasol that looked like a cocktail umbrella. Ali was sitting in a corner, sunglasses covering his eyes, sharing a pot of coffee with a handsome man. No, it wasn't just any handsome man, she realised: it was Matt, the butler from the night before. That was fast work, even for Ali. Maybe Christa was right: you made a decision and made a change. It didn't have to be that hard.

Fortified by bacon and black-pudding, Christa left to catch a cab back to the Big House where she had left her Renault. Zara came across to fill the empty seat.

'How are you this morning?' she asked, putting her hand over Sophie's.

'Surprisingly alive,' said Sophie. 'Last night was a bit like a ghost train. Things kept leaping out of the dark at me, but now it's all over, it doesn't seem anywhere near as terrifying as it was. In fact, I'm feeling a tiny bit positive.'

'Only a tiny bit?' Zara looked meaningfully at the

jacket draped over the back of Sophie's chair. 'And would it have anything to do with the owner of that suit?'

Sophie let out a long sigh. 'No. I'll admit I thought Adam Stowe might be different, but he turned out to be just as unreliable as all the others.'

'And would 'all the others' include Rich Jameson?

Sophie rolled her eyes.

Zara grimaced. 'I'm not sure if I should tell you this, but last night I heard him boasting that he was on a promise with you.'

Sophie's eyes opened wide. 'Rich Jameson? With me? God no!'

Zara nodded in agreement. 'I'm glad to hear it. Although I don't know what Adam must have thought of it.'

'Rich said this to Adam?'

Zara nodded. 'After the fireworks, by the cloak-room.'

Sophie felt an unpleasant adrenaline spike in her chest and jumped up, grabbing the jacket. 'Sorry Zara, I've got to go.'

Adam hadn't got the wrong end of the stick, had he? Was that why he hadn't come back up to the cupola – because he'd believed Rich Jameson's lurid fantasies? She ran out of the breakfast room and out into the lobby.

The woman with the severe hair was at reception, radiating her customary hostility.

'You are checking out?' asked the woman.

'Yes, no. Well, not right now,' said Sophie.

'Check out is eleven o'clock,' she said crisply.

'I know. But it's only ten past ten,' she said pointedly. She really did need a lesson in customer service.

The woman glared at her as if she could tell what she was thinking.

'Anyway, I wondered if I could leave something for a guest to collect. This jacket,' she said, putting it on the counter. 'It belongs to Mr Stowe, room eight.'

'You mean your husband.'

'Adam Stowe is not my husband,' she said firmly.

The receptionist cracked a thin smile as if to say 'you wish'. Sophie gripped the jacket, wondering if she should let it go. It felt like the only lifeline to him, the only reason to get back in touch.

'Mr Stowe has gone,' said the receptionist, turning back to her computer monitor.

Sophie felt her heart bump with panic.

'He's gone? Where's he gone?'

'Customers do not share their plans with me.'

Sophie stood there glaring at her and the woman finally let out a heavy sigh. 'He left twenty minutes ago. He said he was going to catch a train.'

THERE WAS ONLY one bench on the platform at Playborough station, but then Adam and his father were the only people waiting. It surprised him, given there must have been over five hundred people at the wedding, but he was grateful for the quiet, as his head was still banging from the night before.

‘It’s good of you to drive me, lad.’

‘I couldn’t risk you getting a local taxi Dad,’ said Adam, remembering the crazed Fiat driver from the stag do. ‘No telling where you’d have ended up.’

Instead, Ali had generously lent Adam his hire car, on the slightly less selfless condition that Adam drive him back to London afterwards. Adam didn’t have much choice: Ali’s vast intake of intoxicants meant he was unlikely to be sober enough to drive himself for a number of days. Adam was not entirely surprised to discover that Ali’s ‘rental’ was a slick white Porsche Carrera that felt like driving a rocket-powered go-kart. Despite the growling engine and feather-light accelerator, Adam had mostly kept to the speed limit. Mostly.

‘Good to see Ali’s doing so well, eh?’ said Graham.

Adam nodded; he had no intention of correcting him. Graham went fishing with Bill Jameson and Jennifer had mentioned they were still friends with Ali’s parents. Ali needed to deal with all that in his own way and on his own terms.

‘Haven’t been in a car like that in years,’ he added, nodding towards the Porsche in the tiny station carpark.

‘In years?’ said Adam. ‘I’ve never been in a car like that my whole life.’

‘The waste disposal business didn’t set my heart on fire,’ said Graham. ‘But it was well-paid so I had a few flash motors in my time.’

‘Alright for some,’ said Adam, briefly feeling his old animosity to his father flare up. ‘Until a couple of years ago, Mum was still driving that ancient Mini Metro she bought the week I started Cubs.'

'You do know your mother sent back all my cheques,' replied his father. 'I kept sending them though: never wanted you to go without anything.'

Adam looked down the train tracks into the distance, not wanting to pick another fight. He'd enjoyed spending the morning together – Graham had even picked up the tab for the room. The least he could do was not be bad-tempered.

'So how's retirement?' said Adam, moving to safer ground. 'What's your plan?'

'The fishing up the park is better than I remembered. And I've been thinking about going back to DJing.'

Adam laughed, but noticed Graham wasn't joining in.

'Wait – 'going back' to DJing? You've done it before?'

'I was spinning the platters that matter before you were born, lad.'

'You're kidding me.'

Graham shook his head.

'Disc jockeys were all the rage in the late sixties, seventies. Twisted Wheel, Wigan Casino, the Top Rank in Sheffield. Thursday night was the big night in Sheffield, payday at the steel works for some reason. Fridays in the foundry were hell.'

Adam felt a surge of emotion. For so long, his father had been a remote figure in his life, and yet now he felt sure that he was where he got his love of music from.

'So why didn't you keep it up?'

'My dad would never have stood for it. Your Grandad was a very traditional man, with very traditional attitudes. I only went into the foundry in the first place because that was where he'd worked all his life and it was what he expected.

'But you did leave.'

Graham raised his eyebrows.

'I think you mean I ran away.'

Graham shifted in his seat. 'I found solace in work – and in money if I'm honest. It was comfortable for a while. Too comfortable. It insulated me from the things I was missing. The things that I loved. I regret that now.'

He fell quiet and then put an arm around Adam's shoulder.

'I have an idea for my retirement. How about we go on a trip?'

'A trip?'

'Golf, great wine, good food.'

Adam started to laugh. 'Please, no golf.'

'What's wrong with golf?'

'Tim likes golf.'

Graham nodded in solidarity.

'Right you are. Just the food and wine then. Like that movie, *Sideways*.'

'Which was food, wine and women.'

The two men smiled, although Adam thought the idea of going *on the pull* with his father seemed faintly ridiculous.

'Sounds good. Want me to plan it?'

Graham shook his head. 'We'll end up in Glastonbury or Vegas or somewhere with lobby music so loud they give you ear-plugs to sleep, so no, I'll book it.'

He paused.

'Say, that was a nice place yesterday. Haslop Hall. Can you imagine what the bar bill was?'

'My headache is telling me it was substantial,' replied Adam, still feeling a pulse behind his eyeballs.

'Speaking of hangovers,' said Graham leaning in. 'I saw Rich Jameson sneaking out of someone's room this morning. He looked very sheepish.'

That got Adam's attention. 'Which room?' said Adam. 'Next door?'

Graham shook his head, frowning. 'No, not next door. One of the courtyard rooms near the carpark. I saw the young lady at the door waving him off. I'm not entirely sure but I think it was that scary bridesmaid. Emily was it?'

Adam was about to ask more, but Graham was getting to his feet: the train was sliding into the platform.

'Here,' said Graham, reaching into his inside pocket. 'I've got something for you.'

He handed Adam a white envelope with The Swan's logo on the outside. 'I don't have your way with words lad, so…'

He grabbed Adam by the shoulders and pulled him into a hug, startling him.

'You take care, eh?'

Adam felt strangely anxious as Graham gathered

his things. For the first time in a long time, he didn't want his dad to go.

'I'm sorry, Dad.' Adam looked into his father's lined face.

'Whatever for?'

'For all the time we've wasted.'

Graham nodded.

'But it's not over yet, eh? Napa Valley here we come.'

Adam watched as his dad got onto the train and closed the door with a thump, leaning out of the open window.

'Now go and find that girl,' he called, as the train began to move.

'What girl?' shouted Adam.

Graham laughed. 'What girl, he says…'

Adam watched the train clank down the track, feeling a tugging in his heart. Then he turned and ran for the car.

SOPHIE STOOD AT the top of the stairs, her heart heavy. The door to Adam's room was open, a cleaner hard at work inside, sheets and white towels bundled up by the door. So it was true, Adam Stowe had left the building.

Sighing, she went and packed, peering into the bathroom one last time. She couldn't believe she had made such a fuss over it with Adam. How hard would it have been to share a bathroom for a couple of days? No wonder Adam had chosen to keep his distance from the prudish, uncharitable girl next door.

She bumped her case back down to reception. The room had already been paid for, a credit card put down for any additional charges. Once her key was deposited in the express check out box, that was it. It was over.

'Sophie! Are you off?'

Paul walked over, looking happy and relaxed in jeans and a white t-shirt with a red boat and the words 'Team Atlantic' splashed across the front of it.

'I saw you at breakfast but I didn't want to disturb you,' said Sophie with a knowing look. 'I take it you had a good night then?'

'A gentleman never tells' he said.

'I'm glad it's worked out. Although I am still very sorry about stealing your phone.'

Paul shook his head, a serious look on his face.

'Sophie, that message might be the most important text I ever send, even if I didn't actually send it. Whatever happens with me and Tina, I definitely owe you one.'

'Actually, there is one thing you can do for me.'

Sophie wasn't great at being pushy, at least not these days. Asking for things made her uncomfortable, especially as she had spent so many years depending on others. But this morning, she knew she had to ask, if only to share her excitement. She quickly told Paul about her idea for a boutique travel service for the less mobile.

'I think that's a brilliant idea,' he said. 'Seriously.'

Sophie felt instant relief. It was one thing Christa saying lots of nice things, but Paul did not seem like a man to mince his words.

'I can definitely connect you with some people to get you started,' he added. 'Clients of mine, friends from the army rehabilitation hospital. And I'd be honoured to come along and share my experiences, if that's what you want.'

He handed her a business card, then pointed at her. 'You'd better call.'

'I will,' she grinned.

She walked out into the sunshine and waved to Christa, her dusty old Renault standing out among the shiny saloons and 4x4s.

Christa was talking on the phone as Sophie clunked her case into the back seat.

'Well I'm glad you had such a lovely time with Daddy,' Christa was saying. 'We'll do something nice too when I get home, okay? You want sweeties? Of course I'll come home with a big bag… I love you too darling.'

'What was all that about?' asked Sophie when Christa had ended the call.

'I think Hattie and Dan had a better time than we did last night,' she said with a heavy sigh. She handed over her phone and Sophie scrolled through dozens of messages from Dan. There were pictures of Hattie in the kitchen making flapjacks, Dan and Hattie making a den in the garden with blankets and cushions, even a short movie of Hattie washing her hair, giggling through the suds.

'Do you think he's making a point that he's still a good dad?' said Christa with heavy irony.

'He's definitely currying favour with someone.'

Christa's face hardened. 'Well, he'd better get used to weekend parenting,' she growled, throwing the phone down. Sophie saw tears beading on Christa's lashes and reached out for her sister.

'Christa is this really what you want?' she asked. 'Kicking him out, ending your marriage?'

'What am I supposed to do?' Christa barked. 'Go home, make him a three-course dinner and say, "hey, babe – all is forgiven"?'

'No, and you're allowed to be angry and confused after everything that's happened,' said Sophie gently. 'But don't make any snap decisions.'

A car horn honked and Sophie turned to see Paul and Tina waving at them as they pulled out of the car park. Sophie raised a hand.

'See? There's a couple back from the brink. Paul almost let her go.'

'Paul hasn't been shagging someone from his cycling club,' said Christa with a snotty laugh.

'We don't actually know that,' said Sophie, smiling.

'It's too late, Soph,' she whispered, pulling a tissue from a box next to the gear-stick. 'How can I ever trust him again?'

'Remember mum and dad?' said Sophie, trying to catch her sister's eye.

'There was a road bump in their marriage. It wasn't infidelity, or some American lawyer with a peachy ass. It was a daughter who they had to nurse back to health, a daughter they had to help walk and talk again and get through years of depression. My accident strained their relationship, Chris. We all know that, and it changed things for ever. Dad never became head of Chambers. Mum never became a judge. But they came through it, and now look. I truly think they're happier. Happier than they ever were.'

For a moment, Sophie pictured the fondue parties that her father threw for his old university pals every Christmas, and the raucous garden suppers her parents hosted each Midsummer's night. Mr and Mrs Wallis were no longer obsessed with work and the constant, exhausting striving that she remembered from her youth. Adversity fixed them.

Christa gave a tight, tiny nod.

'Dan says he wants to talk when I get back.'

'Talk?'

'He did sound sorry.'

'Perhaps you heard regret,' said Sophie.

'That's a start, isn't it?' said Christa, gunning the car engine.

'It is, but an even better one is to get Hattie her sweeties, before she clobbers you with her Barbie. Come on, there's a sweet shop on the high street.'

ADAM TOOK THE corner at high speed. Ali's muscle car slid around the bend with nonchalant ease and powered up the lane like a runaway horse. Adam wasn't entirely sure he was actually in full control of the motor, but suddenly he needed to get back to The Swan. His mind was making a series of mental jumps. If Rich Jameson had gone home with a bridesmaid last night, that meant he wasn't with Sophie, which meant, maybe, nothing even happened between them last night. He slapped his hand down on the gear stick in annoyance.

Adam had no idea what went on between Rich and Sophie in the fortune teller's tent but suddenly it didn't matter. In fact it never had. He'd definitely felt a connection with Sophie on the roof, but he'd let Rich Jameson put him off, let another opportunity slip by – like never applying for the *Cream* editorship, or never writing that script when a Hollywood director had asked him to. Deep down, Adam knew that things came easily to him, but when they didn't, he didn't fight for things. Perhaps that was something else he had in common with his father, he thought grimly, wondering how things might have been if Graham Stowe had been more like Mrs Robertshaw and had dug deep for the woman he loved.

He looked at his watch: five minutes to check out. There was a chance that Sophie was having a lie-in, sleeping off the excess of the night before. It was a slim chance, but it was better than none. He accelerated into the car park, narrowly missing a battered Renault pulling out onto the high street, then fish-tailed into the drive, laying on the horn as a family of ducks had the poor judgement to step out from under a hedge.

He ran into the hotel with a sense of urgency. Reception was busy – everyone checking out at the last minute – but none of them were Sophie and in the dining room, empty tables were already being laid for lunch.

‘Dammit’, he muttered, sprinting up the stairs to the eaves where Sophie’s room was being hoovered by the cleaner. Dejected, he returned to the now-empty lobby and rang the bell to get the attention of the receptionist.

‘It is not broken,’ said the woman, walking out from the rear office, moving the bell out of Adam’s reach.

‘Sorry. Have you seen…’

‘The woman who is not your wife?’ she said with a raised eyebrow.

‘Yes, yes,’ he nodded. ‘Sophie.’

‘She was here looking for you.’

Hope flared in Adam’s chest.

‘She wanted to give you your jacket.’

‘She did? So where is she?’

‘She checked out already,’ she said, pointing to the rack of keys beside her.

‘When?’

‘Ten minutes ago.’

‘Well, do you have her number, so I can contact her? About getting my jacket back, of course.’

‘We do not give out the private information of our guests.’

‘But this is important.’

The receptionist gave a small, but decisive shake of her head, the angles of her hair barely moving. Adam could tell she was enjoying the power, but he could also tell that nothing short of water-boarding would get anything more from her. Maybe not even then.

Sighing, he walked away, glancing up at the stuffed squirrel under the bell jar. It seemed to be mocking him with its sad eyes.

'Can I help with anything?'

'Sophie?' Adam spun round, his heart thumping, but it wasn't Sophie, it was Dr Cherie.

'Oh hi,' he said, bracing himself for another bout of disapproval, but Cherie was smiling.

'Looking for Sophie by any chance?' she chuckled.

'Yes – you haven't seen her, have you?'

'No, sorry.'

'Have you got her number?'

'I don't really know her, I'm afraid. Try asking Tim and Vanessa.'

Adam nodded. 'Sure, I'll do that,' he said, knowing it was unlikely he would ever talk to either of the happy couple any time soon. 'Hey, weren't you staying up at the Hall?' he asked.

Cherie nodded over to where Henry the photo-booth guy was checking out.

'I gave Ali my room, so I had to stay with Henry.'

'And how did that go?' said Adam.

'Let's just say I owe you an apology.'

'Apology? What for?'

'I was rude to you about the stunt in the van when I knew you were only trying to help. And, well…it worked. Turns out Henry just needed a push.'

She gave Adam a tight hug. 'Thank you,' she whispered, then briskly turned away to join Henry.

He walked through to the bar where Ali was sitting, slumped in an armchair. His old friend looked crumpled and grey, befitting a man who had narrowly avoided having his stomach pumped, but at the same time there was a lightness to him, an upward tug at the side of his mouth.

'Ads mate, you ready to rock and roll?' he said. 'Ali-kazam got moves he needs to make.'

'Ready when you are,' nodded Adam. His bag was already in the Porsche.

'I'd better get my stuff and check out. See you at the motor in ten minutes, yeah?'

Adam walked out into the car park, half-hoping he would see Sophie, but there was no-one in sight. Shaking his head, Adam walked away from the pub, following a stone-flagged path fringed with sprouting grass, past The Swan's beer garden, down between an avenue of trees, just letting his feet lead him. He needed fresh air, he needed open space, but most of all, Adam needed to think. Historically, it had been something he'd been adept at avoiding, especially when it came to thinking about the future, but right now, the future had finally caught up with him.

Love life aside, Adam was actually feeling positive about his next move. Tim's jibes, his sneering accusation that Adam had failed to live up to his potential, had hit a nerve and spurred him on. Adam knew it was time to take charge of his destiny, and on Monday morning, he was going to hit the phones for a charm offensive with editors. Freelance work was tough, he knew that much, but it was a start, a holding pattern while he planned his next step.

He walked along the path, the sun was slanting

across his path in stripes of gold, a gang of housemartins streaking overhead.

Adam shoved his hands in his pockets, half-hoping he'd find his sunglasses in there, but his fingers touched something else – paper: his Dad's letter. He tore it open, expecting a letter, but inside was a slip of paper and his dad's business card.

EnviroTech Inc
Graham Stowe
CEO

Adam was confused. His father was a semi-retired gun-for-hire waste disposal consultant, not a chief executive. Wasn't he? He turned the card around, looking for more clues but written on the back in blue ink was one simple line:

For new dreams – Dad x

He pulled out the paper slip, but it wasn't a note, it was a cheque. From an actual bricks and mortar bank, like in the old days. Adam's eyes opened wide as he counted the '0's.

'No... WAY!' he breathed, blinking hard then looking back at the cheque to make sure he wasn't dreaming. 'You are bloody kidding me.'

It was enough to buy the premises for the record shop, fit it out and stock it – probably enough to set up the events company and hire Belasco for the launch too. Carefully – very carefully, he replaced the envelope in his pocket, his hands still shaking.

He pulled out his phone to call his dad but for once he was speechless. What did you say to something like that? The truth, of course. But the things Adam needed to say to his father needed to be said in private, not when he was on a train or while Adam was sitting next to Ali. But still – there was one flimsy bar of signal on his phone – enough to send a text. A text to say the one thing he knew he should have said to his father at the train station.

I forgot to say. I love you.

CHRISTA PARKED THE Renault on Playborough high street, jumped out, then popped her head back in through the open door.

'Won't be long,' she said. 'Better get Hattie something to rot her teeth like a good parent. Are you staying there?'

Sophie looked back at the queue already snaking out of the shop. Apparently it wasn't too early for double-decker ice cream cones.

'Looks like you may be some time; I think I'll just stretch my legs.'

'Don't go far,' said Christa.

She crossed the street and took the same sloping lane she had followed the day before. It was still quiet and calm, the sunshine peeking through the leaves. The same waving grass, the same bees leap-frogging from petal to petal, but it wasn't the same was it? Everything had changed since then. The river was still there though, still quietly rushing onwards, still carrying the same spinning sycamore leaves – and today, a straggling line of ducks: mother Mallard and entourage of not-quite chicks, artfully dashing between the stepping stones. Smiling, Sophie walked over to the edge of the water. It was somehow reassuring that despite all the human drama up at the hall, the river still flowed, the ducks still swam and the sun – she tipped her head back, breathing in – well, the sun still shone.

There were no children playing in the stream today and Sophie was glad to have this beautiful spot to herself. She walked to the bank, assessing the distance to the other side. It wasn't that far, was it? Not if you counted the stones. One, three, four… twelve was it? Unlucky thirteen? That wasn't so many, was it?

'Sod it,' she said, and stepped out, her heart jumping as her sole slipped, then held. With a little gasp, she brought the other foot alongside, wobbling, but maintaining her balance. With a spreading smile, Sophie looked around. She had actually done it! She was on the stepping stones.

'One down,' she muttered to herself.

If I make it to the next stone, I'll give up carbs, she thought, leaping forward and making a perfect landing. Easy.

If I get to the next one, I'm throwing out my wardrobe. Sophie took a big step, planting a confident foot right in the centre of the stone. Good. She'd been meaning to have a real spring clean. She didn't need an entire wardrobe of red Dolce and Gabbana dresses, but no more frumpy skirts, no more chunky flat shoes, no more sensible *anything* would be a start.

She already knew what her prize was going to be for reaching the far bank. *If I make it across the river, I'm going to resign.*

On Monday morning, she was going to hand her resignation to Serena and watch the look of disbelief on her Botoxed face.

It wasn't entirely true that Sophie hadn't any savings. In the years after her accident there had been very few outgoings – her parents had always refused to take rent money, her commute was short, cheap, and her social life consisted of museums and the occasional trip to the cinema – everything else had been piled into her rainy-day account and she knew there was enough in there to get her business off the ground.

She took another step and another. With each step, Sophie thought of a new client she could approach. Stuart and Sarah Mortimer in the big house near the Common. Before his stroke, Stuart had told her of his plans to visit the temples in Tulum, on the Mexican coast. Sophie could definitely make that happen now. Then there was Alfie from her rehab group who wanted to swim with giant turtles and Daphne, the lady with MS who'd confessed her dream of seeing the Terracotta Army. Sophie took another step, and then another, her heart growing lighter as she thought not of her fledgling business, but of those lives opening up. And then she was standing on the grass, no more steps, no more stones. She was there.

'Yes!' she said. 'YES!'

'Again! Again!' shouted a voice in her head, a voice she recognised. The voice of the teenage Sophie who loved fast rides at theme parks, who would ride the rollercoasters over and over without fear, loving the rush, loving the feeling of being alive. And looking back at the bank, Sophie began to think up a new challenge. What else did she want?

'Adam,' she whispered out loud.

She closed her eyes, suddenly feeling quite dizzy. Adam Stowe. Flaky, irresponsible Adam. She wanted him.

And I do still have his jacket, she thought quickly, her excitement rising. It was only polite to get it back to him, wasn't it? It wouldn't be that hard to track him down: Jennifer would have his details or there was always that magazine he worked for. *Cream*. She'd find him.

Sophie stepped to the edge of the river, assessing the gap to the first stone.

'Wait!'

Sophie looked up: someone was waving on the other bank.

For a moment she froze. Was she dreaming? Still drunk? No, she thought, her heart bumping. It was Adam! That lopsided smile. Those cheekbones.

'I'm coming over,' he shouted.

But Sophie couldn't wait. Without thinking, her heart rearing, Sophie stepped out onto the first stone, then the next, confidently retracing her steps, no longer afraid, knowing – absolutely sure – that she was going in the right direction.

And looking up, she saw Adam coming towards her, bounding from rock to rock with ease. She stopped, waiting in the middle – and for some reason, Sophie thought of a photograph from her graduation day in Bristol. Tim and her, side-by-side in their gowns and silly hats, grinning, looking to the future. Sophie had often looked at that photo as she lay on her back, convinced that it showed the moment her future had split, the moment her perfect life with Tim had veered off and she had begun moving towards the future with the accident, the future without Tim. But maybe she and Tim were just leaves spinning on the river, destined to bump together, then drift away. Maybe it was all leading her here, to this river, to this rock. To Adam.

'Fancy meeting you here,' she said as he met her in the middle. Sophie knew she was rubbish at flirting, but she smiled anyway, because she was happy. Happy that Adam was here. Happy that they were here together.

But Adam wasn't smiling.

'Listen, I need to explain about last night,' he said. 'I didn't come back to the roof terrace last night because Rich Jameson told me you and he had…'

'Had what?'

He looked awkward.

'Well…In the fortune teller's tent.'

Sophie smiled to herself.

'Adam, whatever Rich Jameson said, let me tell you he was a complete sleazeball in the fortune teller's tent. He tried it on and I almost punched him into tomorrow.'

Adam laughed.

'Well, that's a relief,' he frowned. 'Because I …'

Almost in slow-motion, his left foot went from under him and he was tipping face-first towards the water. Just as quickly, Sophie reached out and grabbed his arm to steady him, until her tread slipped too. They wobbled for a moment until they regained their footing and they clung onto each other until they were steady.

'I got you,' he grinned.

'Funny,' she whispered. 'I thought I'd got you.'

Adam bent his head towards her and kissed her softly on the lips. For a moment Sophie thought she was going to fall again, but his strong arms were around her.

'That was worth the wait,' she smiled, as they slowly pulled apart.

'Oh, yes it was.'

She suddenly felt embarrassed. 'So, are you heading back to London?'

'I have to get Ali back to his hotel in Chelsea.'

'And then what?'

'No plans.'

'Me neither.'

'Maybe we could do nothing together?'

Sophie looked up at the blue sky and suddenly the day felt limitless. Adam followed her gaze.

'Sun's out,' he said.

'Yes,' said Sophie. 'It is.'

She could hear a song in her head, something she

had once heard on the radio or in a movie, a heavy trombone and a sultry, smoky voice that made her shiver even though it was just a memory.

'What are you smiling at?'

'A song. Something about dragonflies and sunshine and birds flying high. A song about a day like today.'

'Ah. Nina Simone. Feeling Good. 1965.'

Sophie nodded.

'That's it. I love that song.'

'So do I.'

'When are you going to start giving me this musical education you keep talking about, then?'

Adam thought it for a moment.

'Sloane Square at two o'clock.'

Sophie laughed.

'Two o'clock today?'

'No time like the present.' he said.

'So where are you taking me?'

'I'll think of something,' he said, one side of his lip curling up in the most adorable way.

'I'm sure you will.'

She held out her hand, palm up.

'Shall we?'

'I thought you'd never ask.'

And together they crossed.

NEW FROM TASMINA PERRY

A major new mystery series from the
Sunday Times bestseller.

The Yacht Party

What happens onboard, stays onboard

Investigative journalist Lara Stone is offered a second chance when her oldest friend Sandrine invites her to join the Collective, a network of investigative reporters funded by crusading media player Eduardo Ortega.

But when Sandrine is found dead, Laura believes her death is linked to a story she was working on about Jonathon Meyer, a secretive financier known for hosting glamorous networking parties on his Monte Carlo yacht Pandora.

Six weeks earlier Meyer was also found dead after a violent crime went badly wrong. But Lara soon discovers there are no coincidences: Sandrine and Jonathon were both murdered and that the key to the motive lies onboard Pandora.

What secrets are hidden onboard Meyer's yacht? What deals were brokered that were worth killing for? And can Lara get to the truth before someone decides that she has to be silenced too?

The Last Supper

Murder is on the menu

Erik Wahlund is the darling of the food world, his remote Swedish farm-to-table dining hall Kluven is known as one of the most exclusive restaurants in the world. Situated on an isolated peninsula, it is only accessible by boat and there is only one communal table for 12 lucky people.

When Lara Stone snags a reservation, it promises to be a meal of a lifetime, but the chef is not the only one sharpening his knives. Erik is found dead and everyone spending the weekend at snowbound Kluven has a motive. As a storm closes in, Lara must track the killer down and discover the secret they would do anything to protect.

Made in United States
Orlando, FL
26 June 2023

34543117R00202